THE IRON MASK

The Last Shadow Epic, Book Three

by

AJ Cooper

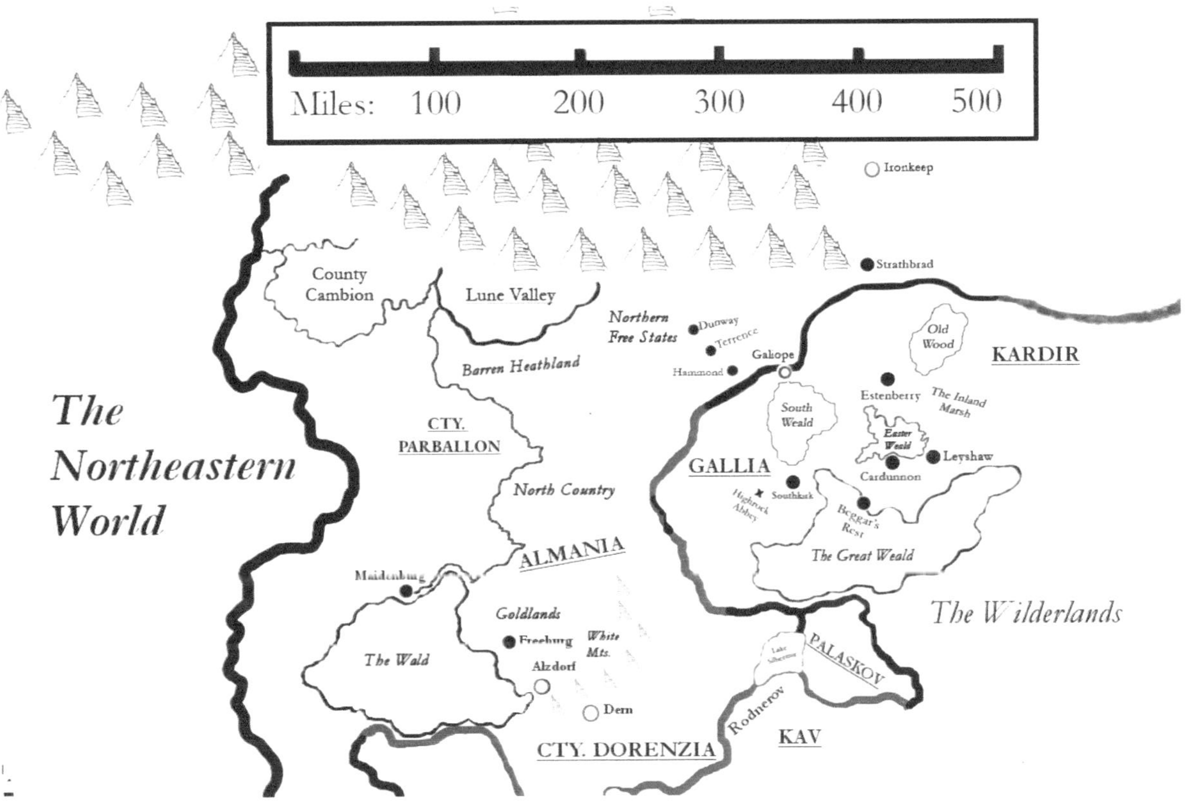

The Northeastern World
Miles: 100 200 300 400 500
Ironkeep
County Cambion
Lune Valley
Northern Free States
Dunway
Terrence
Hammond
Galiope
Strathbrad
Old Wood
KARDIR
Barren Heathland
South Weald
Estenberry
The Inland Marsh
Easter Weald
Leyshaw
CTY. PARBALLON
GALLIA
Cardunnon
Highrock Abbey
Southkirk
North Country
Beggar's Rest
The Great Weald
ALMANIA
Maidenburg
Goldlands
White Mts.
Freeburg
Alzdorf
The Wald
Dern
CTY. DORENZIA
Rodnerov
KAV
Lake Silvermist
PALASKOV
The Wilderlands

GALIOPE

Garrick's Gate
THE ELVEN QUARTER
MARKET DISTRICT
SELWYN'S PARISH
Hawk's Keep
Strathbrad Gate
Tower of Pythor
Horn Keep
MIDDLETOWN
WODENSCROSS COURT
LONEN TOWN
GREENWATER
Bridge O'er Galios
RIVERSIDE
CATHEDRAL DISTRICT
Godsgate

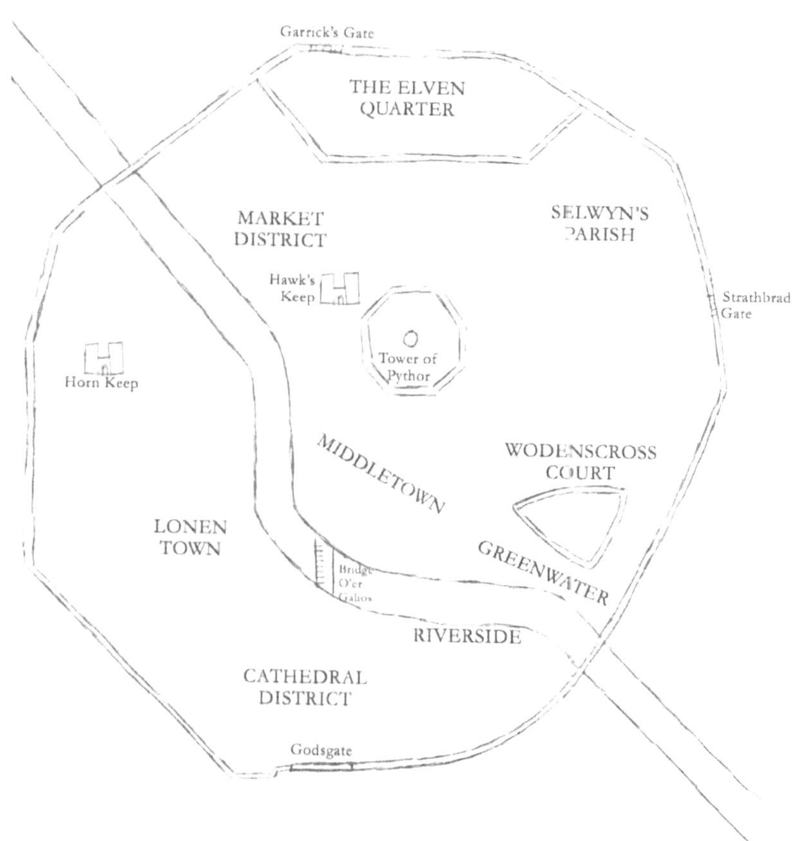

Chapter One:
Caster

Reev Nax walked down High Street in late autumn, headed to the well for water, and watched more of them arrive.

Mountain Folk they were, men—and sometimes women too—bearing swords and axes openly at their sides. Occasionally, even the children were armed. They wore armor even here, in the City of Galiope that had welcomed them. The metal of their swords and axes gleamed. Some of them wore suits of mail, others clumsy leather vests. But the most defining feature of the Mountain Folk was their stench; they did not consider cleanliness a virtue as did the flatlanders, and they considered flatlanders beneath them.

For the people of Galiope, the feeling was mutual.

Day after day they had been passing through Godsgate—men and women, children, entire families—people fleeing their homeland, a place where they were no longer safe, for a place they didn't belong.

Reev fell back to the side of the road, his empty pail in hand. He had heard rumors that the rokahn in the Dragonteeth Mountains were pouring out of their holes in such numbers the normal defenses the Mountain Folk relied on—fortresses and walls and watchtowers—were no longer sufficient. If rokahn were said to appear in times of ill portent, if their number was said to increase in bad times, then these were the worst times yet seen.

"Reev!" The voice of his friend Wrinn stunned him out of his pondering. The elf's bright blue eyes gleamed in the sun. He was dressed in a brown tunic and downy, rugged trousers. His quarterstaff was strapped to his back. "Fancy seeing you here."

The Mountain Folk pushed by, rudely forcing their way through the street.

"So many…" Reev said. "So many of them."

Wrinn smiled. He drew back away from the Mountain Folk, the hundreds pushing through.

"It seems," Wrinn said, "that it isn't our city anymore."

"Our city"—that's what it had become, though Reev had grown up in the town of Norwood in the hinterlands of the Empire, a land so far away it was like another world. Wrinn was a recent arrival as well, from the Kingdom of Zarubain, an elf, once a slave.

"They aren't so populous in the Arcades, I hear," Wrinn said.

The Arcades, a district in the northeastern quadrant of the city, was known for its shops and small shrines. The thought of escaping these burdensome Mountain Folk was so tempting Reev dropped the pail. He could buy another one, and his thirst no longer seemed like his most pressing problem.

"Let's get out!" Reev said as the stench of the Mountain Folk swirled about him. "Show me the way…"

~

From Middletown they walked, through Galiope's cobblestone streets, in the shadow of the Tower of the Pythor. It was high noon, and it seemed there was no hope of escaping the Mountain Folk. At a street corner, a bucktoothed man was playing a fiddle, and his ten children surrounded him, sitting by his side. His collection bucket was empty.

Most offensive to Reev were the tents that had been erected in City Square, where once merchants had sold their wares and entertainers had swallowed their swords or juggled their knives, but who had been replaced. Now, to some in the city, there was a terrible feeling, the thought of the end of Galiope or of the Gallian League itself. If the rokahn poured out of their mountain holes in such numbers, their hungry stomachs would eventually take them to the lowlands. Commerce and entertainment were now secondary to the sense of growing dread, the feeling it was the end of Galiope, or perhaps the world.

They walked in the shadow of the Tower of Pythor, and when they reached the arched, covered corridors and mounting terraces of the Arcades, it was apparent Wrinn had been wrong about the Arcades. As soon as they reached the district, a Mountain Folk child rushed up to beg for coin. Reev offered her a penny, but when he looked up he could see the streets and narrow alleyways were filled, like the rest of the city, with Mountain Folk. And they had brought their stench with them.

"So much for that," Reev said.

Wrinn walked off, leading him down a dark alleyway.

In the darkness, Reev remembered the events of the last year, how he'd been given a chance to depart Galiope and venture to the land of the elves. He had insisted on remaining in Galiope, and now he was faced with great discomfort—and soon with imminent danger, once these voluminous amounts of rokahn formed warbands and ventured into the lowlands after the spring thaw.

"Wrinn!" he shouted. "You're getting ahead of me!"

The alleyway was wet with recent rain. Above him were the Arcades' traditional arches, letting in little light.

But the stench was fading, and when Wrinn at last stopped his hurried walk and turned to face him, they were alone.

"See," he said. "I was right after all."

They were alone in a small space, away from the Mountain Folk for the first time in many days.

"You were right," Reev said. "I admit it."

By proclamation of the Lord Mayor, two-thirds of all rooms in every inn were to put up a Mountain Folk family. The Dragonpaw Inn had never been the same after Glenda, the innkeeper, caved to the pressure. No longer was it Reev's sanctuary. No longer was it a place to escape. This dark alley was the first respite he'd had in days.

What did Wrinn have in mind? As he stood there, noises rose

above the city sounds—the roar of a crowd. Ahead of them was a little green doorway, above it in crude writing, the words The Fattened Pig. It was a tavern Wrinn had in mind, then, like always, or so it seemed.

But Reev did not like taverns, and what time he had, he didn't like to spend drinking. Ahead of Wrinn, another door down, was an open set of red doors, and above them, inscrutable writing carved into the stone, which had faded with time.

"Let's try something else," he told Wrinn, and pushed ahead.

Whatever this establishment was, he had no idea; but it was a roll of the dice, and it was certain not to be a tavern.

It was dark, and the stone chamber beyond the red doors was lined with shelves.

These shelves did not contain books, but instead objects of differing size and type.

"What is this?" Reev said, partially to himself, and Wrinn walked ahead of him.

Wrinn's eyes were fixed on a black ball.

And a man appeared there, pale and thin, with dark eyes.

"Welcome to my shop," he said. "Is it your first time in the Arcades, young elf? Is it yours, young human?"

The shopkeeper had wiry gray hair, and was clearly some mix of man and elf. His ears came to points that were just slight, and he was short and thin.

He turned to the black sphere Wrinn was looking at, and had begun to touch.

"The egg," said the shopkeeper, "of a black dragon. Calcified… it has shrunken over time. Squeeze it! It feels as hard as a stone, but it is harder than a stone, harder than iron."

"What is this place?" Reev said. "What do you sell?"

"Curiosities of various kinds," said the shopkeeper. "Objects that my servants have found in markets from afar. Objects that may have little value to the common, but to the erudite and noble are priceless, and worth much gold."

Reev walked closer to the shelf. On it he could see knucklebones, scratched with strange markings. He reached for them, but the shopkeeper exclaimed, "Halt! Those knucklebones belong to a night hag, for use in her divination.

"One of my servants took it from the Murk Swamps. If you touch those knucklebones, the night hag might grow angry, and appear to you in dreams."

The Murk Swamps was a name Reev was familiar with. He had struggled through them years ago. They lay in the north of the Empire, and in them, a hag was not the worst thing a traveler could face.

As Wrinn held the calcified dragon's egg, wondering at the light that seemed to gleam from within it, Reev walked deeper into the shop. Would it have been better to go to the tavern and indulge Wrinn's vices? He supposed he had made his choice and couldn't back down now.

On the shelves were the preserved paws of creatures Reev had never seen before, coins of kingdoms he did not recognize, and stone tablets in scripts he had never read. All on the shelves seemed of little value on their own, but to an antiquarian, or someone who adored strange things, they would be worth paying for.

As he reached the last of the shelves, full of fluid-filled jars, something caught his eye in the dim candlelight, a stone table that looked like it had been forcibly removed, and on it, a checkered surface with Elvish runes. He approached it, and was overcome with a terrible feeling of dread. Yet curiosity pushed him on.

He sensed the presence of the shopkeeper behind.

"What is this?" Reev asked.

"This," said the shopkeeper, "is not for sale."

"I didn't ask to buy it," Reev said. "I asked what it is."

Wrinn was approaching from the shadows of the room.

"This belonged to the elvish caster Sonori, of whom—I

believe—I am a distant relation," the shopkeeper continued. "In the Elven War, the Zarubes pillaged the town of Banarion, not far from the capital, where Sonori lived in ancient days.

"The knights took this, his caster's table. They played games on it and were said to become afflicted with a curse. For that is not the purpose of the caster's table. It is about finding one's true purpose, about finding, on the deepest level, who you are."

Reev wondered at the markings on the checkered board. He noticed a gray stone sitting on the table's edge.

"I want to know who I am," Wrinn said.

"Are you sure?" The shopkeeper stepped up to the edge of the caster's table and took the gray stone in his hand. "You might not like knowing who you are. You might not like knowing your destiny."

"It's a chance I'm willing to take," Wrinn said.

"One penny for my trouble," said the shopkeeper, and Wrinn instantly began finagling through his coin purse.

Wrinn flipped the silver coin at him and it gleamed in midair before landing squarely in the shopkeeper's hands.

"I am a caster of sorts," said the shopkeeper. "The ability to cast is passed down from father to son. On behalf of my ancestor, I will do this for you…?"

"Wrinn Finnis," Wrinn said.

"Wrinn Finnis… Who are you?"

He cast the gray stone on the table, and it landed on an A-rune.

He continued to cast the gray stone.

A-d-a-r-i.

"Adari," the shopkeeper said. "Helper. That is what you are." He looked to Reev and asked, "And you?"

"Reev… Reev Nax." He did not want to do this, but he felt some compulsive force was driving him forward, the inescapable momentum of destiny.

He reached for his coin purse, but the shopkeeper stopped him:

"No, no, Reev Nax… for you, it is free."

The shopkeeper cast the stone onto the checkered board.

The stone landed on "E."

He cast it again. "L."

And Reev wondered if a caster was not one possessed with wisdom or one whose hands were guided by the gods, but instead a man who could deftly cast a stone in the right place. Was the shopkeeper tricking him? He could see no other explanation.

But the air in the room changed, and Reev's breath quickened. The light in the candles seemed to flare, and the shop became brighter.

The shopkeeper fell back in fear, and the stone began to move of its own accord.

"T," read the stone, then darted by itself to "E."

"L."

"A."

"N."

The shopkeeper's face had turned a shade of white.

"T." "A." "R." "I."

"Telantari," Wrinn said.

"El Telantari," Reev said.

"You are 'the' *telantari*," Wrinn said. "What does that mean?"

In Elvish, "the" was not used often. It meant the consummate, or the ultimate. But did the first casting count?

"Begone from my shop, you!" The shopkeeper was hysterical. "Begone, and take whatever vile magic you possess with you."

But Reev was not a sorcerer, nor was Wrinn. Sorcery had not moved the stone on that checkered board.

Panic turned to anger. The shopkeeper's face darkened to red. "Begone!" he hissed. "Begone, you!"

The room had become brilliant in its luminescence. Reev and Wrinn turned and fled, and in the light, Rev thought of that strange word.

Telantari was Reev's identity. But what was *telantari*, and what force had moved that stone?

Chapter Two:
The Arrival

Gastreel waited beside Godsgate, in view of the wheat fields and cattle farms, and looked down at the little shadow next to him.

Bala Rabaam was by his side, a toddling little child dressed in a robe of ash gray, still wearing that top hat because wise men had to choose their battles, so Gastreel had relented.

What lay ahead for Bala was of more consequence than his little mind could comprehend. To the wizarding world, he had achieved the status of "grave petitioner," but that was about to change. Bala, whose gift was necromancy, had found a teacher. As far as Gastreel knew he would be the first apprentice ever of such a young age. The pressures on the little boy would be immense.

But all was for a purpose, a grave purpose, a purpose little Bala could not understand.

In the cold, Gastreel waited for a sign of Bala's new teacher, dwelling on what lay ahead.

The Six Servants of Seymus, phantoms of the ancient world, had been given false life by the workings of a necromancer. A spell had been cast on their iron masks, the last vestiges of their existence. The Servants had been destroyed, but the magic lingered on those masks and they would reconstitute if left untouched. Only by necromancy could the spell of necromancy be thwarted.

Bala was the wizard order's hope. Bala, yes, little Bala Rabaam, half human, half vampire, the son of Nocturne Rabaam and a woman who was not fit to be a mother.

Bala was stirring in his little ash-gray robe. He had recently eaten, and he had been tended to, but Gastreel knew little children were fussy, and didn't like to wait.

"Bala Rabaam," Gastreel said, "do you know what lies ahead of you?"

"I'm going to learn magic," Bala said. "Right?"

If only it had been that simple. The one who had laid the spells over the iron masks had been the most talented wizard of his generation. Jerek the Necromancer had caused such destruction that necromancy itself had been banned, until just now. His heart had been as dark as the Void. He had declared himself the Dark One's Hand, but that had proven false—the identity of the Dark One's Hand, Seymus's deputy in the mortal world, was not yet known.

"You're going to learn magic," Gastreel said to Bala. "Do you remember what I said? Do you remember? Will you try as hard as you can, for my sake?"

"Of course, Mr. Gastreel," Bala answered.

Gastreel had known Bala only a short while, and he could tell little Bala had a mischievous streak, and that he rarely took things seriously. But he seemed genuinely excited to become a wizard, and Gastreel supposed that was cause for hope.

As for Bala's talent, there was no room for questioning. Talent Bala had in abundance, perhaps more than the vile necromancer who had imbued the Servants of Seymus with false life. He was young, and if he grew old, he would be far mightier than Jerek. But the crises in the mountains and the rumors of far-off war made Gastreel wonder if his time in Galiope would be short.

Gastreel stood there in the cold, uncomfortable. When he breathed, fog formed. The trees in the forests far away had turned brilliant shades of red and gold.

Where was Bala's teacher? Where was Aleksander?

Aleksander, the one necromancer who had not been purged, the one who had survived and remained a member of the wizard order thanks to heroic acts that had built trust, was not talented enough to undo Jerek's spell. To unmake magic, one had to peer into the heart of the one who made it. Only someone pure and innocent, like Bala, was up to such a task.

Aleksander had announced he would arrive at about this hour. Gastreel knew the way from his home in Palaskov was difficult. But could a wizard like Aleksander be overcome by common bandits or Forest Giants or ravenous bears? Could a man of Aleksander's mettle go back on his promises, or possess ulterior motives? No, of course not.

And yet, in the brief moments Gastreel had come into contact with Aleksander, there had always been something that bothered him. Something about his eyes, the way his hand twitched when he held his staff…

His reputation with the Council of the Twelve was impeccable, but to say he was an odd bird was an understatement.

"Where are you, Aleksander?" Gastreel said, so softly that Bala couldn't hear.

Bala was stretching and twitching. He yawned. "How much longer?" he asked. "How much longer?"

If only Gastreel knew.

And then he saw it, rolling down the road, a black coach pulled by four gray horses, rattling on its wheels. He knew that coach. Gastreel took in a deep breath, and his hands became clammy. He realized he was unready for this moment, unprepared for this meeting, which he himself had set in motion.

From the crags of Palaskov, Aleksander had come… Aleksander, the last necromancer allowed to practice his craft. From Palaskov, a land that many considered cursed, he had traveled for many days and weeks, all for the chance to meet his apprentice.

Poor Bala… what had Gastreel done to him?

The coach drew near. At last, the horses halted their stride. The door of the coach opened, and out stepped Aleksander.

The years had certainly worn on his already-strange appearance.

He was thin, emaciated, and yet so tall he had to duck under the doorway. He looked, almost, like one of his necromantic creations. His eyes were dark and beady, his face pale, featureless and plain. His staff was of dark black wood, and topped with red feathers. His robe was pitch black, the marker of his order.

And as he approached, his hand twitched annoyingly on his dark staff, his beady eyes darting this way and that, seeming to reflect a nervous soul.

"Gastreel," he said. "Archwizard. A pleasure."

He bowed just slightly, and Bala grabbed Gastreel's knee with both hands, and began to cry.

Oh, dear, Gastreel thought. When was the last time a toddling child was a grave petitioner, let alone apprenticed? And yet Gastreel did not blame Bala for his reaction. Gastreel would be afraid, too.

But Aleksander was not as he appeared. He was not an imminent danger to society. At least, that was what Gastreel and the wizards had long thought.

Aleksander stooped down, and he was still almost as tall as Gastreel. From the pockets of his robe, he drew out a piece of sugar candy, and offered it to the crying Bala.

His wailing turned to a weep, and then a sob. Out went his little hand; he took the candy, and popped it in his mouth.

"I know it is a hard day for you," Aleksander said. "For today, things change. You are but a child, but there is magic in you. I can sense it even now."

Bala's sobbing had ceased, but Gastreel had begun to worry about leaving him alone in Aleksander's presence.

"A lesson," Aleksander said. "A lesson is what I will give you.

"I will hone you into a master… and you shall be like me, or better."

Bala waddled out of the protection of Gastreel's leg. He reached out his little hands and cupped them. "More candy, please?" he said.

Chapter Three: The Look

Ever since fall arrived the days had not been kind to Ambrass. The trees were cloaked in splendor, the frost spread in white ripples over the grass, the clouds rolled in… and other things rolled in, too.

In the Dragonpaw Inn, there they were, a Mountain Folk family in the booth, rudely cursing and treating Ambrass like a serf. Showing no care for etiquette, the father of the family wore his sword at his side, indoors. The mother of the family shouted at her children while others, their cousins, sprinted around the Dragonpaw's great hall, playing tag.

They breached rules of etiquette and decorum, but at such a rate and with such brazenness that Ambrass had endured so much so fast she was standing in the corner with her broom in hand, watching the chaos and pandemonium unfold, resigning herself to it.

Glenda was staring at her in the corner. It seemed they had both given up.

But the Mountain Folk needed Ambrass and Glenda. The other towns of Gallia, with the exception of Southkirk, had refused to take them in. The Lord Eventide had demanded the Dragonpaw, as with all inns, put up the Mountain Folk families. They'd been paid a small sum, but it was not enough.

Ambrass tried to focus, tried to think about all that had transpired. She tried to regain control of her own emotions, and tried to remember that she was not just a serving girl but a taskmaster too. She was responsible for order in the Dragonpaw Inn, especially in its great hall. She was more than a serving girl; she was Glenda's right-hand woman.

"Enough!" she screamed, and the Mountain Folk cousins

stopped their running and the Mountain Folk family looked up from their bread and whey.

For just a moment, there was quiet, a few precious seconds without chaos and utter disorder. For one precious span of time, not long enough to utter Ambrass's name, there was peace. And then the cousins began to sprint around again, playing tag, and the family turned back to their food. The Mountain Folk mother began to shout again, and all was as it had been once more.

Ambrass had been defeated.

And Glenda was approaching from the corners of the room.

"It's not worth it," she said softly. "Let them have the run of the place. One day our city will be back to what it was."

But would it? These yokels wouldn't be returning to the High Country, to burnt-down homes and ravaged farmsteads. The rokahn wouldn't slink back down into their spawning holes. No, they'd form war bands and raid Gallia.

To believe these Mountain Folk, the war to come would be worse than the Wars of '41 and '42, when the very existence of Gallia was threatened. It would be worse than those wars, still remembered by the people of Galiope almost ten years later, wars in which Ambrass's former love fought, and in which her current love fought as well. As she watched the Mountain Folk run about, she could see no way out of this.

She stepped out of the way as another Mountain Folk family entered the great hall, and demanded bread and whey.

How could it end? How could it possibly end?

"Ambrass!" Glenda snapped. "Food…"

Food… She would have to get this family food. Bread and whey, the meagerest of rations, was served to these unwelcome guests. But bread and whey would allow them to survive, and at the rate the Galiopean government was putting them up, survival was all that was owed.

She remembered her plans for this night. There would be a

small, brief respite. Nocturne Rabaam would come to the Dragonpaw—Nocturne, her love—and whisk her away. Then, at dawn, the pandemonium would continue.

"Bread. Whey," she uttered under her breath. Bread and whey… the Mountain Folk were unwelcome, out food was what they would get.

~

Dusk was setting in. The daylight was waning. The Mountain Folk cousins had run off outside, and the families had eaten their dinners and retired to their rooms. The Dragonpaw's great hall was empty and silent when a shadow appeared at the door.

Nocturne, her love, was there, tall, pale as the moon, his hair as black as the space between the stars. She still found him unnerving sometimes, especially when he smiled and she saw his prodigious fangs. But the two unlikely lovers had been drawn together, and Ambrass could not escape him now.

"Nocturne," Ambrass said, and Nocturne beckoned her.

"Have a good time," Glenda said. Her eyes seemed to narrow. "Stay safe."

~

Hand in hand, they walked into City Square. The whole city knew of their love, Ambrass a human of barely twenty, Nocturne a vampire, aged eighty-nine but who appeared so young.

As dusk settled in gloaming colors, they turned down High Street, heading southward. She wondered what Nocturne had in mind so asked him.

Nocturne smiled. "I hear the Mountain Folk aren't so numerous in Market District."

Ambrass had heard such a thing many different times, said in different ways. "We can escape them in the Arcades." "They aren't everywhere in the Cathedral District." "Their stink isn't so common in Lonen Town." She was ready to be disappointed again. She had resigned herself to the fact that the city was overrun, that squalor would reign. Galiope was no longer theirs, it was different now, and what hope was there that things would ever return to normal? What hope was there that things would ever be the same?

"I doubt it," Ambrass said, "but I'm willing to try."

Beyond, to the south, High Street stretched, piercing the city north to south, from Middletown to Godsgate, straight, unbending. It appeared quiet, even eerie in the fading light.

~

In Market District, as she'd thought, the Mountain Folk were ever present, running amok through the streets, and what's worse, their crude tents had been erected in places that had heretofore been unfathomable, in the middle of the street or beside fountains.

"I was wrong," he said, "but we'll find a place. Quiet. Peaceful."

When Nocturne set his mind on something, it was impossible for him to cease his efforts until it was achieved. Giving up on something was alien to his mind, and Ambrass wasn't sure whether it was healthy.

He turned down a side street, and Ambrass, hand in hand, went with him.

The shops and homes that leaned over the streets, the innumerable market squares where merchants hawked their wares even this late in the day, began to fade away. Darkness was falling.

Up ahead was a great red gate. Ambrass gasped and stopped. For in the crowd she saw two eyes peering at her, two eyes she recognized.

It was some cousin she barely knew, and she thought his name was Ariak. He was dressed in dreary gypsy clothing, and wore a feather cap on his head. Ambrass hadn't realized they'd drawn so near to the gypsy enclave, Selwyn's Parish, a place she had taken great pains to avoid. She had not spoken to her brothers in months, since she'd left the gypsy world, and in so doing invited the enmity of her family. Many, if not most of her relatives would never forgive her.

Her cousin's eyes hardened, lighting with anger. Ambrass let go of Nocturne's hand, and felt herself go white.

"What is it?" Nocturne said. "Are you all right?"

"I… *ehrm*… let's leave," Ambrass said. "The other way, please… to your house, maybe."

"Already?" Nocturne said.

"Yes."

~

In Lonen Town there were no Mountain Folk. The Lord Eventide had not yet imposed on private homeowners. Nor was there any way her cousins or distant relations or gypsy former friends who now scorned her could see her, or know what she was doing.

Nocturne poured her a glass of wine. It sparkled in the glass.

"What happened?" he said. "Why did you become so afraid?"

"My old life," Ambrass answered. "I thought I had escaped it. But it seems like I can't escape it. Maybe escaping it was always impossible."

"Silly talk," Nocturne said. He poured himself a glass, the remainder of the bottle. "You are a free Galiopean now."

"My cousin's eyes… I saw him in the crowd. He looked so angry."

"I will protect you," Nocturne said.

And for the first time since Ambrass saw her cousin, she felt herself relax.

~

She left Nocturne's house at dawn. The sun was rising and light was just beginning to spread. She left, convinced that try as she might, she could not avoid her past. Her cousin had seen her hand in hand with a *kallowen*, a non-gypsy, and what's more a vampire. Her cousin had no love for her and his lips were loose. The rumor would spread to her brothers and beyond.

Why had she been born into that life?

Why couldn't she escape it?

Chapter Four:
To Be A Wizard

As the morning sun arose, Bala followed the scary wizard-man outside the city, through the great open gate.

The grass was wafting in the wind, and Bala did not know what to expect, but ever since he had begun learning magic, like Mr. Gastreel asked him to, he had been afraid. Meeting his teacher had made things worse.

Mr. Aleksander was taller than anyone he had ever seen, and he was so thin Bala could see his cheekbones. He had a strange smell, like some foul oil or rancid mixture. The red feathers on his staff looked like no bird's feathers Bala had ever seen.

But this was what Mr. Gastreel wanted. Mr. Gastreel said it was very important. So he followed after Aleksander, down the road called the Royal Road, in view of the farms and pastures.

Aleksander turned, and down another road they walked until they reached an iron fence with an open gate, and beyond it a cemetery—rows and rows of gravestones, miniature mausoleums, and large stone tombs.

Bala didn't want to go in. But Aleksander was walking inside. He felt like crying, but he tried to hold in all his feelings. Mr. Gastreel said it was very important...

He walked on, through the open gate, and when he had walked a while and they were near the center of the cemetery, Aleksander stopped, and turned to face him.

"Bala," he said, "what is this place?"

"A graveyard," Bala answered.

"What is its purpose?" Aleksander said.

Bala's fear was rising. His eyes were watering. He wanted to be home with Dada Reev, or even his first dada, Nocturne. But he couldn't, and he had begun to realize it.

And so he tried to say, in as many words, what he knew to be true. "A place where dead people live," Bala answered.

"Death," Aleksander said. "A necromancer cannot truly reverse death. A necromancer can only give motion to flesh and bones, to imbue it with some semblance of raw intelligence. And a skeleton that walks or a ghost that howls... a necromancer cannot always control his creation."

Bala's lip was trembling. He feared he was about to lose control. He shut his eyes. A tear dripped down, but he remained calm. He wouldn't weep, he wouldn't sob. He would remain as he had been.

"What do you feel, Bala, when you stand here?" Aleksander said.

"I feel," Bala said. "I feel..."

The wind was gently blowing. The sounds of the city were in the distance. But something else was rising up, a feeling, cold air, goose-prickles formed on his skin—and a taste, sweet yet sickly...

"I can't describe it," Bala said.

"Open your eyes," Aleksander said.

Bala opened them and twin nimbuses of purple light were glowing around Aleksander's hands.

"Magic is what you felt," Aleksander said. "You see what lies about my hands? This is my craft. This, around me, is raw energy to give motion to dead bones, to give animation to dead flesh, to strike the healthy with weakness and the undead with strength."

The nimbuses of light faded to nothing, but the icy feeling lingered. Goose-prickles had formed anew all over Bala's hands and legs.

"To give motion to dead bones, to imbue a body with rigor— that is what most necromancers do. But there is a different reason why you are here, Bala. For necromancers can also do something far worse.

"Many years ago, a man of our disposition wandered the earth.

With the assistance of rokahn and wicked humans, he stole six iron masks from the elves' safekeeping. The iron masks belonged to the Servants of Seymus, fiends of the ancient world. By the spell he cast on the masks, he returned the Servants to bodies, not bodies like yours or mine, but bodies of a kind.

"Those Servants, at a fraction of their former strength, were terrible foes. They were destroyed by a friend of yours, Reev Nax. But the spell of the necromancer Jerek lingers. And you must undo it."

"Why me?" Bala's lip was trembling again. His eyes were watering. He wanted to bawl. "Why can't you do it, Mr. Aleksander?"

Aleksander stooped down to one knee and took Bala's hand in his. "Bala," he said, "do not be afraid. I am your teacher… I mean you no harm."

"Why can't you do it?" Bala said. "Why does it have to be me?"

"I am old," he said. "I am strong in the ways of magic. I cannot safely stare into the abyss… but you can."

Bala began to sob. He could control himself no longer.

"There, there, Bala," Aleksander said, patting Bala on the back. "It is all right. One step at a time, and at the pace you choose. Shall I take you back to the Dragonpaw Inn? Have we done enough for today?"

Bala bit his lip. His teeth had lately felt sore. He stepped back and wiped his eyes. He straightened his back. He took a deep breath.

"No," he said. "I will be a wizard, like you or Gastreel. Teach me, Mr. Aleksander. Teach me magic."

Aleksander stood up. He was like a giant shadow. His face again became grim.

"That is what I like to hear," he said. "You will be a wizard, Bala Rabaam, far sooner than you know."

Chapter Five:
The Troubled Vale

Amid the arches and austere stone architecture of the Galiope Town Hall, the Council of Brightleaf 1152 was meeting for the tenth time in as many days.

Gastreel, as archwizard, was considered a stakeholder in city affairs, though the Tower of Pythor, the nation-state he presided over—the smallest in the known world—was considered self-governing. The late morning light was shining, just barely, through the high windows. The faces of the council, as always, were grim.

The Lord Eventide, the mayor of Galiope who had become a despised figure for his unpopular but, in Gastreel's mind, necessary decisions, stood directly across the room. His keen eyes gleamed as the Rector of St. Sigmund's, Bartholem, delivered the invocation.

"Alabaster, gods in heaven, give us wisdom in our words and decisions, patience in our hearts, and concord with each other. So let it be."

"So let it be," the members of the council, city masters and aldermen, said in unison, and Gastreel followed, a moment late.

The Lord Eventide began speaking. "We have begun a mustering in preparation for the expected war," he said. "We have asked the towns of Gallia to provide what men they can."

But ten thousand soldiers, young men from all across Gallia, had already been sent to fight a war against a human nation, the Empire, and so the strength of those ten thousand had been spent.

"I will not try to put any of this lightly," the Lord Eventide continued. "Reports I've heard are alarming… Rokahn in numbers that are unheard of. Warbands forming in the thousands. But the walls of Galiope are strong. They are being reinforced by the Mountain Folk who've come here will fight with us as a condition of our hospitality."

The Lady Llewyn of Leyshaw began to speak in her cutting tone. "Not all of us can afford to spare our young men. Our towns are important, and they are less fortified than Galiope. Galiope is the chief town of the league, our heart, but the men and women of Leyshaw are no less important than you."

"No one has said otherwise," the Lord Eventide said. "Certainly not me."

The tension in the room seemed to grow. Everyone was on edge, and Gastreel knew it. A disaster was coming after the spring thaw, when the rokahn came to the lowlands—the only question was how great a calamity it would be, and if it would spell the end of the humans of Gallia forever.

"I have brought with us a dear public servant," the Lord Eventide said. "Niall has returned from the mountains. He shall give us a report... Niall?"

A young man stepped forward with bright gold hair and brilliant eyes, dressed in a leather tunic and rough leggings. He was thin and muscular, and had the look of a warrior. He bowed, gazed around the room, then faced the Lord Eventide.

"My liege," Niall began, "honored members of the council... aldermen and alderwomen representing the various towns of Gallia... I rode, with a contingent of warriors, as swiftly as I was able, to the fortress which is in the Valley of Aíl. There, the hold-lord told me what he knew.

"The towns of the Valley of Aíl have all been evacuated. A small fraction of people have foolishly refused to leave, but thankfully, they are in the minority. The hold-lord is preparing to leave with his men in a few days.

"But almost half the people of the High Country live in a place called the Vale of Ahorne. The hold-lord there is a man named Maerrick. Some are saying that he is refusing to let his people escape. No Mountain Folk family has been seen leaving the Vale of

Ahorne, even as conditions rapidly deteriorate, and the time is coming when the way down will be snowbound. If the rumors are to be believed, the hold-lord Maerrick is endangering the people he is entrusted to protect—committing murder, in my opinion—and for what?"

It was grim tidings. Gastreel could not believe what he was hearing. He knew of the Vale of Ahorne, a deep network of valleys in view of a peak called the Matinberg. It was from the Vale of Ahorne that the family of Simeon Nax, Reev's father, was said to originate, he remembered.

"How can a hold-lord keep all his people from fleeing?" Gastreel said. "The Mountain Folk have strict codes of honor and liegeship, but the danger—it must be apparent. The High Country is being overrun."

"I think you underestimate, Lord Gastreel, just how much the code of honor means to the Mountain Folk," Niall replied. "The word of their hold-lord will keep them bound. The people of the Vale of Ahorne will remain in place."

Such a strict, almost religious view of honor was unthinkable to Gastreel, but the danger was apparent.

"This council has sent him letters," Lord Eventide said. "Letters demanding he begin evacuations. Strict orders… it is the law! He must evacuate his people from the High Country."

"Law, perhaps," Niall said, "but he has refused to obey it. Or so it seems.

"The Mountain Folk are mostly illiterate. Maerrick, I suppose, would have a scribe. Perhaps he does not take much stock in a letter from the council, even one sealed with the city's seal."

"We must send an emissary…" The Lord Eventide's eyes glinted. "An emissary demanding at penalty of death that he begin evacuations."

"If he would not obey a letter," Gastreel said, "would he obey a man like Niall, or myself?"

"A bond of blood," the Lord Eventide said. "My son."

And suddenly Gastreel noticed another face among the dozens of lecterns, young, hale, with his father's eyes and his mother's red hair, dressed in a black tunic and long trousers… the son of the Lord Eventide and the Lady Fiona, a city master and a warrior, Ethelbert. He was twenty years old, known for his bravery and sense of honor.

"I will go," Ethelbert said, a bright face among the darkness of the town hall chambers. "I will go, if this council will have me go."

It was apparent to everyone in the council that time was short. The snows would begin in a matter of weeks, the roads become impassable, and no one could leave the mountains even if Maerrick had a change of heart.

"A bond of blood…" Niall said. "That may work better. He will heed the voice of Lord Eventide, or his son… or else he is a madman and a traitor."

"If you will do it," Eventide said, "I propose that this council agrees."

Gastreel had a bad feeling, but he had to choose which battles to fight and which to abandon. What other option did they have? What else was left to try? Many thousands of souls lived in the Vale of Ahorne, and whether the word of Maerrick or something else prevented them from escaping, they were in grave danger.

No one spoke an objection in the council; the pronouncement had become law.

"I will saddle up," Ethelbert said. "I will depart tonight."

"Gods be with you," said Bartholem, Rector of St. Sigmund's Cathedral. "So let it be."

"So let it be," the council repeated, and this time Gastreel joined with them, on time.

Chapter Six:
Telantaren

Telantari, what was *telantari*?

Reev and Wrinn were in the main hall of the Dragonpaw Inn, and thanks to the city's rationing, feasting on meager morsels of bread and butter.

"Telantari," Reev said. "What does it mean?"

Wrinn looked at him askance. A foamy mug of beer was in front of him, and in front of Reev a cup of cold water. *"Adari.* Helper. I put no stock in it.

"Do you think that man was anything except a crook? He probably mastered throwing that stone at the right letter, and making words. He's an illusionist, nothing more."

"But didn't you see what happened?" Reev said. "The way the stone moved by itself, to 'T,' to 'E,' to 'L'?"

The Mountain Folk in the main hall were loud, but they had become background noise. They smelled of dirt and sweat, but Glenda had begun pleading with them to bathe, and so one by one the smell had begun to lessen.

"Telantari," Wrinn said. "Elvish, clearly. Pity I don't know. Maybe we should ask Gastreel."

But then Reev remembered something, how sometime in the last year Gastreel had procured the old prophecies, dusty copies created not long after the prophecies' origination. One of the prophecies declared that the Sage, the Hand of the Gods, the one— it was said—who would defeat Seymus, would be *telantari*. Gastreel had read the word, and been as baffled as Reev.

"Gastreel wouldn't know," Reev said. "Some things are too obscure. I doubt it's even in a lexicon."

"So how would we find out something," Wrinn began, "that no

one knows, that no one remembers? Sorry to say it, Mr. Reev, but I think the way that stone moved was probably an illusion too. Maybe there were secret gears and wheels underneath the shopkeeper's table. It makes more sense than anything else."

But it didn't… *telantari* was an obscure word, and how would the shopkeeper know anything about Reev, or about the old prophecies?

Not long ago, Reev and Gastreel had ventured to a great library, a library of impossible size, holding the knowledge of the ages. If Gastreel hadn't been able to find what *telantari* was among so many scrolls and books and shelves, there was little hope of Reev ever discovering its definition.

From the corners of the room, Glenda approached, dabbing her hand in a cloth. "How are you two enduring all this?"

"We're doing well, Miss Glenda," Wrinn answered.

"So some of us are," Glenda said.

The world at large seemed to have fallen apart. The chaos and war of the wider world, which Reev had heard in rumor, had at last come to Gallia. And in the town of Galiope, overrun with refugees, he no longer felt secure or safe.

"I hope you're finding some time to yourself," Glenda said.

"We are," Wrinn said. "We're trying to uncover a puzzle."

"A puzzle?"

"*Telantari*," Wrinn said. "What is the meaning of *telantari*?"

Glenda seemed to stiffen. Amid the pandemonium of the great hall, time seemed to stop, and there was only Reev, and Wrinn, and Glenda's bright green eyes.

"*Telantari,*" she said. "Hmmm…"

~

Reev had never been in Glenda's room before. It was ornately decorated, and the walls were painted bright pink. Her bed was lined with silken red sheets with a mountain of pillows in the back. There were bookcases and potted flowers growing in the windowsill. There was a great wardrobe, a medicine cabinet, a table with chairs, and what looked like a war game, with miniature soldiers aligned across a checkered board. It was clearly the best room in the house, and it was tucked away down a staircase at the end of the main corridor, so well hidden it was difficult to notice.

"Telantari," Glenda said, "a riddle. I like riddles."

Reev wasn't sure if it was a riddle, but at the sound of the word Glenda's entire demeanor had changed, and she had invited Reev and Wrinn into her private chambers, into this space that was rarely seen.

Glenda walked up to her bookshelf and picked out a codex, on whose spine was written *Elvish Grammar*.

She sat down on her bed and let the codex fall open. Paging through the book, she continued to say, *"Telantari. Telantari...* a riddle."

Reev and Wrinn sat down by her feet.

"According to what I remember..." Glenda began. "Yes, that's right—" her index finger was pointing to an entry—"*-ari*, it says, the root coming from the *-as* declension. A *telantari*, by that logic, is a person of Telantas, or by Gallian convention, Telantis."

"What is Telantis?" Reev asked.

It was clear that no one in the room knew.

But a slight curl came to Glenda's lips. Her eyes became dead serious. She said, "A person of Telantis. By Gallian grammar, a Telantine.

"And I recall someone else who identified himself as a Telantine... Fortunato."

"Fortunato?" Reev said, utterly confused. "What does he have to do with all this?"

"When you said the word *telantari* I remembered," Glenda said, "a story he told me, so long ago I can hardly remember the details.

Telantari sounds an awful lot like Telantine. And Fortunato said his mother called him a 'Telantine.' Perhaps… you should go find him. Talk to him."

"Maybe," Reev said. But he realized in that moment he hadn't seen Fortunato in a long while, in many days, maybe weeks.

Still, that seemed as good an idea as any, though solving this problem didn't seem quite so imperative now that refugees were pouring into the city, and in the world at large, war drums were beating in every direction.

"Wrinn," Reev said. "You know the way to Fortunato's place. Will you take me there?"

"Of course," Wrinn answered.

Adari. Helper. Maybe that casting-stone had been right.

~

They reached his rented room hours later. A rain was falling over the city as they ascended the steps, and a fork of lightning blazed in the distance. The wind was picking up speed.

Reev knocked, though he was convinced now, more than ever, that spending his time on this futile endeavor as the city and the world about him fell apart was likely ill-advised.

He knocked again—and there was no answer.

"Wrinn," Reev said. "You are close to Fortunato. When did you see him last?"

"Ten days ago," Wrinn answered. "I came by once before after that. He didn't answer then, either."

Reev touched the doorknob and twisted lightly. The door fell open, unlocked.

And beyond, Fortunato's upper room had been cleared. The chairs and tables, the ornamentation as spare as it was, were gone.

"Fortunato?" Reev said. "Where are you?"

Chapter Seven:
Charged

At dawn, like before, Ambrass was returning from Nocturne's house. She was walking unsteadily in her shoes, as the last night's rain sparkled on the cobblestone. The stately homes lining High Street surrounded her as she crossed the Bridge-O'er-Galios into Middletown.

She was walking purposefully, under the sky, wondering what she was doing with the entirety of her life, wondering indeed where her future lay, the town pariah, locked in a deadly embrace with Galiope's most notorious man, unwed yet unable to break from his spell. Her cousin's eyes reminded her that she was a gypsy, yet. She had not truly shed her identity in view of her family, in view of the gypsies of Selwyn's Parish.

And as she walked, faces in the crowd were staring at her, judging eyes, knowing of her ill repute. But she ignored them, she ignored those faces. And as she walked, for some strange moment she thought of Fortunato, her former love.

Then the Dragonpaw Inn appeared, the Dragonpaw with its signature sign: All Races Welcome.

And Ambrass, though she knew not her future, or her direction, though the days seemed to blend all into one and she could only face the sunrise and sunset on their own terms, passed through the double doors and resolved herself to a day of hard work cooking, cleaning…

~

But in the light of dawn, Glenda, the innkeeper, her overseer, seemed changed. She was holding something.

"Ambrass," she said. "A letter arrived for you last night. A young man was here… asking for you."

But she had been in Lonen Town, with Nocturne.

She took the letter in her hands, and when she saw the seal she almost fainted.

The insignia was in the sign of a wolf. Not just a wolf but a stylized one—the very image of the Vidowa, the street patrols, the self-proclaimed judges and juries of the gypsies, a secret police force that operated thanks to the cowardice of the Gallian government.

Panic consumed her as she laid her eyes on the seal, pure panic and torment. Why were the Lord Eventide and his privy council such cowards? Why did they refuse to enforce Gallian law and allow another law to exist side-by-side?

She broke the seal, aghast, and the folded letter came undone. Black ink—severe in handwriting. Words:

Two charges of treason against the gypsy people. The punishment: Death. How do you plead?

Treason… against her people. One for Fortunato, who no longer loved her. Another Nocturne—and that was that.

Her door in the Dragonpaw had locks. Her window was airtight. If she remained a shut-in, the Vidowa wouldn't snatch her. They wouldn't be able to get their hands on her. If she remained indoors at all times, she would be safe.

~

At night the rain started again, and there was thunder in the distance. In her bedroom was a windowsill garden of Grayman's beard, a prayer book by her bedside table open to a request of safety. Anew, she began to dread the Vidowa.

The door to her room opened and Glenda was there. Lightning

flashed and bathed her face briefly in blue light. And Ambrass saw to her alarm that Glenda, for the first time Ambrass had seen, was carrying a weapon in her hands—a dagger.

"What is this?" Ambrass said.

"A weapon," Glenda replied. "And I know how to use it. I read the letter. I'll protect you as best I can."

But the sight of her overseer carrying a weapon of war did nothing to soothe her.

"I've secured most entryways," Glenda said. "Maybe you had best not go in or out. At least, keep a watchful eye when you leave. No more meetings with Nocturne."

No more…

And the Vidowa had won. No more meetings with Nocturne, no more lackadaisical walks throughout the city. It seemed wise, but Ambrass wasn't sure if it was possible. She thought of him even now, and felt tears forming in her eyes for lack of him, for the situation she had fallen into, for the cowardice of the Gallian government, for the nest of vipers that now sought her as their prey.

Vidowa… a curse on them. She would overcome them. She was a free woman, and nothing less.

Chapter Eight:
A Memory of Darkness

"Power. Control. Focus." The voice of Aleksander was not comforting, but Bala was doing his best, for the sake of Mr. Gastreel, for the sake of the mission he had said was important.

Masks… phantoms. "Fiends." An "ancient world." None of it made sense to Bala, but he had tried not to cry, tried not to be overcome with emotion. He was on his best behavior, and if Dada could see him now, he would be proud.

On a high hill the wind kissed his cheek. His eyes were shut. The air was cold, but the ash-gray robe he wore was keeping him warm, and his tufts of hair protected his ears.

"Power. Control. Focus." Aleksander was nearby, and Bala could smell the strange oils and offensive perfumes that wafted from his body.

"Raise your hands, little Bala," Aleksander said. "Clench them."

He raised them, and balled them into fists.

"Power. Control. Focus," Aleksander said. "Do you feel the power within? Waiting to be released? What do you sense? What do you think is happening?"

Bala was trying not to stir, trying—as Aleksander had said—to clear his mind from all distractions. As he balled his fists, he did indeed sense something, the strange airy feeling of magic within and all around him. But the magic he felt on this hill had a lingering aspect.

Bala saw two terrible dark eyes, black and featureless as a wolf's, empty, evil—as vile as the abyss, devoid of light or life or love.

He screamed, and opened his eyes, for he could endure it no more.

The day was sunny and bright, and through a thin veil of fog,

Bala could see the snowcapped purple peaks of the Dragonteeth Mountains in the distance.

"I sensed something evil," said Bala. He was proud of himself for not crying again. He could now endure a lot without so much as a sob, without so much as a tear streaking down his cheek.

"Jerek's feet once walked on this hill," said Aleksander. "In fact, it was here that the ceremony of induction took place, where he was first admitted to the wizard order. Jerek is the one who imbued those six masks with false life. On this hill, here, he went from apprentice to full wizard. And do you know who his master was? Gastreel."

"What do you mean?" Bala said. The pressures, the troubles, they were conspiring to overwhelm him with emotion, but he tried to gain control of himself, tried to remember why he was here, and who he was doing this for.

"Jerek was Gastreel's apprentice for a short while," said Aleksander. "And yet Jerek disguised his true nature.

"Darkness was brewing in that time. There was war and tumult, like today but on a lesser note. There were rokahn in the mountains—not as many as now. There were conspiracies, assassinations. The Lord Mayor of Galiope was killed on the street, in cold blood."

That did it. Bala's eyes were watering. His lips were trembling. He was about to lose control.

"Jerek was nursing a delusion that he was the long-prophesied Dark One's Hand. He was nursing a delusion that he was the Dark One's deputy in the mortal world. And that delusion inspired him to act on his own, to make his delusion true by his own hand. As he gained power and prestige in the wizard order, he began to make journeys to the mountains."

Aleksander motioned to the jagged snowcapped peaks.

"The rokahn welcomed his entreaties, and for that reason, his delusion grew stronger. He became convinced what he thought about himself was true. And when he was strong in the ways of magic, advanced in the hierarchy of wizardry, he struck… with his rokahn allies, and with his followers, he stormed the elven keep of Vadras Henion in the Shield Mountains. He stole the iron masks, and when he had taken them back to Gallia he cast a spell."

Bala bit his lip. He didn't want to do this anymore. He didn't want to be a wizard anymore. No, he did not. He didn't want to be anything other than a child, anything other than the son of Nocturne and Mama.

"Jerek is gone now," Aleksander said. "His delusion was proven false. Even the spell he cast was for naught. But we must make sure it is for naught. That is up to you, Bala Rabaam."

Why me, he had said more times than he could count. Why me, he had said, but it didn't matter, because it was him… all this had been placed on his shoulders, on him, Bala Rabaam, who wanted nothing more than to tag along with Reev and Wrinn, maybe kick a ball, have some bread to eat and some milk to drink.

"Close your eyes," Aleksander said. "Close your eyes. Focus. Try to summon magic from deep within."

Bala shut his eyes and lifted his hands. He ignored the stain of Jerek's presence.

A gentle wind was blowing, cold on its face, and for some reason as he stood there, he thought of the mountain snows, of great white flakes drifting through the air. He thought he heard a song, rising above the wind.

He tapped into the magic within him, tried again to bring it outwards. He gritted his teeth; he growled, trying to summon within himself the strength—power within he could sense innately, but his body or his mind or some defect inside him refused to bring into the material realm.

"Patience," said Aleksander. "Patience. You will be a wizard, Bala, far sooner than you know."

Chapter Nine:
Whispers of War

The Council of Brightleaf 1152 continued, convening daily in the shadows of the Gallian town hall.

Gastreel was growing tired, standing behind his stone lectern, but he knew the problems in the Gallian League had never been so severe, the threat never so ominous. The number of rokahn, reliably reported by trusted eyewitnesses, was nothing less than cataclysmic, and he wondered if this disastrous event, these creatures innumerable, portended some far greater danger looming in the future.

The faces in the Gallian town hall were ashen. The city masters and the great dames had attended not at all to their appearance, no rich gowns, no cosmetics of the eye or lip—the Gallian nobility, which loved a party and an ostentatious display of good breeding, was perfectly aware of the grave conflict brewing, the danger not just to their own lives, but the survival of Gallia itself.

Gallia had survived in many forms throughout millennia, a kingdom and now a league, and now the wise, those who knew what was happening, had begun to fear the destruction of an entire people.

"Have you heard from Ethelbert?" said the Lord Anglesey of Southkirk. Fierce-eyed and fierce-featured was he, dressed in a plain black tunic, his brown hair neatly combed. "He said he would send back a message when he arrived…"

The Lord Eventide, the mayor of Galiope, chancellor of the league and Ethelbert's father, had put on a solemn face. If he had any fears about his son, he would not show them—he knew not to show them.

"I am certain he is capable," the Lord Eventide said. "He

brought with him a hundred men-at-arms. The message is probably on its way right now."

Traveling lightly, in a small group, it was possible to make the journey to the High Country in two days or fewer, if one left at dawn and rode until the night.

Three days had passed since Ethelbert departed. And with the dangers of the rokahn, the refugees fleeing the Valley of Aíl, the treacherous roads that were difficult even in a time of peace, there were many reasons Ethelbert could be delayed. Snows were not uncommon, and each day Maerrick, the hold-lord of the Vale of Ahorne, refused to let his people depart, he was trying fate. The roads could be snowbound early, the people trapped—helpless prey for the rokahn.

"And if the hold-lord refuses?" said Lord Alden, a city master with red hair and grayish eyes, Eventide's right-hand man.

"He will not refuse the chancellor's son," announced Eventide. "To do so would be treason."

Eventide's wife, Fiona, the first lady of Galiope, had not been seen in these council halls since the first meeting many days ago. Of late, she had tried to make a show of strength, visible displays of grit and courage, feeding the Mountain Folk refugees on street corners, exaggerated exhibitions of kindness to make an example. She was probably putting on such a show right now.

And yet something else was on Gastreel's mind. Something lingered on the surface… a mission these bright faces in the Council of Brightleaf 1152 seemed to have totally forgotten. "And the Empire…"

"What of it?" said Eventide. He did not seem to want to discuss the topic.

Ten thousand men had been sent to fight the Empire, the most powerful nation in the world… an intervention in the lands of the west. The reckless decision had been bothering Gastreel ever since it occurred, and now, after this new terrible crisis had been foisted upon them, it seemed to have been forgotten.

"We must remember that we have declared war," Gastreel said.

"One crisis at a time," the Lord Alden said dully. "If some calamity had befallen our men, we would know it. The Empire has conquered savage men of the forests and of the desert… they have never faced before the full strength of the North."

And yet Gastreel had a feeling the Lord Alden was wrong. He looked into Alden's eyes, and for a moment, thought he saw guile.

The kingdoms of the west had been joined with Gallia in a show of strength against the Empire… and the day after those ten thousand young men departed Galiope, the following morning, this crisis had erupted. The first of the refugees began arriving, the Council of Brightleaf 1152 had been declared, and Gastreel had not gotten a wit of sleep. All his energies had been focused on this, and presiding over the wizards had become the least focus of his work.

He realized he had not seen his pupil, Reev Nax, since the council was declared. But he trusted Reev would be kept safe, if not by his friend Wrinn, then by Glenda the innkeeper.

"Gastreel Osiris," said Eventide, "are the wizards prepared for war?"

"They have all been made aware of the situation," Gastreel said. "If they do not love the city, they love the tower. They will defend Galiope, in one measure or another."

For a while, silence returned to the Galiope Town Hall. Then the Lady Llewyn of Leyshaw spoke. "What shall we do if we do not hear from Ethelbert in a manner of days?" Her voice as always was cutting, and drained the energy and spirit from the room.

Eventide's steely resolve seemed to crack just a bit.

It was his son they were speaking of—his and Fiona's—not just an emissary sent from Galiope. To Eventide, he was more than an ambassador.

"We will hear from him," he said. "I know it. His messenger is probably on the way right now."

This time, in the second telling, he did not sound so sure.

39

Chapter Ten:
In Pursuit

The sun was shining through a mix of white clouds, Reev and Wrinn were in Market District with loaves of sweetbread, and for a moment it seemed—despite the Mountain Folk everywhere—that there remained a little bit of enjoyment in life.

If they searched for it.

Telantari—Reev's interest in uncovering the meaning of the word had waned. But as he and Wrinn stood in City Square, eating sweetbread in the morning light, a thought returned to him: Fortunato's rented room, completely empty.

Fortunato had been with Reev ever since Reev left his hometown of Norwood. And as he finished off the sweetbread and licked his fingers, he had a gnawing feeling. "Fortunato's room was empty... you don't think he's left, do you?"

Wrinn's mind seemed to be in another place altogether, carefree and thinking of nothing beside the honey-baked, sugar-covered morsel he was devouring. But after he had eaten the remainder of the sweetbread, a new look appeared in his eyes: concern.

"You know," he said, "now that I think of it... it is rather odd. Shall we go back and see if he's there, one last time?"

~

They knocked on the door of the rented room, and waited in the cold morning, shivering. Reev tried the knob, and this time it was locked—a sign, perhaps, of hope.

Behind the door, someone began to fiddle with the locks, and the door opened.

"Fortu—" Reev began, but swallowed the word.

It was a woman there, an elf with dark brown hair. Behind her in the distance stood a young man, and a gaggle of children ran around the room. The furniture had been replaced with tables and beds and chairs, fitting for a family.

"I'm sorry," Reev said. "I was looking for Fortunato—"

"No one by that name lives here," the woman said, and she slammed the door in Reev's face.

Now worry had been planted in Reev—the thought of Fortunato leaving was a savage blow.

"Maybe he's living somewhere else, now," Wrinn said.

But Reev had his doubts.

"I can think of someone who might know," Wrinn continued.

~

The Green Girdle was a tavern that, according to Wrinn, Fortunato loved to frequent.

In the morning, its booths and barstools were empty, and the barkeep, a woman with curly red hair, seemed to want nothing to do with them.

"Gertha," Wrinn said, and when the barkeep turned, she was looking at them with almost a snarl.

There were dark circles under her eyes—a late night, perhaps.

But she and Wrinn, it appeared, were on a first name basis.

"It's about Fortunato—have you seen him?"

Gertha put down the rag she was carrying, but which it seemed she wasn't using. Her snarl had become a scowl. "Last night he was here… never seen him in such a state," she said "I had to call the town watch on him."

"What happened?" Wrinn asked.

"He was despondent," Gertha began. "Beside himself. Kept talking about someone named 'Ambrass.' "

Fortunato had departed his rented room and cleared it out. And

Reev knew that Ambrass and Fortunato had once been enamored with each other; but now Ambrass was often seen in the presence of Nocturne Rabaam.

So where had he gone after his incident with the night's watch? And where was he living now?

"Do you know where I can find him?" Wrinn asked.

"No idea," Gertha answered, "but he kept saying he hated living here… hated Galiope. I told him he should leave."

But would he leave? Would he abandon Reev, Wrinn, Gastreel? Did Ambrass have such power over him?

"Well, you shouldn't have said that, Gertha," Wrinn snapped.

The snarl returned.

"Now I've got to find him before he makes a decision he'll regret."

~

The city prison had no record of Fortunato. His drunken incident had apparently not resulted in so much as a lashing.

They asked Glenda where he could be, to no avail. Then, from the morning to the afternoon, they searched his favorite spots, from garden parks to the lowliest tavern.

But there was no sign, no sign at all. And a feeling grew in Reev that he would never see Fortunato of Ríva again.

Chapter Eleven: Warned

"It's past noon," said the Lady Llewyn of Leyshaw, in the dark of the Gallian town hall. "Shall we take a rest?"

"A rest," Eventide said. "We are all hungry. I suppose we have made all the decisions that can be made today. All in our power, all our deliberations, the full force of our arms, careful planning… the rest is in the hands of the gods. I move we adjourn this day's meeting."

The faces in the Galiopean town hall were for the most part weary. They had spent hours deducing how much food was stored in the granaries, and how many mouths would have to be fed, how many swords and axes and suits of armor had been forged and how many young men were available to wield them. They had gone over their best estimates of when the rokahn warbands would form and when they would descend into the lowlands for hunger.

They were tired, annoyed, at each other's throats. But Gastreel knew of one thing the Council of Brightleaf 1152 had not discussed in depth today.

"I object," Gastreel said.

There was a sigh, scattered hisses, the Lady Llewyn's cheekbones turned a shade of pink.

"One matter we haven't discussed," he said. "A matter I fear will strike us in the back if we do not make preparations."

"And what is that, Lord Gastreel?" said Eventide, Mayor of Galiope, in almost a sneer.

"The Empire," Gastreel said, "that we have declared war on."

Lady Llewyn looked like she was about to pick up her notes and cast them at Gastreel. Eventide rolled his eyes. Sneers and jeers greeted Gastreel, but he was confident in the wisdom of his words.

"Rokahn are one thing," Gastreel said. "They are by their nature stronger than humans, and taller. But the weapons they wield are crude and inferior to ours.

"We have declared war on the Empire. I pray that somehow, we gain our victory. I pray that somehow the joined forces of the Northern World can repel our foe. But what if they do not?

"One crisis at a time, we say. But we are ignoring what I think is a much greater threat. Thousands of legionaries, steel-forged swords and glossy breastplates, machinery and ballistae and catapults whose accuracy we cannot replicate. What will we do if the Empire comes to our doorstep?"

"They will not," said Eventide. "I guarantee it."

But a guarantee from Eventide was not worth much. Eventide had been wrong in so many matters before. There was no guarantee of anything in a time such as this, no guarantee of success, only a likelihood of failure.

"The war is far from here," said Lord Alden, red-haired and gray-eyed, Eventide's right-hand man. "The war in the west, if it comes to our doorstep, will take a long while to spread… enough time to beat back the rokahn threat and take control. The Imperials are nowhere near Gallia. And if by chance they do stray here, the Almanians have agreed to protect us."

But Gastreel did not trust the Grand Duke of Almania to honor his oath. The Almanians were warlike and strong, more numerous than the Gallians, and the entirety of their land was fortified. They had made a promise, but they had never been Gallia's true friend, never ones to call on in Gallia's times of need.

The war was far… and precious little news of the west reached Galiope. But in a sense, Lord Alden was right. The Empire was distracted, fighting far away. Gallia had announced itself as the Empire's enemy, but before total war crossed the river Galios, first the Kingdom of Zarubain would have to be defeated, and Ardogne. Only then would the peoples of Gallia face the full force of the

Empire's might. Only when the war in the west was lost would the war go east.

"Time," Gastreel said. "Precious time. Perhaps an entreaty to the Duke of Almania could be made… a coordination, a mustering of our troops."

"One crisis at a time," said Eventide. "Right now, Lord Gastreel, we could face our own extinction.

"And all that can be said has been said this day. The fifteenth of Brightleaf, 1152, has produced all the fruit that it can. Again, I move to dismiss."

And Gastreel did not raise an objection. There was a limit to what he was willing to do, a limit to his appetite for stroking the hornet's nest. The matter was not resolved to his satisfaction, but they in the council refused to take it seriously.

The war in the west was far, but unless by some miracle Gallia and the Northern World prevailed, it would one day come near.

~

From the halls of the Galiopean town hall out through the great brazen double doors, Gastreel found himself in the narrow, crowded streets and ancient buildings of Middletown. Tents had been erected just outside Town Hall's steps, dozens of tents where Mountain Folk families slept. It was a hazard to the public health, a great hazard as well for pedestrians to walk. But if all inns in the city were packed to capacity with Mountain Folk, still there would not be enough room. The tents were illegal, they were unsightly, but the town watch would not destroy them or arrest those who erected them.

It was a piteous sight, but nothing could be done about it.

The council and thinking about the council had consumed Gastreel's every thought since the month of Brightleaf began. Sometimes he forgot he was old, and that he needed to rest.

Gastreel Osiris, sixty-four years of age, gray haired and gray bearded, was more active and busier than he had been in his twenties.

Cataclysm was all about him, disaster untold. But perhaps it was time to stop thinking of such matters. Perhaps it was time to forget. Perhaps it was time to act the part of an old man for once.

From Middletown to Greenwater, Gastreel walked, through the great open gate into the mansions and townhomes of Wodenscross Court. When he entered into his house at Rosetree Manor, it was the late afternoon, and clouds were moving in from the west. From his hearth he grabbed his pipe. He stuffed the pipeweed within, started a fire, set it alight.

And he was sitting on his rocking chair in the light of the fire, pipe in his mouth, beginning to drift off to sleep, when there was a loud knock on the door.

Deafening was the knock, terrible, frightening, like some hellish toll-keeper had come to collect his due. Gastreel's pipe fell out of his mouth. His heart trembled. He had been having a happy dream, of his childhood, when the knocking stirred him out of half-sleep.

He got up and brushed his green robe. He grabbed his white staff then tossed the pipe on the floor and hurried to the door.

When he opened it, he was greeted by a face he recognized. It was the castellan of the Tower of Pythor, a mouse of a man, thin, petite, always quiet. His dark hair was neatly combed, and he seemed apprehensive about being where he was.

As archwizard, Gastreel was, if not the ruler, then the chief citizen of a nation-state entirely enclosed within Galiope's walls. He governed the order of wizards from their base at the Tower of Pythor, he and the other eleven members passed laws that were binding on magic weavers throughout the Northern World.

The castellan, Avan, supervised all that went on in the tower. He was charged with its maintenance, and ensured everything went smoothly, from the kitchens to the hospital to the arcane armory.

"Milord," said Avan, "a word?"

Avan took a seat before the fire at Gastreel's request. Gastreel had not yet prepared dinner, though he supposed he could fetch something quickly from the larder. It was rude not to offer a guest food, but Avan seemed like he was in a hurry.

"I do not like being in the city, I confess," Avan said. "I am a creature of the tower. And I know you are busy, milord, with the disaster that Galiope faces, but—but—"

"Out with it, Avan," said Gastreel.

"I am rarely seen by those that work in the tower… to the wizards that come and go I aspire to be invisible. But people who are invisible have ears… they hear things they do not even intend to hear. And your absence from your duties as archwizard, your meetings with this council, your focus on the safety of Galiope… I fear there are some in the wizard order who are plotting against you. They are calling you a false archwizard in private conversations. They are saying you do not belong in your position. And what's more, your position that the mundane and the magically gifted are of equal value, it is causing secret anger even in the tower servants."

"Hadn't your mother taught you not to eavesdrop?" Gastreel said. But he believed the man's words. Gastreel was skilled in magic, powerful in the arts of the arcane, but to his fellow travelers, his fellow wizards, he never felt as though he fit in.

"I am sorry, milord," Avan said. "I am a mere servant of the tower, and in the ways of magic I am far inferior to you. But I consider you the rightful archwizard. I consider your appointment to the position legal and legitimate. And I love the changes that you have made, the integrity and humility you have brought back into the ranks of the wizards. That is why I am doing my best to help you. I am doing my best to ensure your rightful place as archwizard endures.

"But this focus on the city, this absence from the tower… I fear you are unwittingly encouraging some sort of coup."

Now Avan had pressed a little too far. Gastreel did not respect eavesdroppers or spies. All that he had said was not surprising, even if it was disappointing.

"Let me worry about these things, Avan," Gastreel said. "All that is required of you is to keep the tower in shape. Whether I live or die, succeed or fail, it isn't up to you."

"Some people I overheard," Avan said, "were talking of murder."

~

Murder… murder…

The murder of the archwizard. The resentment of the wizards to Gastreel ran deeper than this council, declared at the beginning of the month. Gastreel had begun to realize now the depths of that resentment.

Gastreel had brought Avan some salted meat to eat, and poured him a glass of wine. The archwizard nibbled at his own meal, but Avan's words had changed things. A coup, not just the Council of the Twelve turning against him, but murder… No scheming would-be archwizard had resorted to it in the history of the order.

"Who spoke of a coup?" Gastreel said. "Who spoke of murdering me?"

"Milord," Avan said, "I do not know their names, or even the robes they wear. I was cleaning the Chamber of Mysteries diligently, and through a peephole I heard scattered voices I did not recognize. They were in the seventh story parlor, which is right next to the Chamber of Mysteries. They spoke of killing you in cold blood. They spoke of replacing you with Ariya the White Wizard."

Ariya… Gastreel had not heard that name in more than a year. When, long ago, the former Archwizard Syrion marched against the city, she had been one of his greatest allies.

During that war, the wizards' great shame before Gastreel

became archwizard, the order had—with the assistance of rokahn—besieged Galiope. But those traitors had failed. They had died. He had assumed Ariya had perished with the rest of them.

Ariya the White Wizard was an accromancer, with power over speed and increase; she had spoken so endlessly of the pacifism and peace for which the Order of the White Robes advocated. And then she had joined in. The wizards had fought against the city, and she had become ferocious and depraved, spurning all her talk of nonviolence. But she and Syrion had failed. The city yet endured.

"Ariya," Gastreel said. "A name I had almost forgotten. I assumed her dead. But if she is alive, that would make her a renegade. By the laws of the wizard order, renegades who continue to practice magic are to be hunted down and killed."

"Yes," Avan said. "I thought she was dead, too. But if she is alive, that fact must be known to some... some, whom I overheard, who were plotting to kill you."

After the wizard order was defeated in their war against the city, the Lord Eventide had proclaimed Gastreel archwizard. That had never been done before... the city declaring the rightful ruler of the tower.

Avan's words troubled him, but Gastreel knew his life and his position were not the top priority, not now.

"Thank you for telling me this," he told Avan, "but I cannot abandon Galiope in her darkest hour, or refuse to give her my utmost. I will exercise caution and restraint. You are a good castellan, Avan. Report to me if you hear anything else."

Chapter Twelve: Friends and Foes

The afternoon shadows were falling over the Dragonpaw Inn, and Reev felt as though he couldn't relax. If Fortunato was long gone, Reev would never see him again.

All this for Ambrass—all this because she rejected him.

Sitting in a booth with Wrinn, Reev couldn't help but glare a bit at Ambrass as she swept the main hall. She was there with her broom, dressed in a dreary brown gown, dark-featured, beautiful indeed but not worth the cost of abandoning your friends.

Fortunato of Ríva—the thought of losing him was a terrible blow. On Reev's journey north, Fortunato had traveled with him. While Reev lived in the Northern World, he had never been far away. And now, it appeared, he was gone.

Wrinn had a flagon of ale before him. On the table, a war game had been set up, a checkered board, Wrinn playing the knights, Reev the barbarians. As Wrinn puzzled over his next move, as he had for the past few agonizing minutes, Reev tried to think of anywhere he had not yet looked, any place Fortunato could be beside his rented room, his favorite tavern, the garden parks and the alleyways he frequented.

He had been despondent—all for the sake of that young woman, sweeping next to Reev. He had declared his hatred for living in Galiope. Had he fled away somewhere, or had it all just been talk? The sale of his rented room indicated he had been serious.

So where could Reev look? Where could Reev go? What part of Galiope was left to search?

Wrinn moved one of his knights directly at Reev's barbarian chieftain. He knocked the barbarian chieftain off the board. "I win," Wrinn said.

And Reev wasn't sure the move was legal, but he supposed he didn't really care.

"If you were Fortunato," Reev said under his breath, "if you were terribly sad, terribly disappointed, where would you go?

"If you were planning on running away from your problems, but you hadn't decided, where would you last be?"

"Fortunato doesn't seem like he'd run from his problems," Wrinn said. "He would confront them."

And the problem, it would seem, would be Nocturne Rabaam, who had taken Ambrass from him. Was Reev crazy enough to go ask Nocturne about Fortunato's whereabouts? The very thought of his fangs and his startling demeanor caused Reev's stomach to writhe. But before Fortunato left, maybe he would have confronted Nocturne Rabaam… maybe Nocturne would have seen him. It was a crazy idea, but it was the last thing Reev could think of to try.

Was Wrinn crazy as well? Crazy enough to join him?

~

Even in the streets of Lonen Town, once pristine and well-swept, the cleanest and most diligently cared-for part of the city, there were still Mountain Folk wandering around. For their part, the elves of Lonen Town made clear the Mountain Folk were not welcome, and as Reev and Wrinn walked, some Lonen Town residents were openly heaping insults on the intruders. Those that did not confront the Mountain Folk verbally would only glare.

The sunlight was taking on contours of red and orange, the sun was dipping low in the sky, and Reev was questioning the absurdity of what he was doing, when the Bloodmoon Inn appeared in the distance and the narrow alley Reev had been to long ago came into sight.

Reev's stomach twisted in knots at the foolishness of this

decision, but who else would have seen Fortunato, what other place remained to search? He felt in his heart that Fortunato was gone, that he would never see Fortunato again, and it was all thanks to that serving girl, all thanks to Ambrass.

Butterflies seemed to dance in his stomach as he drew near the tenement house, the home with the blue door and the balcony. Reev and Nocturne were by no means friends, and the first time they met had been a night of terror.

And yet, who else could possibly know where Fortunato might be?

He approached the door, and with prayers said under his breath, he began to knock.

He remembered Wrinn had brought his quarterstaff. He reminded himself that Nocturne's natural thirst for blood did not mean, on its own, that Nocturne meant him harm.

He knocked again, and he waited. And the door opened just slightly; two dark eyes twinkled.

The vampire of Night Owl Way was there, confused at first, but a sadistic smile dawned on his face when he saw Reev's fear.

"Nocturne," Reev said. "It's Fortunato… have you seen him?"

"Why would I have seen him, Mr. Nax?" he said. "He and I aren't exactly on speaking terms, for obvious reasons."

Why would he have? Why would he have, indeed? It was foolish to begin with, a desperate proposition born out of losing Fortunato—and Reev had lost his friend, forever. He knew it now.

"You and Fortunato were once friends," Reev said. "Now, no one can find him. No one knows where he is."

"Why did the two of you *really* come here?" Nocturne said. The sadistic smile seemed to have grown. "Tell me the truth."

Reev took a step back. This had all been useless.

"You've really hurt our friend, Mr. Rabaam," Wrinn said. "We don't appreciate it."

There was commotion behind Nocturne, the barest hint of a

voice. But maybe, it was just Reev's imagination. Nocturne looked back, but just briefly.

"I haven't seen your friend, Fortunato," Nocturne said. "But while you're here, can you deliver Ambrass a message?"

He puckered his lips in a kiss.

Wrinn balled his fist and said some curse.

Nocturne backed away, smiling, and as she shut the door, in the shadows of his house Reev caught sight of a woman, dark-haired and dark-eyed.

Chapter Thirteen: Master and Apprentice

Aleksander guided Bala down the country road.

They were farther from Galiope than Bala had ever been, and in the distance, in the gloaming twilight, was a chicken coop, and on the far side of the road, a fenced-in pasture where cows were roaming.

Bala's gums were getting sore and his teeth were aching. He had not drunk blood in many days, not since Aleksander arrived and began teaching him. The sight of those heifers and bulls, wandering amid the grass, was bringing his natural desires as a vampire to the fore.

As a child, his father had told him not to drink the blood of sentients, but only cows and sheep and certain other animals. If he drank the blood of anything else, he had said, he might get addicted, and do things he would regret.

"Come," Aleksander said, "what we are about to do is not altogether legal, but you are but a child; you will not be punished."

His words seemed ominous.

~

In the shadow of a country church was a small cemetery, fenced in by wood.

"What are we doing?" Bala said.

"I did research these past few nights, while you were sleeping," Aleksander said. "A mausoleum is here, a mausoleum for a merchant's family. The patriarch died in 776. Most importantly, there are no living relatives."

Bala didn't like what he was hearing. But he had a mission,

which Gastreel had placed on him. He had a mission, and he had to stick to it.

The mausoleum, he saw, was a large stone edifice, relatively plain, with words written above the lintel that Bala couldn't read.

"The Laventer family," said Aleksander. "They aren't going to like what I'm about to do, but they can't do anything about it."

~

Underground, the mausoleum was dark and dank. The stone floors were moist; the air was cold and terribly stuffy. Bala was having a difficult time breathing.

The coffins were of stone as well. There were about a dozen, and most were open, exposed to the air. In them were dry, desiccated skeletons and mixed bones.

"Bala," said Aleksander, "for the past few days, I have sensed your weave growing stronger. I sensed you are at the cusp of being able to use your magical ability, of transforming what is inward outwards.

"So strive hard this evening. Shut your eyes. Focus. Bring to this effort all that is in your strength, all that is in your power."

Bala shut his eyes and balled his fists. He remembered all the lessons he'd been taught, all the points of advice and all the exhortations he had listened to. And he sensed a power within as he stood there, magic, waiting to burst free, a potent energy eager to break free from its chains. The power was not something he knew how to describe—raw force, a shell of something—and as he stood there his fingers begin to tingle, and the air in the room grew cold. Bala's heart began to tremble, and it felt like an icy hand was gripping it.

Then—pain. Sharpness. His hand was bleeding.

Brilliant purple energy burst from that hand, brilliant purple and black. Aleksander was now holding a switch.

"There," said Aleksander, "the magic came free."

And Bala began to sob in pain, and he wanted nothing more than to abandon this quest.

Yet the energy in the room was not dimming, and the brightness lingered, motes of light swirling about the air.

There was a crunching sound—a skeleton's jaws snapping open and shut—and Bala screamed. He backed away as one of the skeleton's bones slammed rigidly together, and a hideous creation began to move.

"Ada Laventer," Aleksander said. "She would hate the look of herself now."

There were purple lights in the skeleton's eyes, and its jaw did not cease its opening and shutting. Its bone legs moved. It stepped out of the coffin.

Bala turned and ran.

But the doors of the mausoleum slammed shut, and Bala turned back to look, weeping.

Aleksander's staff was now in his hand. He had shut the doors. He had trapped his pupil.

"Why? Why, Mr. Aleksander? Why?"

The skeleton of Ada Laventer was now standing upright. Its false intelligence radiated from the beacon-like points in its eye sockets.

"It is your creation," Aleksander said. "Do not be afraid."

The skeleton was continuing to click its jaws.

"Your progress is remarkable," said Aleksander. "From a baby to an adolescent you have gone in so short a time. You are almost ready to take your next step.

"Now dismiss the magic, Bala! Dispel it, like I taught you before. Dispel it, or we are never leaving the mausoleum, or Ms. Ada Laventer."

Bala was weeping bitterly, but the clicking of the skeleton's jaw brought immediacy to the effort. He raised his hands and gained control of his emotions. He balled his hands into fists, and swallowed a scream. He summoned all the energy that was in him. He felt the magic coursing all about him and within, and he opened his eyes with determination and focus, and cast his right hand out.

"Away with you!" he shouted. "Be destroyed!"

The lights in the skeleton's eyes flamed out. Its jaw ceased its snapping. And then, within a moment's span, it collapsed in a pile of bones.

"Good," Aleksander said, and his grin was ear to ear. "You are ready... ready to try. Ready to make your first attempt to disrupt the magic of those iron masks."

Aleksander raised his staff; the doors of the mausoleum ground open.

Bala wondered whether, if he did what Mr. Aleksander said, he wouldn't have to be a wizard anymore.

Chapter Fourteen: Under Shadow

With a gasp, Gastreel startled awake. The fires of his hearth had turned to faint embers. His mutton chop, half-eaten, had grown cold. It was the dark of night, and he had fallen asleep on his rocking chair. His pipe, no longer smoking, was still in his mouth.

And he had a sense of something terrible, some great danger making itself known. His dreams had been troubled, and those dreams lingered. He dreamed of a yawning mouth of many fangs, of winter snows, of starved, skinny bodies and icy cold. And he dreamed, most strangely, of an eerie song, a lullaby that was not soothing.

And through his house he felt a draft, an open door, an unsecured window. Shadows were dancing in the light of the embers. He thought he heard a voice, the vaguest whisper: *"Cast yourself into that fire."*

Now wide awake, he grabbed his staff, summoned his magic and the power of the weave. He stood up, and he sensed darkness had come to his house, the power of Shadow. It was a sense he had not felt in more than a year, a sense he had felt in the presence of the Six Servants of Seymus, they that wore the iron masks.

But they had been defeated; their power had been ended. Reev Nax, the Sage, had smote them to dust. And now Bala was being trained, and soon he would finish the job, erasing the remaining traces of the spell on those masks.

He felt the draft again; the embers flared, raging into brightness. The sense of Shadow grew tenfold, and he thought he heard another whisper, *"Slice open your wrists."*

He began to shout: "Out! Out, powers of the Dark One. You are not welcome here. You were not invited."

And in a panic, he wondered if he had acted too late, if the magic of undeath had returned to the six iron masks, and that now the Servants of Seymus were wandering the city of Galiope, or were just outside his door.

He called up the weave, and activated the starstone on the tip of his staff. Light began to pour forth, bright blue light, as he walked through the hallways of Rosetree Manor, illuminating his path wherever he went.

But as he scoured the rooms and forgotten corridors, he began to gain the sense that this power of Shadow was far removed from him, that its originator was impossibly distant. And then he began to wonder if in some faraway forgotten kingdom, the Dark One had achieved physical form.

No, such an event would be too dolorous. At such an event, the mountains would quake, the deeps rise up, and the stars fall from the heavens.

The sense of Shadow was all around him. There was another draft—a cold wind—and he saw his front door was wide open. *"Remain in Galiope."*

At the command, he felt assailed, a suggestion that he wished to take, but why would he not remain in Galiope, and why would he not stay there? Of course he would remain in the city.

"Be gone, power of the Dark One!" Gastreel shouted. "You are not welcome! You were not invited."

And he walked outside, shutting the door behind him.

The blue light of his staff cast eerie shadows in his front garden. Wind whipped about him. Rain began to pour, turning to sleet. A storm had fallen upon Galiope so suddenly he wondered if it was unnatural somehow, if it had been sent from afar, to accompany this power of Shadow.

"Be gone!" Gastreel shouted again. "Be gone!"

He felt as though this assault was coming from the northwest, in the direction of the mighty mountains. Wind assailed him, and his robes were twisting and wrinkling.

"Be gone!" Gastreel shouted. "Be gone!"

"Stay where you are!" the whisper now was stronger than all former whispers. *"Stay where you are! Kill yourself!"*

"Be gone, powers of the Enemy!" Gastreel shouted. "Be gone! *Illunitari! Illunaddori! Illuné vadila!"*

The winds ceased. The sleet stopped.

The Shadow was gone, and Gastreel was left standing there, panting and utterly confused, but convinced now beyond all doubt that Galiope did not fully realize what it was facing.

The rokahn were pouring from their mountain holes, but something darker was here.

Chapter Fifteen:
The Woman

It was night when Reev and Wrinn returned from Lonen Town. Glenda was in the main hall; Ambrass, too.

"Where did you go, my babies?" Glenda said. "Your dinner is getting cold."

Reev turned to see two plates of baked chicken and a loaf of bread at their favorite booth.

"We went to see Nocturne," Wrinn replied.

"And why?" Glenda asked, aghast.

"Reev thought he might know where Fortunato was," Wrinn said.

Ambrass had looked up from her sweeping.

"He was with a woman," Wrinn said.

"A what?" Glenda replied.

Reev winced. He edged toward the booth, to the dinner that had been prepared for him—a better dinner than he had expected in the wake of the city's rationing.

"Well," Glenda said, stunned for a moment but clearly recovering. "You two had better stay indoors tonight. That's an order. There's talk of a bad air about… some sort of foul wind. Trouble. You'll want none of it."

"We don't intend on leaving tonight, Miss Glenda," Wrinn said.

Reev could see Ambrass had frozen in place, apparently stunned by what she had heard. Wrinn just couldn't keep that tongue of his in check. A woman had been there—and it could have been an aunt, a cousin… Now Ambrass was distressed, but as Reev sat down and took to his chicken, he thought of Fortunato, the friend he had lost forever, and he had no regrets about upsetting her. Ambrass had taken Fortunato from him, so maybe she had best suffer a while.

Fortunato… where was he?

He was gone.

He had felt it in his heart. Now, he knew it in his mind.

Chapter Sixteen:
Into Danger

Ambrass worked all night, barely keeping herself together. She watched Wrinn and Reev retire to bed. It was coming close to the end of her day of work. She had not been at all outside the Dragonpaw, never venturing into the street or visiting Nocturne at his home.

The Vidowa was after her. They had charged her with treason. She was in danger. But another woman… another woman…

Wrinn was young, perhaps he did not know what "another woman" meant.

Ambrass had decided to lay low for a while, until the Vidowa forgot about her. Nocturne had agreed it was wise.

Did he then betray her?

Another woman… another woman.

It was what she had long dreaded in her heart. Some called Nocturne a whoremonger. His bad reputation was universal.

Another woman… another woman…

The sun had set. The church bells in Cathedral District were ringing, ten hours after noon. Glenda was eyeing Ambrass from her desk.

Ambrass set her broom aside and went her room. She lit a candle. Her prayer book was open to a prayer of safety. Should she open it to a prayer of calm?

How far she had fallen, how low. She remembered the man she had first been betrothed to, Gaius, a gypsy. He had been harsh, sometimes cruel, quick to anger, disdainful of non-gypsies. She had never been happy in his presence, but he wouldn't do this. Ambrass could never even conceive of the fact that he was with another woman. He was cantankerous, rude, loveless… but pious.

There was a knock on the door and Ambrass winced. She did not want to hear from anyone, not right now.

But she knew she could not stop Glenda from entering her room. The door opened a crack, and her overseer was there, golden-haired, green-eyed, her ears coming to the slightest of points—half-elven.

"Ambrass," she said, "don't do anything rash."

I tried to warn you—it was on the tip of her tongue. *I told you so. I said Nocturne Rabaam was bad news.*

And she had been a fool. But Ambrass wouldn't let this go.

"Before you act out of anger," Glenda said, "remember that you're being hunted."

It was true. The Vidowa did not hesitate in carrying out sentences of death. The town watch feared a gypsy riot, and so were too cowardly to resist. A parallel law existed alongside Gallian law, and therefore Ambrass was a second-class citizen, with fewer rights than non-gypsies.

But Nocturne…

Nocturne, if he had betrayed her, if he had scorned her in this way, then Ambrass could catch him in the act. It was a crazed thought, because it was after dark, and even those who were not at risk of being abducted by the Vidowa would refuse to walk alone. At night, the robbers and bandits came out, and the wicked performed their foul deeds without the clarifying light of the sun.

"I am aware I am being hunted," Ambrass said. "Don't worry about me, Glenda. I won't do anything rash. Just leave me be. I want to be alone."

Glenda looked skeptical. Something seemed to be hovering on the tip of her tongue. But she said nothing, and let the door shut.

And Ambrass turned her prayer book to a prayer of success and quick feet.

~

The church bells rang eleven o'clock. Ambrass was crouched by the door, dressed in her winter cloak, a knife dangling from a sheath in a makeshift rope belt. She put her ear to the door, listened for the sign of any dull murmuring, any sign that Glenda was awake. She counted from one, to two, all the way to thirty. There was no sound. The way, it appeared, was clear.

She opened the door and found a darkened and empty hallway, and beyond, a main hall lit by the dying embers of the hearth. She was alone. Glenda was nowhere in sight.

Out she walked, into the gloom of the Dragonpaw Inn's main hall. In times that were not troubled, when the city was not filled with refugees, Glenda would probably be up, there would be patrons still in the booths—a party every night, until the early hours of the morning. It was not so now. No one had time for parties or revelry, or happiness or joy, only darkness and fear.

She knew she went into danger, but the thought of Nocturne betraying her overpowered all concern. She would catch him in the act and then—well, then… What would she do?

~

The streets were inky black but there were still lights in windows, candles burning, hearths glowing. There were scattered far-off figures in City Square, prostitutes perhaps, or people of ill repute.

And as she stood there, there was a flash of white light, like sunlight cast into a mirror, dazing her, blinding her for but a moment. More flashes appeared in the distance—a strange thing indeed, but she ignored them, and left, exiting City Square down High Street.

At the Bridge-O'er-Galios, moonlight glittered in the river below. There were dark figures at the edge of the bridge, and as she hurried south, she thought she heard a jeer, a crude whistling. She ignored it, and touched the hilt of her knife to make sure it was still there.

She was drawing near Lonen Town. She could see its buildings.

And there were loud running footsteps, a cacophony of footsteps, and trouble and danger fell upon Ambrass in the turning of a moment. In the span of a second, she was likely to lose her life.

~

The torches the Vidowa bore revealed the face of her cousin, and a few relatives she had not seen in years. All were dressed in leathers and feather caps. All had quick-blades in their hands, and saps.

"Ambrass Saida," said the brawniest of them, a young man with bushy black hair and a harelip.

She knew him as the leader of the Vidowa. What was his name? Bruno.

"You are a traitor," Bruno went on. "Two counts of treason. Add to that a count of resisting justice. Combined, that could be a sentence of death."

"I am a Galiopean," Ambrass hissed. "A free woman. Don't come near me, Bruno."

She drew her knife.

But she could not overcome all these young men. She could not. She did not know how to wield her knife. Perhaps she had only taken it along to reassure herself.

"A free woman," Bruno said. "I can't imagine what Gaius would think to hear you talk like that."

"Gaius is nothing to me!" Ambrass hissed. "We are not wed. We will never be wed! I walked away."

"You walked away," Bruno said, "but you are bound from birth. It will be you and Gaius… or it will be death."

A shadow stepped in front of Ambrass. That shadow began to hiss.

She stepped back, and Nocturne was there, Nocturne pallid as the moon. He drew his two knives from their sheaths.

The hiss was guttural, a warning, like an animal, like that of a jungle cat. Bruno began to back away. The others followed. Their bravado had vanished in the span of a moment, and Bruno's eyes were growing shallow and wide.

"Step back, little man, if you know what's good for you," Nocturne said.

Little man… He knew how to goad Bruno, he knew how to taunt him.

"These knives have killed men just like you," Nocturne said. His fangs had swelled noticeably; he was ready to strike.

He jerked forward, Bruno screamed and ran, and the other members of the Vidowa broke and fled in every direction.

Ambrass let out a wail, allowed the fear to leave her, allowed the relief to settle in. She fell upon Nocturne and met him in an embrace.

"Why?" Nocturne said. "Why so foolish, Ambrass? Why?"

"I heard you were with another woman," she said.

"It was Drassané, my little fool. Drassané."

Drassané, plump, plain, middle-aged… Nocturne's business partner, the other owner of the Bloodmoon.

And Ambrass wanted to strike herself for being so foolish.

But she was unnerved, rattled, for a different reason now.

She had seen Nocturne with anger and bloodthirst in his eyes, fangs prodigious, knives in position and wielded like an expert.

She recalled the rumors that had spread around town, the gossip that followed Nocturne wherever he went. Some called him the High Street Slasher. Some said he was the murderer from all those decades ago.

Nocturne, the High Street Slasher. It was ridiculous, she knew.

"Come, my little fool," Nocturne said. "Come home with me."

And half-carrying her, he led her away, down the street, and to his house in Lonen Town. She had been a silly little fool, but as she walked, she remembered Nocturne in that new guise.

The High Street Slasher…

It couldn't be Nocturne. It couldn't be.

Chapter Seventeen:
The Message

When morning dawned on the sixteenth of Brightleaf, a lone figure was riding through Godsgate.

To the citizens of Galiope, who didn't normally pay much attention, it seemed a mere rider. But as it clopped on down through High Street, in view of the churches and spires of Cathedral District, shouts began to rise up, and an alarm was raised.

It was Ethelbert.

Ethelbert, they said.

Eventide's son.

He had been beheaded, and his head had been sewn crudely to his left arm to mimic him carrying it.

"Ethelbert!" cried the chief nun of Hildegert Abbey.

"Ethelbert! It is Ethelbert!" said Abbot Clearey.

The monks and nuns were the first to see the sight, at this early hour. They stopped the horse's weary clop. They summoned the authorities. And the sight, and the news, spread like a forest fire. By late morning, the people of Galiope talked of nothing else.

A note had been sewn to Ethelbert's patches of dead skin.

The Council of Brightleaf 1152 was called forth again, right away.

~

Eventide was still weeping when, amid the stone grandeur of the Galiopean town hall, the letter that had been sewn to Ethelbert was read.

Gastreel was struggling not to weep himself. He had hardly known Ethelbert, but what a loss it was, for Eventide and for all

Gallia.

" 'To the arrogant Eventide and the arrogant council,' " the Lady Llewyn of Leyshaw read for all to hear. " 'It is I, Maerrick, hold-lord of the Vale of Ahorne, who decides whether my people leave or stay. And stay they shall. We are of the High Country, and we will remain of the High Country. A pox on your head, Eventide. Forthwith we declare our independence from the Gallian League.' "

The Lady Llewyn was the least emotional face in the room, the one most able to read.

Eventide looked up. Through tears, there was rage, unbridled, all-consuming rage. "So be it. Let the people of the Vale of Ahorne die."

Some of the other city masters growled their agreement.

But a different feeling was dawning on Gastreel, one not of vengeance but of alarm. He remembered the assault of Shadow that had fallen upon him last night. And he knew all was not as it seemed.

And he knew that whatever wickedness the hold-lord Maerrick espoused, there were good people in the Vale of Ahorne who were innocent and did not deserve to die. Shepherds, cattle-herders, freeman farmers… They did not deserve death, even if their master did.

"I concur," said the city master Lord Alden, Alden red-haired and gray-eyed. "The hold-lord Maerrick has chosen death. Let him have the death he wants."

"He chose death," Gastreel said, "and murder and war. The people of the Vale of Ahorne did not."

There was scattered grumbling. The lights in the high windows seemed to flare.

Would wisdom or emotion win the day?

Chapter Eighteen: Where Is He?

In the main hall of the Dragonpaw Inn, Reev had not even begun to think of breakfast. Last night, he'd had a dream of Fortunato, of Fortunato of Ríva and the wolf he rode.

And for that reason, in the light of morning, before Wrinn could drag him into meaningless games or fruitless searches for adventure, Reev pulled his friend aside.

"I can think of one last thing to try," Reev said. "One last way to find Fortunato. It's crazy, but it just might work."

~

Telantari. Adari. He began to think that caster's table really portended the truth. Through Middletown Reev led Wrinn, up Mersey Street, heading due north. And then, not telling Wrinn anything, he led him into the Arcades, down the crowded streets filled with tents and Mountain Folk, down that narrow alley, past the Fattened Pig.

"Reev!" Wrinn snapped. "You've got to be joking!"

But Reev had made up his mind, and for some reason, he had awoken with a terrible bout of hope.

"One last thing," Reev said. "The only way I can think of left to try."

~

The shopkeeper began to shout. "I told you to keep out of my shop! I told you to leave me be!"

"Sir," Reev began, "you are the last person I can turn to. My friend is gone, and no one knows where he is. You are my last hope… please."

"I told you!" the shopkeeper howled, in view of the shelves of bizarre trinkets and bewildering *objets d'art*. "Out! Out, or I will call the town watch."

But Wrinn stepped forward, and from his coin purse drew four pennies. When the shopkeeper's eyes widened, Wrinn offered him a fifth.

~

Before the caster's table, the shopkeeper took up his gray stone. Satisfied by the transaction, he began his work, uttering something under his breath, and then casting the stone.

"Th," it read. "R."

Th-r-o-n-i.

"D," it read. "A."

D-a-n-o-r-e-n.

"Throni Danoren," the shopkeeper said, satisfied by the money but clearly still bothered by Reev and Wrinn's presence. "Gate of the Gods."

"Godsgate," Reev said. He turned, and with Wrinn, sprinted out of the shop as fast as they could go.

"Don't come back unless you pay double the price!" the shopkeeper called after them.

~

In the brisk autumn air, they ran at a sprint, filled for the first time in many days and weeks with hope. Down Mersey Street they ran, through Middletown and its crowds, over the Bridge-O'er-Galios, pushing through the pedestrians. Down High Street they ran, through Cathedral District, in view of the towering churches, in the light of the sun, under the clouds.

They were at Godsgate, at the entry point of the city.

Beyond was the Royal Road, and emptiness.

Fortunato was nowhere in sight.

"I told you he was an impostor," Wrinn said. "I told you."

But Reev still had hope, inexplicable hope.

Chapter Nineteen: Closer than a Brother

"We clearly can do no more," said the Lord Eventide, mayor of Galiope and chancellor of the league, before the gathered faces in the town hall. "Maerrick has made his decision. His people will die.

"I sent my own child, the blood of my blood, the flesh of my flesh. No more can be done.

"The people of the Vale of Ahorne, if they hold to such a sick view of honor, deserve death too."

The emotion had cleared from his voice, but his words were bitter gall.

"Your Honor," Gastreel said, "I have lived many years. I have seen many things. I have spent my life as a wizard, and I believe I have a seat among the wise.

"Something about this does not add up. Maerrick's behavior… his people's refusal to leave. Something is not right. Something dark is at work.

"Some fifteen thousand innocent souls live in the Vale of Ahorne, in scattered villages. Their lives are precious. We cannot abandon them."

"Maerrick killed my son," said Eventide. "I wash my hands of this."

The Council of Brightleaf 1152 seemed too stunned to do anything, too frightened to act or react. Gastreel felt as though a great burden had been placed on his heart, an incomparable burden, fifteen thousand souls whom the people here in this great hall were now abandoning. Fifteen thousand souls, and Gastreel knew things were not as they appeared, that something strange and something frightening was at work.

"With the blessing of this council," Gastreel said, "I will go to the Vale of Ahorne. I will confront Maerrick. I will depose him. And I will evacuate his people, with or without his approval."

Eventide looked up, incredulous. "You're joking."

"I do not think it is wise," said the Lord Alden, Alden red-haired and gray eyed.

"Precious few days remain before the Vale of Ahorne is snowbound," Gastreel said. "By deceit or by force, Maerrick is keeping his people there."

The fate of fifteen thousand innocent souls had been placed upon his heart, and a deep conviction that something was amiss in that high valley, something darker than Maerrick, and more meaningful.

"With your blessing, I will go."

"Alone?" Eventide said.

"No," Gastreel said. "I will not go alone. I will take one other person with me. One who is closer to me than a brother, the heart of my heart, the sword to my spell. Fortunato of Ríva."

"Then you should abort this folly at once," said Lord Alden, who seemed so eager to foil Gastreel's plans. "Fortunato of Ríva announced this morning that he is heading back to the Empire. He is returning to his homeland."

"Gods," Gastreel said. "You must be joking."

Gastreel would find him; he had to.

The vote was eighteen to one, with Alden voting against, for Gastreel's new mission. As soon as that mission became law, Gastreel bolted through the Galiopean town hall's brazen double doors, in pursuit of Fortunato.

Chapter Twenty: Leaving

Reev and Wrinn had been standing in Godsgate only a few moments when, in the distance, a familiar shape appeared.

It was black, as black as the wine-dark sky, with eyes a bright red and fangs a bone white. Tied to the black wolf, Tyra Jade, was a saddle.

And through the great gate another familiar figure was walking—Fortunato of Ríva, heaving several saddlebags in his thews of arms. He had shaved his beard.

He passed by Reev and Wrinn, not noticing them, and Reev and Wrinn were too stunned to follow. For many days, they had sought him, and now it was apparent he was leaving, departing Galiope forever.

"Fortunato! Fortunato!" Reev called after him.

Fortunato had begun to sling the saddlebags onto Tyra Jade. There were so many, it was clear he had stowed all his possessions in them.

Fortunato turned, and set the saddlebags on the ground. The slightest of smiles appeared on his face as Reev and Wrinn ran toward him.

"Where are you going?" Reev said.

"You aren't leaving us, are you?" Wrinn said.

And Fortunato's slightest of smiles became noticeable and large. "I am leaving, indeed."

"You shaved your beard—" Reev started.

"In the Empire, a beard is the mark of a barbarian," Fortunato said.

Reev hated to hear him talk like that. "You can't leave us. You can't!"

If there was any lingering pain over losing Ambrass, any heartbreak that remained, he showed no sign of it. He appeared supremely confident, bordering on brash. And it seemed he was humored by Reev and Wrinn's desperation.

He began to sling the saddlebags onto Tyra Jade once more.

"I am glad for my time in Galiope," Fortunato said. "I am glad for my time here. I learned a lot. But I also learned I don't belong. The Empire is my home, I realize… not Gallia."

All this because of heartbreak… but he showed no outward sign of it.

"You can't leave us," Wrinn said. "What will we do without you?"

Fortunato's smile grew. "You will manage, Wrinn. You have Reev here. You have Bala."

Bala… But Reev had not seen Bala in more than a week.

"I beg you," Reev said. "Stay with us. Stay in Galiope."

But he knew his words fell on unwilling ears. Reev had no power over him, nor did Wrinn. And what a tragedy this was… to lose a friend. He would likely never see Fortunato again, not as long as he lived.

He felt his eyes water. Fortunato had slung the last of the saddlebags onto Tyra Jade. He was about ready to go, and he showed no regret, no sadness over leaving all his friends behind, departing Galiope and leaving the city to its fate

And despite his emotion, despite his grief, there was something Reev would never be able to ask again if he did not ask it now.

"Before you go," Reev said through a film of watery eyes. "What is a Telantine?"

The brightness of Fortunato's smile grew larger, if that were possible. His eyes twinkled.

"A Telantine is what my mother said I was," Fortunato began. He rested his hand on Tyra Jade's head. "If I spilled milk and caught it just in time… if I staggered out of the way right when a cart was about to run me over… if I found an unattended coin purse, or got some unexpected windfall… then my mother would say, 'That's because you're a Telantine, Fortunato. That's why all this good happened to you.' I began to think it meant that the gods favored me, that I could do things other people couldn't.

"When she said it, I'd roll my eyes. I never asked her what she was talking about," Fortunato said. "I guess you could say I was too full of myself to care to know."

The puzzle remained. What was a Telantine? According to Glenda, it was a "person of Telantis." Fortunato, apparently, wouldn't be able to illuminate the matter.

Reev wiped his watery eyes. Fortunato had decided to abandon them, to abandon Galiope and the cause in general. There was no stopping him now. It was clear the love Fortunato had had for his friends was only an inch deep. He showed no sign of grief, no sign of sadness, for losing them all.

The pounding of hooves echoed behind them. Reev turned and Gastreel was there behind, them mounted on Ivy, his white staff in his hand.

And Fortunato's demeanor changed. The smile vanished; the brightness disappeared from his eyes.

"Fortunato of Ríva," said Gastreel, looming above Reev, Wrinn, Fortunato… looming above them all. "You are abandoning us? You are abandoning the cause?"

"I am sorry, Gastreel," said Fortunato.

"All for a young woman," Gastreel said. "All because a young woman rejected you."

"You don't understand," Fortunato said. "You don't understand the hurt. You have never loved someone."

"And you have shaved your beard," Gastreel said. "Ah, Fortunato, you may be an Imperial by descent, but you will not be any safer in the Empire than I would be."

Fortunato's outward wall of confidence had crumbled. He

seemed to have shrunken.

"The adamant knife you bear, you took from an Imperial legate," Gastreel said. "You gave aid and comfort to the Zarubes on many occasions."

"Silence, wizard!" Fortunato said. "I am not a traitor. I have not betrayed my people."

"No," Gastreel said, "you have betrayed something else. You are a traitor to something that matters beyond the costliest of silver and the most priceless of gems: the cause against Seymus and his servants in the mortal world.

"Fortunato, you were a boy when I first met you. I sensed in you greatness and I sensed compassion. For sixteen years, we have fought and striven together; and now Ambrass will cause you to discard our friendship?"

"You don't understand," Fortunato said. "You don't understand at all."

"Fortunato," Gastreel said, "I am going to the mountains. I thought you would come with me. Galiope is in danger, and the magnitude of that danger cannot be overstated. If something is not done, the city could well fall… and danger could be brought near. The one you say you love may die."

Fortunato's demeanor seemed to soften; his eyes grew dim.

"Fortunato," Gastreel said, "we have been allies so long. Do this one last thing for me. If, at the end of this quest, you still wish to leave, then go. You will have my blessing."

Fortunato now appeared resigned. "One last quest," he said. "One last quest for you, Green Wizard. Then, I will depart."

"So be it," Gastreel said.

And Fortunato swept himself onto Tyra Jade's saddle.

"You aren't going without us, are you?" Wrinn said.

"You and Reev should remain here," said Gastreel, astride Ivy. "It would be the height of folly for you two to come with us."

But Reev recalled something as he stood there, how, in this past year, his aunt had told him of his family's origins in the mountains, how his grandfather, Kal Nax, was still alive. Winter Ridge, that was its name.

Winter Ridge was the town in the High Country that his father and his aunt had grown up in.

"Gastreel, please let us come with you," Reev said. "You may have need of us. You may have need of Wrinn's staff and my sword."

A sword was not really what Reev offered. What Reev offered was something else entirely, and it appeared at the most unexpected of moments, like when power had overcome him in the Black Pass, and he had destroyed the six reanimated Servants of Seymus.

Gastreel pursed his lips. "The rokahn are in great number," he said. "We cannot risk the Sage being harmed."

"But it is the Sage's command," Reev said—and that's what Gastreel and others believed him to be. "Will you disobey the Sage?"

Gastreel's silence was consent. Wrinn ran off to procure his horse Noble from the stable. Reev put a finger to his lips and began to whistle an undulating song.

Within minutes, his horse, Cobalt, golden-horned and red-haired, came galloping from the wheat fields.

~

It was still morning when they departed, and the sun shone on them as they rode from the Royal Road to Strathbrad Road. Farms continued apace, but when the shadows lengthened and the sun was advanced in the sky, the foothills appeared, mountainous unto themselves, behemoths of rock and earth and forest that were the herald of something awesome or terrible.

At night, they had begun to ascend the mountains proper. The air grew cold, and Reev wondered if it would snow.

Tyra Jade was huffing and puffing. Fortunato seemed resigned to this one last task. Wrinn seemed apprehensive, even fearful. Only Gastreel was calm.

As they began to ascend switchbacks, passing by fleeing Mountain Folk families, clouds rolled in, obscuring the moon and stars.

When they stopped to set up camp, it had begun to snow.

Chapter Twenty-One: Out of Place

In the dark, Bala was led through the great courtyard before the Tower of Pythor. The doors of the tower were open, and Aleksander guided him in.

Bala was trembling, barely holding himself together, but Aleksander said it was time to try, time to make an effort, to "unseal the magic" from the iron masks, and then "dispel it."

Through the open doors, Bala walked, and as he and Aleksander reached the vestibule, Bala could see other wizards, grown-ups in variously colored robes, walking through this doorway or that. On the black marble floor there was green light, a portal shining with the power of magic.

"Do not be afraid," Aleksander said.

When Aleksander said "do not be afraid," it only made Bala more fearful. And he said it often.

"To the eighty-third floor we must go," Aleksander said, "far longer than the sane should walk. Step in, Bala, and think of the number 'eighty-three.'"

Bala, still trembling, did so, though such a number was far greater than he had ever counted to, and so he thought of the word itself, the sound of it rolling off the tongue.

The green light enveloped Bala, and when he stepped into it, he shut his eyes.

When he opened his eyes again he found himself in a room high above the city. The lights of the city could be seen through a dark window, and in front of him was a giant black door.

Aleksander's light-wreathed form burst into existence next to him. The sight of Aleksander's red-feathered staff was a stark contrast against the darkness of the room.

"A little while more," Aleksander said. He stepped forth toward the black door.

Aleksander raised his bony white hand and lights appeared in ornate patterns, ghostly white veins of light like the light of the moon. In the center of the door, a face was outlined in that light, and then pieces and parts of the door seemed to fold back, disappearing, laying bare the room beyond.

"This chamber," said Aleksander, "is secret, known only to the highest-ranking members of the wizard order. Be thankful you were blessed with such trust, little Bala."

And Bala stepped forward.

On a dark table of wood were hideous iron masks, and at the sight of them Bala lost control and began to bawl.

Aleksander stooped down and put a hand on his shoulder, and offered him a piece of candy from the folds of his pocket.

"No," Bala said. Candy wouldn't stop the pain. Only doing what he had come here for would stop the pain.

He walked forward, wiping his eyes. He looked up.

He noticed something.

One, he counted, two, three, four, five.

There were five masks on the table. There were supposed to be six.

He looked up at Aleksander and held up the five fingers of his right hand, plus the index finger of his left. "You said there were this many," Bala said.

He held up the five fingers of his right hand alone.

"But there are only this many."

And something new fell over Aleksander, something Bala had never seen in him before: wide eyes, a trembling lip—fear.

"You are right, Bala," he said, "and I'm not entirely sure what this means. But we had best go. Without all the masks together, it would be pointless to disrupt the magic. We must go... we must leave at once. Our quest is canceled. I must uncover what has happened."

And what had happened? Why was one mask missing? Bala wasn't sure he wanted to find out.

84

Chapter Twenty-Two: The Son of Simeon

The sun was waning, and the afternoon light was shining, when, on the second day since Reev, Wrinn, Gastreel, and Fortunato departed, they ascended a rocky outcrop and the Vale of Ahorne appeared below.

The valley stretched into the interminable distance, greenery and vibrancy and life between two mountain ridges, and impossibly far away, a rocky peak that appeared almost bent, rising titan-like from the ground, crowned in snow, dominated the landscape.

"The Matinberg," said Gastreel.

Reev had heard the people of Galiope talk poorly of the "bumpkins" who lived in the High Country, even before the refugees began to arrive, but to see the valley now, the brilliancy and life, the beauty, it seemed the mountain-dwellers were the ones who were blessed, and not the city folk.

"My family lives here," Reev said, gazing at the towering green hills and verdant high pastures in wonder.

"They once did," Gastreel answered, "but no longer."

Gastreel did not know what Reev's aunt Ramona had told him, how he had a grandfather, Kal Nax, in Winter Ridge, and that he was still alive.

"Such beauty," Fortunato said. "Such beauty, my eyes water."

"Looks are deceiving," Gastreel said. "The rokahn threat has never been so severe."

Throughout the journey, travelers had told them of the abundant rokahn, the attacks on villages and even forts. There were no reports of them attacking travelers on the roads, but surely on the slopes of the mountain ridges and peaks to the left or right, perhaps even on the slopes of the Matinberg, the rokahn were pouring out of their spawning holes and preparing to strike.

Gastreel galloped off on Ivy, down the road toward the Vale of Ahorne, toward the green grass in view of the snowcapped peaks. Fortunato followed a moment later, then Wrinn, then Reev.

~

The afternoon light was waning. The sun was low in the sky. Far in the distance, a flock of sheep were grazing on a green hill. The dirt road was winding throughout the landscape, taking a meandering route in view of the towering peaks. On some hills were villages of stone houses, with smoke rising up from their chimneys. Everywhere, walls were being constructed, hastily-built walls of wood. The people knew their danger—but why weren't they leaving? Why hadn't they accepted the generous offers of hospitality from the Lord Eventide?

As the four of them galloped, in view of the peaks, there was a crisp horn blowing, the peal of a trumpet, and Reev felt his hand move to Doomblade's hilt.

"Stop!" he shouted.

And Gastreel, surprisingly, obeyed, bringing Ivy to a halt, Fortunato a moment later, and then Wrinn.

Reev's sense of danger was confirmed moments later when the riders appeared, men on horses with steel barding, draped in suits of mail, tabards of night-blue hanging over their chests—and on the tabards, the sign of a white eagle.

Gastreel drew his sword Maderias, Fortunato Danenhir.

Would they be robbed in the daylight?

But no, these were not common bandits, but men of arms, warriors—soldiers, perhaps, of the Vale of Ahorne's hold-lord. They were approaching with wrathful countenances, their swords and spears drawn.

They halted just feet from where Gastreel rode.

One of the riders lifted the visor of his helm, revealing a set of green eyes. In his hand was a double-edged sword, in the other a heavy shield painted with the sign of the white eagle.

"Flatlanders," said the man, "I thought we made it clear your entreaties are not welcome."

"You did more than that," Gastreel said. "You committed an act of treason, and made a declaration of war."

Reev wanted to back away. Silently, he began to count the number of riders. He thought there were about thirty.

"Have you decided to join Eventide's emissary in death, old man?" said the chief rider.

"You would be wise to put down your arms," Gastreel said. "I am not just an innocent emissary you can betray and cruelly kill, but a wizard, the archwizard, the leader of the wizards of the north."

"And I am Cerdic, son of the hold-lord Maerrick," said the rider with green eyes. He removed his helm to reveal flowing brown hair. "I am the Master of Horse and the leader of his army. Three thousand men answer to me.

"You may be able to cast spells and bewitchments, but I do not think you can overcome so many."

"No," said Gastreel, "maybe not. But the rokahn appearing in the mountains will certainly put an end to those three thousand, and to all your people."

Cerdic's eyes gleamed. "Who have you brought with you, wizard? Two men, an elf…"

"Fortunato of Ríva." Fortunato brandished his sword. "I will be your end, if you draw any nearer."

"Wrinn Finnis," Wrinn said, and removed his quarterstaff from its brace. "The same."

"Reev Nax," Reev said.

And Cerdic's green eyes widened. "Reev Nax," he said, "are you, perchance, related to Simeon?"

"What is it to you?" Reev answered.

Cerdic lowered his sword. A wind was blowing, gusting from the high peaks, and the mountain asters and wildflowers on the hills bent before it.

"His name is still revered here, here in the Vale of Ahorne," Cerdic said.

The other riders began to lower their weapons as well.

"He was a page in my father's court, for but a short while," Cerdic said. "A man of war he was. I was but a babe when he fought alongside my father. Nevertheless, he is remembered."

"And will you strike down the son of Simeon?" said Gastreel. "Will you kill those who accompany him?"

When Cerdic's eyes turned to Gastreel, a look of wrath replaced the gleam of wonder. "You are not welcome here in the Vale. The people will not leave; it is my father's command. For now, we shall let you live. But if you ride anywhere near Aerie Hold you will face the same fate as the one who came before you. It is you all who shall ride headless through the streets of the flatland city."

Cerdic turned and galloped off, and the other thirty riders followed him. The sound of their hooves was like a thunderstorm.

The sun was drawing near the horizon. They had at long last arrived at the Vale of Ahorne. But if Gastreel intended at all to force Maerrick's hand, to uncover what plagued the Vale, they had not come close.

The turn of the seasons was growing late. Soon, it would snow, and these people, these shepherds and cattle-herders in these idyllic villages, would be left to their fate.

~

That night, Fortunato fashioned a fire in the thin mountain air. They had hidden themselves in a stand of mountain pines. Gastreel had brought plentiful road-bread, and large portions of salted pork. The stars appeared; the moon arose above the mountains, a waning crescent. Here, in this unspoiled land, on the roof of the world, the air was fresh, and the nights were cold.

In the light of the fire, Gastreel took a seat and distributed the road-bread.

Quietly, Reev began to nibble it, in between sips from his waterskin. "What will we do now?" Reev asked.

"We wait for Maerrick to make a mistake," Gastreel said. "At the right moment, we confront him at Aerie Hold."

"It will snow any day now," Wrinn said.

The air at night had a wintry chill as the heat of the sun departed from them.

Fortunato had finished his road-bread. He took a deep gulp from his waterskin. "We should put the fire out before we sleep," he said. "I am sure there are stray rokahn wandering the Vale, even if they have not yet formed warbands."

After the rokahn emerged from their spawning holes, there was a precious delay. They would become self-aware; they would join a tribe. The tribe, in their dark-holds and scattered settlements, would forge swords and spears and armor. Then hunger and bloodthirst would drive them to violence. Large numbers of them would join in groups. They would invade first the mountain valleys, and then descend, after the spring thaw, into the lands below.

That was the pattern. And Reev knew, sitting in the light of the fire, that if the way became snowbound, if they lingered too long, then all of them—he, Gastreel, Wrinn, and Fortunato—would die. They would be unable to escape—easy prey for the innumerable host, easy prey for the rokahn. They would join the people of the Vale of Ahorne, and Maerrick and his nobles in their high-hold, in death.

"Have you been to Aerie Hold?" said Reev to Gastreel.

Gastreel was gazing into the fire. "I know the way. It is built on a high cliff on the slopes of the Matinberg. It is the most impregnable of all the mountain fortresses, but it too will fall when these rokahn are organized in their full number."

"Then we must hurry," Wrinn said.

"We must hurry slowly," Gastreel answered. "We must be wise."

After they had finished their road-bread, and after Fortunato had erected their three tents, he ordered them to douse the fire in water. They retired to bed not long after, and Reev and Wrinn—sleeping in a tent together—lay awake a while, speaking quietly.

Eventually, Reev drifted off to sleep.

~

It was dark when Reev awoke. Wrinn was fast asleep beside him. He thought he heard a noise outside, a faint voice, straining under the wind, like birdsong.

He opened the tent flap, and with Doomblade's hilt in his right hand, walked out into the camp.

The wind had picked up. The stars were advanced in the sky. It was almost dawn.

The song was still audible, so faint it could be construed as his imagination. He walked off in the direction of the song, amid the wind.

With each step, the wind seemed to grow. Reev left the security of the stand of mountain pines, and the song was now audible, a wordless tune that rose and fell.

And in the dark of night, illuminated by the far-off light of a village, he saw it—a figure in a robe, a mask of iron that he recognized, the chief of the Six Servants… Gogg.

Reev began to scream, and there was a commotion in the tents, first Fortunato storming out then Gastreel.

"What is it?" Gastreel said as he ran up to him.

But when Reev looked back to where he had seen Gogg, the chief of the Servants had disappeared.

"It's the mountain air," Reev said. "I thought I saw something. I thought I heard something.

"I was wrong…"

Gastreel laid a hand on his shoulder.

"Don't be so sure it was an illusion," he said. "Something ill is at work in the Vale.

"What did you see?"

"Gogg… the chief Servant of Seymus," Reev said. "But his robe looked different."

"In what way?"

Reev did not know how to describe the difference in the robe, nor the difference in the way the person he thought was Gogg had carried himself. He had appeared and disappeared so suddenly.

"Something ill is at work," Reev said. "I know. I sense it. But maybe it was some sort of delusion, some sort of trick of the light."

Fortunato walked ahead of them. The gold pommel of Danenhir glinted in the moonlight from its sheath.

"Do you hear, Gastreel, the voice?" he said. "Listen."

And together they were silent, and under the wind, Reev again heard that strange wordless song, rising just slightly above the ambient night noises. It was distant, so soft it could well be imagined. But what were the chances that all three of them had the same delusion?

"A song," Gastreel said, "a sighting of a man that resembles Gogg. A hold-lord issuing mad decrees. Something ill is in the Vale of Ahorne, and I do not know what."

"We should get on the move," Fortunato said. "We shouldn't remain in place for very long. I don't want Maerrick or the Vale-dwellers to know where we are."

~

By the time the day dawned they were on the move, as

Fortunato requested. The clouds were low in the sky, obscuring the snowcapped peak of the Matinberg. Rain was drizzling down through the veiled sunlight, bordering on sleet, and the wind was whipping again, and it seemed to Reev that there was a promise of a storm.

Down the road they traveled, drawing nearer and nearer to the Matinberg.

At noon, they passed over a high hill. The mountains on either side of the Vale had pressed in. Ahead of them, on another hill in the distance, was a village of stone houses. And along the green grass were dark shapes, bearing red standards, moving toward the village proper.

"Rokahn!" Fortunato shouted, drawing his sword.

But Gastreel, on Ivy, put a hand on Fortunato's shoulder. "No," he said, "we shall leave them to their fate. Else we will die, and there will be no hope of driving out whatever ails this valley."

What ailed this valley seemed to be the hold-lord Maerrick, whose baffling decrees had kept his subjects bound. Reev watched as the rokahn moved on the village, dark shapes in crude dark armor, bearing dark spears and dark swords. A few of them rode black wolves, and it struck Reev at that moment that his dear friend Fortunato rode a black wolf, too—a contrast of dark and light, of evil and good.

"We must save them!" Reev said, bristling at Gastreel's restraining words. The men of the village, young and old, were running out of their houses with swords and axes, and the women were joining them, bearing daggers in their hands.

"We must save them!" Reev said.

There were about a hundred rokahn and about fifty villagers. The rokahn would slaughter them without help.

Reev drew Doomblade. "If you won't help them," he said, "I will."

And he galloped forth on Cobalt to cries of "What are you

doing?" and "You fool!"

He had not traveled fifty paces before Gastreel, Fortunato, and Wrinn were ahead of him, galloping for the rokahn host.

~

They fell upon the rokahn suddenly, Tyra Jade grabbing a large rokahn in her teeth and casting him to the ground, Fortunato dismounting and impaling an armored rokahn on his sword in one smooth motion. Wrinn hopped off Noble and did battle with his quarterstaff, striking at and missing a slimy-skinned rokahn as the rokahn grabbed hold of a Mountain Folk man and sank his yellow fangs into the man's tender flesh.

Reev engaged with the rokahn on Cobalt, fending off their strikes feebly, trying to revive the Mountain Folk's spirits, trying to kindle in them passion. And the villagers fought furiously.

A purple-faced rokahn pierced a Mountain Folk woman with his spear, sending her entrails flying. He turned his yellow eyes to Fortunato, his face now smeared with blood, and howled and hooted a war-cry.

A green rokahn, his rancid black hair piled with a headdress of human skulls, smashed Wrinn across the arm with his spiked club, opening up a gash.

Fortunato engaged the purple-faced rokahn, smiting him with Danenhir as the rokahn struck him across the face with his spear-shaft.

Gastreel, in desperation, called down spears of lightning and hurled balls of electricity at the gathered host.

And Reev's heart shuddered as he looked to the hills and saw in the cloudy light another force of rokahn, twice as large as the first, headed right at them. At the fore, rokahn warriors hoisted pikes on which human heads were impaled, still bleeding, so fresh Reev wondered if they might blink. The coming rokahn force was chanting, and amid the guttural words Reev could not understand, he thought he heard "Seymus! Seymus!"

Reev fought against panic, fighting every inclination of his body to turn around and flee. He uttered prayers under his breath and renewed his resolve, but the villagers were falling, one after another. A few yards away, the purple-faced rokahn was knocking Fortunato back and forth with his spear.

Reev turned amid the confusion and saw Wrinn was bleeding profusely from his gash. He would die without help.

What a fool Reev had been, not listening to his mentor, not listening to words of wisdom, instead acting purely out of emotion and blind compassion.

The other force of rokahn was drawing near. Reev saw that some of the rokahn had doused themselves in human blood. It dripped from their faces. Others had painted their beastly bodies with the shapes of skulls. And others wore necklaces of human bone.

Ten of their foul brothers lay bleeding, perhaps twenty scorched dead by Gastreel's magic. Reev had not so much as wounded one.

But over the hills, from another village, a rabble of Mountain Folk perhaps a hundred strong were joining in the battle, girt in suits of mail and bearing many blades. They engaged with the other host and battle swept over the hills in the valley.

A burly Mountain Folk woman went down with a cry, pierced by a rokahn's axe. Some five of her fellow Mountain Folk had fallen to the rokahn.

Fortunato dodged a blow from the purple-faced rokahn and, taking Danenhir, beheaded him in one smooth stroke.

Wrinn at last landed a blow, spearing the green rokahn in the face with his quarterstaff and sending him flatly to the ground.

Bolts of lightning, bursts of brilliance, strikes of force, and Gastreel was swiftly whittling the rokahn down. But his power seemed lessened, and the energies he used appeared dimmer than before. He seemed to be growing exhausted, a strange sight for Reev to witness.

A gray-skinned rokahn with towering horns slashed at Fortunato with his dagger, and it grazed his rib, opening up a bleeding wound.

Wrinn's movements were growing slow and labored as he bled from his gash.

Reev charged into the fray, panting in exhaustion, but grew confused as the bodies massed against each other. The rokahn were too numerous, and it appeared they would claim the victory.

Reev looked back and there was a deafening boom. A blue flash erupted across the sky; and a rokahn lay black and sizzling near Gastreel, stricken dead by lightning.

A storm of lightning erupted, ten stricken dead by ten bolts and in that instant, to Reev it seemed, amid the deafening roar of shouts and iron clanging against iron, that the air of the battle was changing. The morale of the Mountain Folk rose as the morale of the rokahn began to splinter. More Mountain Folk were dying by the minute, but together, they were forcing the host back.

Fortunato, still bleeding, plunged Danenhir into the heart of the gray-skinned rokahn who had wounded him, then turned about and chopped the rokahn standard-bearer in half. The red standard, whipping in the wind, fell to the ground.

The rokahn host began to disintegrate, and then, in the span of a moment, broke in a panic, fleeing in every direction.

The Mountain Folk women were crouched beside their dead husbands, weeping. Fortunato rushed to Wrinn and began to dress his wound. Gastreel appeared staggered and dazed.

Victory…

But this was but a small force of rokahn, a foretaste of what was to come. Outside this valley, the number of rokahn was unfathomable.

And someone was approaching Reev from among the twitching rokahn bodies and the corpses of the Mountain Folk. "Heroes," said the portly old man dressed in overalls and bearing a clean, bloodless spear. "Were you sent from the gods?"

~

In the center of the hilltop village, a fire was made, and the wounded Fortunato and Wrinn took a place of honor. Warm blankets were laid over their shoulders, and the women brought them mugs of ale and slices of buttered bread, and platters of cheese—but they did not seem to want to eat.

The man in the overalls, Reev learned, was the parish priest of the village of Ethelwhite. He beckoned Reev and Gastreel to sit down as well, and they too were offered buttered bread.

The taste was strange—barley. The cheese was salty and hard.

"In all my time," said the parish priest, "I had not seen rokahn come so close. We had best hurry our preparations. A wall, a wooden fort!"

"Why will you not leave?" said Gastreel. "The flatlanders, as you call them, have offered to house you at no cost."

"Our hold-lord has demanded we stay," the parish priest continued. "We are bound by honor, and he says too that if we disobey his commands, we shall be killed."

To Reev, that was murder. Maerrick had committed an act of murder against so many people, against all that dwelled in the Vale of Ahorne.

The rains had cleared, and in the changeable mountain weather, the sun was now shining through light clouds, and the Matinberg's peak was visible, glittering white.

Far away, Mountain Folk were piling the bodies of the rokahn in a great heap, preparing to burn them.

"You came from the flatlands," said the parish priest, portly and gray-haired. "I had thought you were forbidden from entering.

"You saved the lives of I and all my family… Anything you ask for, we will do. Any way to repay you, just ask and it's yours."

"How about a word of wisdom?" said Gastreel. "A piece of advice. A bit of rumor and intelligence. How long has the Vale been troubled? How long has an evil power been at work here?"

"An evil power," said the parish priest in the light of the fire. "I wouldn't call it an evil power, but sometime last winter our hold-lord Maerrick fell ill. Days of mourning and prayer were assigned. We thought he was at the threshold of death, but he made a rapid recovery. There were days of celebration and I… I…"

"A word alone?" Gastreel said.

The parish priest's voice had grown hushed. Reev looked up.

Gastreel had stood up from his seat.

Chapter Twenty-Three: Malison

Gastreel withdrew with the Mountain Folk priest to the edges of the village. In the distance, the bodies of the rokahn, heaped in a great pile, had been set alight. The smoke was wafting upwards, a black tendril rising into the bright blue sky.

He had sensed in this priest fear, hidden underneath the surface, an unwillingness to talk. Beneath his shell, there was dread in his heart.

Far from prying ears, Gastreel asked again: "What plagues the Vale?"

"Last winter, when Maerrick grew ill," the priest said, "some began to hear a song in the wind.

"We called it Malison, after a folk curse. Some reported strange illnesses. Those illnesses never came to Ethelwhite, to my village. But I heard they were terrible—poxes and diseases of the limb.

"Some claimed the singing was coming from a place called Council Rock. That's deep in rokahn territory, but every once in a while, our warriors will venture there to clear the dark-holds and cull the population.

"They said they heard it coming from Council Rock, and that a fire was set there, a ritual fire like those of the ancient days.

"A person in a mask… a strangely-colored robe. A stunted man beside him."

"Who told you this? Who saw this sight?"

"At inns and at festivals," said the parish priest, "the rumors surely swirl."

"How do I get to Council Rock?" Gastreel said. "Can you show me the way?"

But a trumpet blew, and a commotion overtook the village of

Ethelwhite. The parish priest, without a word, hurried back to the fire and the gathered crowd.

Gastreel had learned something. It could have just been idle talk. Perhaps, it did not hold the key.

The voice had not just been in Gastreel and Fortunato and Reev's imaginations. Soft, faint, it was… but Gastreel had a feeling it was important.

Council Rock. A mask. A stunted figure.

Gastreel would think this over.

~

In the light of the fire, they had company. Cerdic, astride his horse, was among the villagers and his company of thirty riders had swelled to about fifty. Over their armor were night-blue tabards, and in their hands were keen weapons of steel.

"People of Ethelwhite," said Cerdic. "Flatlanders." He lifted his visor. When his green eyes met Gastreel's, they bordered on murderous. "Tell us what has happened. Who is your village's chief elder?"

The parish priest stepped forward. "Your Honor," he said, "at about noon, we spotted rokahn battle standards. I raised the hue and cry, and together we gathered our weapons and met them head on. The hue and cry was raised in Drury Village, and they joined us in our fight.

"With the help of these flatlanders, we defeated the rokahn."

Cerdic's horse reared up slightly. His eyes hardened.

If he were impressed by the people of Ethelwhite's bravery, he showed no sign. And he glared at Gastreel. "Flatlanders," he said, "you were told not to draw near to Aerie Hold."

Gastreel looked up to the glittering peak of the Matinberg. On its slopes, the hold-lord Maerrick reigned. That had been their goal. It remained so.

"I have been patient, more patient than you deserve," said Cerdic. "I shall not kill you, not now. Draw but a bit nearer to my father's house, and I will cut you down, and spill your blood."

How swiftly Cerdic and his men had ridden here. Aerie Hold was now not far.

"But a bit closer," Cerdic said, "and we will put an end to you. Simeon's blood will not save you."

Gastreel did not know what to say.

Fortunato, still draped in the blanket, stood up. His face had been cleaned of blood, but lacerations were visible on his cheek and jaw. He was still battered. Danenhir gleamed in its sheath.

"We saved your people's lives, Cerdic."

Cerdic turned to glare.

"We came to rescue them while you left them to die."

The gathered villagers of Ethelwhite seemed to give no disagreement.

The parish priest appeared to have drawn backward.

"I think a bit of reward should be offered," Fortunato said. "Perhaps… a meeting with your father, the hold-lord."

Cerdic drew his sword.

"Draw but a bit closer to Aerie Hold," he said, "speak one more word, and these swords will fall upon you." He looked to the villagers. "You shall speak to these flatlanders no more, nor shall you put them up in your homes. You will not offer them comfort. You will not offer them food."

Cerdic looked again to Gastreel.

"Do not travel any further," he said. "Do not draw any nearer to the peak or to my father's house. That is the law."

Gastreel said no more. Fortunato remained silent. Wrinn seemed to be struggling not to say a word in response. Reev, sitting by the fire, was still.

"Out," said Cerdic. "Out of Ethelwhite. Flee from this village, the four of you.

"If we meet again, it will end in blood."

~

The four of them departed Ethelwhite in the morning light. Wrinn's left arm was now bound in cloth. Gastreel feared infection or worse, but he knew all he could do was hope and pray.

On Ivy, he rode away, away from Ethelwhite and Drury Village, through the high hills and verdant pastures, drawing no closer to the peak but also no farther away from it.

In view of the mountains, the four of them traveled, plotting their next best move silently, among themselves

They had prevented a slaughter of so many innocent lives. Cerdic, galloping at full speed, had not been able to protect his people. As Gastreel sped through the High Country on Ivy, he wondered what he should do next.

He knew his time was not unlimited. He knew that soon it would snow, the ways become impassible, and traveling to the lowlands impossibly difficult. If he did not act swiftly, if an opportunity did not arise, if he could not with all speed uncover what ailed this valley, it would not just be Maerrick and his people who would die, it would be Gastreel, Fortunato, Wrinn, and Reev. If they did not act swiftly, all hope not just for the Vale of Ahorne but for the world would be gone.

Chapter Twenty-Four:
To Be a Blackguard

On Tyra Jade, riding swiftly over the hills, Fortunato had a taste on the wind. He knew that taste, and by the stillness of the trees, and by the waning nature of birdsong, he believed a storm was coming.

Amid the mountain asters and wildflowers, in view of the Matinberg, he was following Gastreel.

Following Gastreel—that is what he had been doing for many days. He had made plans, he had set a course for his life; if he had had his way, he would be on a journey back home. He would be past Hammond by now, maybe as far as the Lune Valley or County Cambion if he had ridden swiftly. But his plans to return to the place of his birth, to where he knew he belonged, had been thwarted by Gastreel's words. The Green Wizard knew the art of speechcraft; he knew how to manipulate Fortunato, how to get him to do what he wanted.

And Ambrass—he no longer cared for her. His reasons for leaving had been many. He no longer wanted to live in this barbarian land.

But here he was, riding, in view of the mountains, under the blue sky. He could taste a storm on his tongue, but there was no sign of it for now.

The hills were ascending. They were drawing near the slopes of one of the mountains.

Far in the distance something took shape, and Fortunato gasped in wonder.

Up on a high hill, surveying the valley far below, was a circle of standing stones, immense monoliths of rock the size of buildings, eight in number.

"What is this?" Fortunato said.

In the center of the standing stones, Ivy had halted her stride. Gastreel turned to look at him.

"This, I assume, is Dweorg-work." Gastreel gazed up at the high stones. He was an ant before them.

"The Dweorg once lived here?" Reev said.

"In the time of the elves," Gastreel said, "the Dweorg were widespread throughout the world. And they had a kingdom here, high in the eastern Dragonteeth.

"That kingdom was in the mountain valleys, and it was under the mountain, too. The Kingdom of Ëarno. Some in the High Country still find their coins—square in shape, made of steel. Those coins are useless now.

"They called the Matinberg sacred, but they had another name for it."

"What happened to them?" Wrinn said.

"Their fall was sudden," Gastreel said. "And as for its cause, I am not sure.

"Humans claimed the High Country. The name Ëarno vulgarly become 'Ahorne.' But signs of their stone-craft endure—and these stones, I assume, are one of theirs."

Fortunato turned and looked to the sky. The taste in the air was growing stronger, and the perfect stillness foretold danger. He would not yet raise the alarm, but he could feel the temperature dropping too, growing colder by the moment.

"Wrinn," Gastreel said, "look to the Matinberg. Peer carefully. Tell me what you see."

Wrinn walked up to the edge of the standing stones, the edge of the hill, and stood there a short while. He seemed to be straining his eyes. "I see cliffs," he said, "Billy goats on the cliffs' edges."

"Look to the center of the mountain, near to the ground."

"A great fortress," Wrinn said. "A splendid thing."

Wrinn's keen elven eyes could see far, much better than human sight. His hearing was heightened too, but he didn't seem wise to the danger Fortunato was sensing now.

"It's on the edge of one of the cliffs. I can't imagine any army being able to besiege it. There are stables, and there are many warriors marshalling around it."

"Aerie Hold," Gastreel said. "The seat of the problem. Now, your eyes have seen it. Now, we must venture there. But we cannot, not now."

Fortunato withdrew, walking to the other side of the standing stones. To the south of the standing stones was another deep valley, brilliant green, stretching into the distance. He looked up, past the peaks, and for the first time saw the approaching storm clouds.

"A storm!" Fortunato shouted. "A storm is coming!"

Hurriedly, he began to give orders, and furiously Reev, Wrinn, and Gastreel worked, erecting tents and building a fire. By the time the tents had been erected, the clouds were overhead. The winds began to pick up, and in the wake of the wind, the mountain asters and wildflowers in the valleys were wafting, and the pines far away twisted this way and that.

At first, rain began to fall, but the air grew colder and there was snow—snow in thick, coin-sized flakes, drifting from the heavens. Fortunato feared the ways would become snowbound already, though by his reckoning they would have had, at worst, a week left.

The fire raged, the winds blew. Snow drifted onto the grass. There was a horn, and in the southern valley, pouring down to a collection of villages, was a mass of black shapes with red standards—instantly recognizable.

"Rokahn!" Fortunato shouted. "Put out the fire! Put out the fire!"

And with their feet and with their waterskins, Wrinn and Reev did just that. Into their tents they retreated, Wrinn with Gastreel, Fortunato with Reev. Each young boy had a protector.

~

Reev was silent in his bedroll. Fortunato had his hand on Danenhir. The horns were audible at times against the raging of the wind and the fervor of the elements. The rokahn Fortunato had seen would have had to number in the hundreds. The people of those villages would die tonight, and no derring-do from Fortunato or anyone else would save them.

For the rokahn to be so numerous, to go boldly into those fortified villages, confirmed everything the Galiopean government feared. The spawning pits were active on a level beyond anything in recorded history.

Gastreel had not just drawn Fortunato into a new adventure; he had drawn him into a death trap.

~

Hours passed, and Reev had fallen to sleep. But Fortunato could not rest if he tried. The horns continued.

He did not want to alarm anyone; he wanted to guard against panic. He opened the tent flap, stepping out into the waning daylight, hoping to see if the rokahn had drawn near.

But the snow was falling so heavily it obscured all sight. He could scarcely see Gastreel and Wrinn's tent just feet away.

Horns blew, louder than before, but these were not crude rokahn instruments carved from goat horns, but instruments of brass—trumpets.

Cerdic, or perhaps one of the hold-lord's other minions, had met this force head on, attempting to protect the villages.

Cerdic had shown no sign of madness or delusion. Bound by that nearly religious sense of honor that the Mountain Folk suffered under, he was obeying his father's commands. But surely now he realized the folly. Now, in the midst of a blizzard, trapped in a valley that would soon be snowbound, facing a vast host of rokahn—a vast host that was not a hundredth or a thousandth but an infinitesimal fraction of what he would soon face.

Fortunato drew Danenhir in the midst of the falling snow, though he did not know why. The trumpets blew again, farther off now. The battle was beginning, and Fortunato did not have confidence in the humans' victory.

Far off, he thought he heard footsteps—near footsteps. He swallowed a scream. The song he had heard before was rising again, rising above the wind, and a terrible feeling of darkness fell over him.

A whisper was audible, a whisper whether of the mind or in the material world, clear to hear: *"Run! Save your life! Flee this valley, Fortunato of Ríva! And leave your friends behind…"*

He walked toward the whisper, wherever it was coming from. The sense of darkness was growing heavier and heavier. The snow had reached his knees. He couldn't see a foot in front of him.

"Run! Save your life! You never wanted to be here! Leave those fools of friends behind!"

Through the snow he thought he saw a gleam of iron, an iron face—a mask. But it disappeared as quickly as it appeared.

And Fortunato sensed a presence behind him.

The light of Gastreel's staff was glowing. "Begone, Dark One!" Gastreel said. *"Illunitari! Illunaddori! Illuné!"*

The darkness faded. But in its wake there was no feeling of light.

"Into the tent," Gastreel said. "Don't linger in this storm."

"There are rokahn about!" Fortunato said.

"They cannot see in the snow any better than we can," Gastreel said. "Let us hide ourselves."

Gastreel's words were not wholly unwise. But someone had to keep watch.

The light of the day was almost gone. It would be a long night.

At last, after standing there a while, in the whipping wind and voluminous snow, Fortunato relented, retreating to his tent.

He slept hardly at all. The horns and trumpets continued after dark.

~

He arose at first light.

The snow in the Vale of Ahorne sparkled. The sun was shining, and the blue skies were clear and cloudless. With his hand on Danenhir's hilt, Fortunato walked to the southern edge of the standing stones and looked down into the south-facing valley.

The buildings of the villages had been set alight, and smoke was still wafting upward. The bodies of the rokahn had been set in piles, but even from where he stood, Fortunato could see the corpses of the villagers, and the corpses of Maerrick's men.

Gastreel, Wrinn, and Reev, were fast asleep. It was but a short journey to the battlefield.

~

The buildings were burnt out shells. As Fortunato drew near the village he wondered at the size of the piles of rokahn corpses. Their standards were broken, lying all about the area.

Bodies of Mountain Folk were strewn throughout the ground, frozen solid, hundreds and hundreds of them abandoned to the elements in an act of desecration. Dead horses, and their riders, also frozen solid, lay everywhere.

Fortunato looked to the east and up a slope, the area from which the rokahn had descended, he imagined.

Maerrick's men had not bothered to burn the rokahn bodies. Fortunato drew near one of the piles, of which there were ten, and there saw the rokahn's dark faces, brown, red, and muddy green, mangled and dismembered, armored and unarmored. Piles of their weapons were there beside them, crude works of iron that showed little skill, and together helmets and breastplates of equal crudeness. Warbands were forming, countless warbands. How long until the Vale would be overrun? How long would it be until the rokahn at long last achieved dominance over the High Country, and no humans could be found alive in this place of supernal beauty?

Fortunato drew nearer to the bodies, to the standards that had been discarded. They were colored bright red, and against the red were black serpentine symbols.

He recalled the voice he had heard, but now, in the morning, he was convinced it was a delusion, a product of his alarm and fear, and nothing more.

He looked again toward the rugged mountainous terrain beyond the villages.

There was a gleam of metal.

Riders were galloping toward him, dozens of riders— Maerrick's men. He could not see Cerdic among them, but they were all arrayed like him, in the same attire, bearing on their shields the sign of the white eagle and wearing tabards of night blue. Clearly warriors of Aerie Hold.

Within a moment's time, they had drawn near, and in the distance, Tyra Jade was approaching, speeding toward him, running at Maerrick's men.

"Stop, Tyra! Stop!"

~

One of the warriors held in his hands a great spear. It was clear he was the leader of this battalion.

"Have you come to pilfer from these ruined villages?" he said. "Have you come to rob the dead of their possessions?"

"No! No, I haven't."

Tyra Jade was beside him now, and had begun to growl.

"He has a black wolf as a companion," said another of the warriors. "He is a *blackguard*—a friend of the rokahn."

"I am no blackguard!" Fortunato insisted, but these warriors, returning from culling the rokahn, seemed intent on doing him harm, and Fortunato didn't have the claim of Simeon's blood to stop them. "I am no blackguard, no friend of the rokahn! I raised Tyra from infancy."

"Why would anyone besides a blackguard have a black wolf as a pet?" said the captain of the warriors. "Kill that beast!"

But Fortunato kicked at Tyra Jade, and ordered her to run.

She fled off into the snow, bounding through the hills. A few of the warriors gave chase.

"Lay down your arms," said the captain of the warriors. "We will take you to Aerie Hold for execution. There is no toleration for blackguards in the domain of His Honor, Maerrick."

Fortunato removed Danenhir and handed the captain his adamant knife, Glyrnslayer.

The gods alone could save him now—the gods, and maybe a little of the gods' own luck.

Chapter Twenty-Five:
Losing A Friend

Gastreel watched as, far in the distance, Maerrick's warriors tied Fortunato's wrists in rope. They would take him to Aerie Hold, keep him for a little while, offer him a chance at a defense, and—if Maerrick's capricious and mad rule was any sign— kill him quickly.

What a way for a noble and blessed life to end—and it was Gastreel's fault. Gastreel had drawn him here. Gastreel had come to the Vale of Ahorne out of a misguided belief that he was needed. But recent events seemed to have proven that what ailed the Vale of Ahorne could not be cured. A voice in the wind, a Malison, a hold-lord keeping his people imprisoned—how could the mightiest of wizards right these terrible wrongs?

The sun was out, and the snow was glistening. Fortunato was being forced onto one of the horses.

Gods, to have done this to him. Heart of my heart… the sword to my spell.

Reev had awoken, and shouted as he approached from behind Gastreel, "What's wrong?"

Wrinn followed moments later.

"They've captured him!" Reev said. "We must save him!"

But the force of warriors that had captured Fortunato numbered at least a hundred, and as Gastreel stood there, another force twice as large was galloping down the slopes. Clearly, Cerdic's warriors had pursued their rokahn foes deep into enemy territory.

It was the mountain way.

"Shall we all die, Reev?" Gastreel said. "Or will we wait and be wise?"

He turned and looked ahead, to the north, seeing more faded stonework. "Here is a path," Gastreel said. "A Dweorg path to high altitudes.

"The work of Ëarno is all about us. They did not only leave us henges and dolmens. Their true ingenuity was in their tunnels beneath the earth.

"Maybe, we can find a way into Aerie Hold that Maerrick does not know about. If Aerie Hold is not the work of Dweorg, I am sure that its stone foundations are.

"We find a way in… and we save Fortunato."

Even more riders were galloping down into the south-facing valley; their force had to number a thousand. Some were hoisting the heads of rokahn on pikes.

But as Gastreel looked down into the valley he couldn't help but wince again at the carnage. The villagers had been slaughtered, and the bodies of fallen riders numbered in the hundreds.

Together, Gastreel, Reev, and Wrinn packed up the tents. Reev and Wrinn hefted them on their backs, as Fortunato had.

The riders had taken off, heading for Aerie Hold.

~

On Ivy, Gastreel rode, and Reev on Cobalt and Wrinn on Noble followed him. They ascended as they followed the Dweorg stonework, and as they ascended, the sun's warmth was building. The high ridge they rode upon surrounded the Matinberg like the rim of a bowl. The valley below was impossibly vast.

Late in the morning, just barely visible, Gastreel spotted the rugged path leading to Aerie Hold. Rescuing Fortunato was now his mission. But even he, as archwizard, could not overcome so many men-at-arms. So what could he but wait? He had an inexplicable hope that some opportunity would present itself, that something would fall into his fingers.

"Fortunato…" Under his breath, in the late morning light, Gastreel prayed for his old friend.

Chapter Twenty-Six:
The Hold-Lord's Daughter

With his hands bound and his mouth gagged in cloth, Fortunato rode on a black horse down into a deep valley, and then up the slope of the Matinberg. Rugged cliffs greeted him as the warriors led him to his fate. On those rugged cliffs, mountain goats perched precariously and unsteadily, pine trees clung to the rock faces, and the snow was getting deeper—up to the horse's hocks.

Danenhir had been taken from him; Glyrnslayer, too—an insult. All he once possessed was now gone, and he hoped to the gods that Tyra Jade had escaped, that she had evaded those warriors who had pursued her.

The sun was growing higher in the sky, and the air had warmed significantly, when the warriors turned around a rocky ridge toward a series of staggeringly steep switchbacks, and Aerie Hold appeared before him.

The fortress was massive, twice the size of St. Sigmund's Cathedral, larger even than the temples in his hometown of Ríva. It was built in an older style, with square towers and little ornamentation, on the edge of a high cliff face. From its square towers the flags of Maerrick's men were flapping—a white eagle against a blue field.

Fortunato's horse panted and heaved with exhaustion at the steep switchbacks, as they ascended the impossibly high cliffs in quick succession. The castle's portcullis was open above him.

How could such a castle ever fall? It seemed impregnable.

When at long last they had reached the open portcullis before the castle yard, the hundreds of riders stopped their stride. The leader of the battalion, who had arrested Fortunato, lifted his visor and shouted, "Dismount!"

No sooner had he dismounted then the warriors fell upon him, beating him over the head with a sap.

He slipped into unconsciousness.

~

Fortunato's eyes strained at the light. He was dressed only in a loincloth, and he was shivering. The room he sat in was terribly cold, and there was a window of horn through which he could see nothing, and to his left, wooden bars.

They had knocked him with a sap, and they had delivered him into the castle prison. Here, they would hold him until they arranged for his execution. What a way to go—and if he had refused to listen to Gastreel's speechcraft, he would be past County Cambion, now, if he had taken the northern route, or in County Parballon if he had taken the southern. He would have been on his way to his homeland.

But sitting here, thinking about it, he had begun to nurse doubts as to whether he would have received a hero's welcome in the Empire. He had not seen his father Petro and his mother Alessa since he was a boy. How would the town of Ríva have changed? How would the Empire that he knew have changed?

He supposed it did not matter now, now that he had been delivered to the castle prison, and would be sentenced to death.

A blackguard, that is what they called him. As soon as they spotted him, they had intended to kill him; he was certain of it.

How could he escape? The wooden bars were thick.

The only ornamentation in the room was a chamber pot, and up on a stone ledge, a cot of rough wool.

What did Gastreel think now? Fortunato hoped he felt guilty; he hoped he regretted what he'd dragged Fortunato into. He hoped the Green Wizard was saddened by his fate.

"You there, prisoner." The voice that stirred him from his

thoughts was pure and resonant. He looked up, and saw through the bars a woman in a long green gown.

Her brownish-blond hair was tied in a braid that fell to her ankles. The green of her gown was interwoven with gold thread. She was fair in complexion, and her eyes were a sky blue. Her lips were red and healthy, and there was a healthful luster to her skin. She possessed a quiet beauty.

In her hands was a tray.

"Here is your meal," the woman said. "We treat prisoners well in Aerie Hold. A mountain meal is what you will have. Cheese, bread, and a generous cup of milk."

But when Fortunato drank raw milk, he was prone to bouts of indigestion. He supposed he would suffer through it; he had a chamber pot within arm's reach.

Using her hip and the back of her hand, she opened the latch, and through a miniature slot within the wooden bars, pushed the tray into Fortunato's hand.

The bread was a hard bun, smeared in butter. The hunk of cheese was large and white, and had a dry look. The cup of milk was generous indeed, a tall portion, poured into a ceramic cup.

She shut the miniature slot.

"What is your name, miss?" Fortunato asked.

"Wouldn't you like to know?" she answered. "I am Edith. I am the Lord Maerrick's firstborn daughter, second in the line of succession.

"I have not only come to give you food, prisoner. We in the mountains hold to strict codes of justice. All charged with a crime are given the ability to mount a defense.

"So to the charge of blackguardry, prisoner, how to you plead?"

"I am innocent," Fortunato said. "Innocent, and what's more, I am no blackguard, but probably a bigger enemy of rokahn than any of you."

"That would be a difficult proposition, prisoner," Edith said.

"For in the House of Atheling, which rules the Vale of Ahorne, there are countless branches that have been winnowed out, entire gaps in the family tree.

"I, a woman, am not supposed to be the prison warden or the bailiff. That was my uncle's task, my uncle Dunstan… killed in battle by Barka Bone-Crusher.

"There is no greater enemy of the rokahn than the House of Atheling."

Barka Bone-Crusher… the name seemed vaguely familiar to Fortunato, like he had heard it before.

"And if you are not a blackguard, prisoner, then why do you have a black wolf as a pet?" Edith continued.

"What if I told you, Edith," Fortunato began, "that black wolves are not by their nature the servants of rokahn, but that if you, Edith, took a pup from her mother, she would be as eager and as loving as a dog?"

"Sounds fanciful," Edith said. "Eat your food, prisoner. Your plea is noted. To the charge of blackguardry, you say you are innocent. As bailiff, I am judge. And I am not convinced."

"You will find yourself convinced, in time," said Fortunato.

The slightest hint of a smile appeared on her lips, but she turned and left.

The bread was slightly stale, the cheese salty and dry. But the milk helped wash the taste out of Fortunato's mouth.

The indigestion that followed was minor, nothing a chamber pot couldn't cure.

Chapter Twenty-Seven:
Doomed

On the roof of the world, or, more practically, the roof above this bowl-shaped valley, Wrinn kept his eyes fixed on Aerie Hold, the fortress where Fortunato was now being kept prisoner. The fortifications seemed impossible to breach, not least because of the number of horsemen surrounding the castle.

The snow of last night's storm had slowly begun to melt, and the heat of the day was growing. They had passed by a number of other standing stones and bizarre structures that Gastreel claimed the "Dweorg" left behind. But they had not uncovered any secret tunnel or any way under the earth, something that to Wrinn always had seemed a vain hope, not something to count on.

And so, as he followed Gastreel on Ivy, riding beside Reev on Cobalt, he remembered the power he had discovered in the past year, what the elves of Alonar had called treespeaking. And he tried to get a sense of the plants and vegetation. He knew they were about to fall asleep for the winter, and that now, covered in snow, most were dying or dead. But he got the sense from them that the trouble in the mountains was growing, and that some of their roots touched the spawning pits beneath the earth, from which the rokahn were emerging hourly in great numbers.

As he drew near a stand of pines clinging to a rocky outcropping, he thought he heard them say, *What are you doing here, Son of the Forest? Do you wish to die? Do you not understand the danger you are in?"*

Wrinn did understand, in a sense. But Gastreel was determined, and now Fortunato had been captured. They couldn't just leave.

The ground began to sharply ascend, and then Gastreel halted his stride. At the height of this ridge was a stand of pines. Due southeast was Aerie Hold. They could clearly see the castle, though it was far away.

"What madness ails Maerrick?" Gastreel said. "What sickness of mind plagues you?"

He seemed to be talking to the hold-lord from afar, but the hold-lord was secure behind the castle's giant portcullis, secure behind a force of countless hundreds of riders in glittering mail with swords in hand.

Gastreel gripped the reins of Ivy and led her into the stand of pines. "Here, we will be well hidden. Here, we will wait."

~

Of the three of them, it seemed Reev was the most skilled at making a fire, and amid the darkness of the pines, as the sun began to wane and the light took on properties of orange and red, he used a flint and tinder to set the logs aflame. Marvelous was the fire, and skillful, and as Wrinn sat beside it, he was more comfortable than he had been in many days. He feared the rokahn, for the three of them were at the outer limits of human territory, but he couldn't afford to think about that now.

In a pan of melted snow, he moistened his road-bread and let it soften. He looked about him, and saw perched in the boughs of the pines birds of different colors, mountain sparrows and robins, finches and a bluebird.

"What sense do you get of this valley, Reev?" Gastreel said.

Reev was staring into the fire. "Doom," he said. "All these people will die. Maerrick has made sure of it. He wants them to die—and why?"

"Why?" Gastreel said. "We will not know until we find a way to breach Aerie Hold and confront him."

"Perhaps, even then, we will not be able to change his mind. Perhaps, some dark power is at work in him."

The light of the day was fading. Their camp was well hidden. Wrinn swallowed his moistened road-bread in a few bites and got up to set up their tents.

"I fear that Fortunato is in a place of terrible darkness," Reev said as Wrinn unfastened the poles and stretched out the panels of hide. "I fear he does not understand the danger he is in. He does not know what is at work in that place."

"Let us hope he can hold on a day," Gastreel said. "A day and a dark night.

"Let us hope that with the light of the morning, a way is shown to us."

Chapter Twenty-Eight: The Hold-Lord's Son

The light in the window of horn was almost all gone; night was here, and Fortunato was in darkness.

There was the sound of a door opening, and then footsteps.

Edith was there, in the same attire as before, and there was a candle in her hand. She had dared to smile at him, and the candlelight sparkled in her eyes. "Prisoner," she said. "I have come to collect your tray."

She opened the latch, and Fortunato, smiling in return, pushed the tray through the open slot. Only crumbs and the empty ceramic cup remained. She took the tray, but as she did, her hand touched Fortunato's.

"That cloth…" Edith said. "That cloth about your left wrist. Who tied that cord?"

She let the tray fall. She was touching the white cord of elvencloth, which long ago the elven princess Nenré had fastened about his wrist.

Nenré had called it a gift of remembrance.

"That cloth," Edith said. "It is precious. It is elvencloth. That's what they call it, don't they? Did an elven woman give it to you?"

There was the sound of a door whipping open and then harshly slamming shut, and the hinges whining in protest. A dark figure took shape, a mighty man, and Edith cried out and slid backward.

"You've gotten friendly with the prisoner, haven't you, sister?"

Fortunato knew that voice; and when the mighty figure drew near the wooden bars, Fortunato knew Cerdic's green eyes.

"Father has promoted me to bailiff and to prison warden. I am now bailiff, prison warden, Master of Horse, and marshal.

"Keep disappointing him, sister, and I'll take your job as cook as well."

He began to fiddle with a set of keys. He opened the wood-barred door. "This room has a little too much light, and the bed is a little too soft… for a blackguard."

"You of all people know I am not a blackguard, Cerdic," Fortunato said. "You saw the rokahn that died by my hand."

"So you are accusing me of being a deceiver," Cerdic said. "Add that to your offenses, blackguard.

"You are lucky we in the mountains have such strict codes of law and fair trials. Lord Maerrick of the House of Atheling, hold-lord of the Vale of Ahorne, has heard your plea of innocence and rejected it. He has determined that you are a blackguard, a rokahn's friend, and he has sentenced you to die."

~

Bound again, Cerdic forced him down countless descending staircases. At last they reached a place of inky darkness, and Cerdic—now bearing a torch—offered the only light. The air in Aerie Hold's lowest level, the dungeon, was stale and dead, with notes of must, and the floor was mixed dirt and flagstone.

Fortunato, clad only in a loincloth, had his cloth binds removed, and one of Cerdic's minions slapped iron manacles onto his hands then tied those manacles to a hook in the dungeon ceiling. Fortunato—hanging—could only barely touch the ground with his feet.

"The people of the mountain do not suffer blackguards," Cerdic said, then spat in his direction.

"You know I am not a blackguard," Fortunato said, hanging from the ceiling, his arms straining in pain. "And look into that honor-bound Mountain Folk heart of yours. You know it though you do not say it that your father is a madman, and that if he is not a madman, then he is evil."

Cerdic's iron gauntlet took Fortunato across the cheek. He could taste blood, and the loosening of teeth.

"Mountain justice is coming, flatlander," Cerdic said. "Your last hours on this earth will not be pleasant. Treat the hold-lord with respect, or you will severely regret it."

He turned, and disappeared into the shadows.

Chapter Twenty-Nine: Under the Wind

It was the dark of night, and Reev, attempting to sleep but failing, wondered how late was the hour. Wrinn was snoring beside him, the winds howled outside the tent, and under the wind that strange song, barely perceptible to the human ear.

He knew something terrible was at work in this valley, and that something terrible was at work in the place called Aerie Hold.

The winds were growing stronger, whipping at the tent of hide. For sleepless hours, Reev had lain here, and he knew that there were more dangers than the voice and the power of suggestion in the Vale of Ahorne—there were rokahn pouring out of their spawning pits, warbands forming, and at any hour, any moment, a horn could blow and those monstrous creatures could lay upon the camp, and he and Gastreel and Wrinn would be unprepared.

He was hungry, too. The road-bread softened in water had begun to make him retch, and even when he choked it down, it wasn't enough to sustain him.

Doom was in the Vale; and they that lived there would die, and now, it seemed, because of Gastreel's quest, the four of them would die as well—Reev, Gastreel, Wrinn, and Fortunato.

Reev thought he heard a horn in the distance, but as he lay there he realized it was only the musical song, rising or falling in rapid succession, the song that never ceased to be heard, audible under the wind, in the silence of the night.

"Turn back," a whisper seemed to say. *"Run back to Galiope! And then throw yourself in the river!"*

Reev spat at the whisper and cursed the one who had said it, though he couldn't be sure it wasn't his own imagination.

What hour was it? He guessed it was past midnight, maybe the witching hour. The darkness above him was total. Wrinn and Gastreel were fast asleep. His only companion was the wind.

"Gods guard us," he said under his breath. "Gods guard us, everyone."

Chapter Thirty:
What Is Done in the Dark

Hanging from a hook, Fortunato's arms were straining. It was the middle of the night when a noise awoke him from his foul stupor, a state between consciousness and unconsciousness, between alertness and sleep.

He felt like he had something stuck in his throat. The skin of his wrist was raw and tender against the tension of the manacles. He tried to touch the ground with the soles of his feet, but could only reach it with his toes.

And in the daze of his pain-induced stupor, the fogginess of his vision seemed to subside just a bit. There was a light approaching him—no, the soft illumination of a candle.

A woman was holding the candle, and Fortunato's eyes strained at the sight of her. He saw golden brown hair, tied in a braid, a green gown.

And she was smiling.

She set the candle down on the ground. She drew near him, near Fortunato hanging from the hook.

"You are handsome for a blackguard, prisoner."

Fortunato blinked at the words.

"I am no blackguard." In the fog of pain, the hours spent straining in agony, he remembered at that moment where he was, and the crime of which he had been accused.

He was in the dungeon of Aerie Hold, and this—this woman before him—was Edith, Maerrick's daughter, a noblewoman of the Vale of Ahorne. She looked more beautiful than she had before. Maybe it was the soft candlelight.

"My brother wishes to punish you," Edith said. "I have a different idea."

She began to disrobe, and when she had pulled her gown over her head, she was only in her smock.

She drew up to him, lust burning in her eyes, and touched his arms with her hands.

"What is your name, prisoner?" Edith said.

And despite his pain, Fortunato felt a smile appear on his lips.

"Fortunato," he answered.

Edith's green gown was in the distance, discarded. In her smock, she rose up on her feet.

"Fortunato," she said, "what do you think of this?"

She drew nearer to him, and kissed his lips.

She smelled of perfume and mountain pine.

And Fortunato could feel the pain and fog clearing from his mind, and he knew, hanging there, he was about to do something he could well regret.

Chapter Thirty-One:
A Chance

In the morning light, Reev prepared the fire. The snow had mostly melted, and there were scattered patches of white here on this high ridge, and scattered patches and flowing water in the bowl-shaped valley below.

Far away, at the foot of Aerie Hold, it looked like the cavalry forces had increased in number, and now several hundred riders in glittering mail had gathered there, together with a force of men-at-arms on foot.

"What shall we do now?" Reev asked. "Just leave Fortunato to his fate?"

"No," Gastreel said. "We must act. But first, let us strengthen our bodies. Let us have ourselves something to eat. And then... Then..."

"Then what?" Wrinn said.

If they approached, they would be thrown into prison as well, executed perhaps for disobeying Cerdic's commands. It was apparent, at that moment, that there was nothing that Reev or Wrinn or Gastreel could do except wait, and pray, and hope. Fortunato had been through many dangers before, and had survived them. But time was running out, and it was running out quickly. Soon, there would be nothing they could do.

Why had Fortunato strayed from camp? Why had all this befallen them? Why had the gods allowed such a catastrophe?

As the fire took, Reev had a feeling of disaster he couldn't shake. His eyes turned to Aerie Hold. The sun was shining through mixed clouds. He looked to the east, toward the mountain peaks. In the light of the flaming logs, amid the warming of the sun, Reev prayed under his breath.

Chapter Thirty-Two:
The Blodgarth

At dawn, Cerdic and his men had unhooked Fortunato's arms and dragged him, still bound in manacles, to the edge of the dungeon. They had thrown over his body a rough robe of sackcloth, which they claimed those condemned to die were meant to wear. Then they had begun to force his injured body up the winding stairwells of Aerie Hold.

Cerdic's sister had left not long ago, and after what she had done to him, more than just his arms and wrists were aching. In the candlelight, in the dark, love had been made to him, or rather, lust. And Cerdic did not know it—and Fortunato couldn't help but smile at what had been done without him aware, even as he was forced up and up, to his death. Cerdic, through force of arms, with the help of his underlings, had prevailed over Fortunato; but Fortunato had done something to injure Cerdic before death.

Up he walked, poked and prodded, up the rough stone steps, and Fortunato, battered from his night of endless agony and also bliss, was growing exhausted and haggard, heaving in ragged breaths. This, he supposed, was part of the punishment, the humiliation of being forced up the stone steps, struck when he faltered or tripped.

It seemed an hour by the time they ceased their prodding, and through a wooden door, light appeared—the light of the sun, the outdoors. They were at the highest spire of Aerie Hold, and up ahead was a sheer cliff face.

Fortunato gulped. This was not how he had imagined he would die.

Cerdic's men forced him ahead, and Fortunato lightly resisted; they responded with whips whose thongs were lined with broken glass, and Fortunato fell forward, breathing roughly, at last falling face first at the very edge of the cliff face, and peering down at the countless fathoms below.

The ground was impossibly distant; the cliff overlooked an area of ground that was filled with scattered bones and blood-darkened stone.

"Do you see it, blackguard?" Cerdic said. "The *blodgarth*, where your body will lie in the sun. Crows will pick at your eyes, and your flesh will fall away. You will join there the graveyard of murderers and traitors and bandits, and worst of all, blackguards such as yourself."

"You know I am not a blackguard, Cerdic," Fortunato said.

At the sight of the drop, which had to be at least a hundred feet, he couldn't help but realize his guts were twisting in fear, and that truly there was no way to avoid this. This was how the life of Fortunato of Ríva would end—an ignominious drop to his death. And his body would be treated with the utmost disrespect.

Fortunato turned to face Cerdic's green eyes. The son of the Vale of Ahorne's hold-lord was still wearing his armor. "Please… you know I am not a blackguard."

But there would be no mercy, and Fortunato knew it. There was no sinew of mercy in Cerdic's body.

"Jump," said Cerdic. "Jump, blackguard, or we will toss you."

But through the door there was a commotion. In the distance, a figure appeared, a woman—Edith, who had wisely changed from her green gown to something else, a houppelande of gold.

"Stop this! Stop this, brother!" she said. "The prisoner is no blackguard… He is a good man!"

Cerdic whipped back to face her, and Fortunato could almost hear his snarl.

"Sister," he said. "No one wants to see your face. I am the prison warden, the bailiff. I will carry out the hold-lord's command. And that is for the blackguard to die."

He motioned to his men. "Toss him!"

The warriors moved toward Fortunato, but Edith threw herself forward and cried out, "By mountain law, brother, the law we are sworn to uphold, if a criminal is sentenced to die in the *blodgarth*, an innocent of noble blood may elect to take his place.

"I elect to take his place!"

"Madness!" Cerdic screamed—and Fortunato did not disagree.

"It is my will," said Edith.

Cerdic seemed beside himself. "I will talk to the hold-lord, our father. Go sit beside the criminal, sister."

And Cerdic left with his men.

When they were gone from sight, Edith knelt down, beaming quietly. "Father will not allow me to be killed… and therefore you will be spared, prisoner."

"Fortunato," he corrected her.

The gambit seemed crazy. But without her brother in sight, she took his hand in hers, and she kissed him on the cheek.

~

Minutes passed, an hour, and early morning turned to mid-morning. Cerdic reappeared, his face ashen.

"Father has ordered the death of you both. "Both of you will die on the *blodgarth*."

Edith shrieked. "Brother, will you kill me?"

"My loyalty is to the House of Atheling," Cerdic said. "My loyalty is to the law… to the Vale of Ahorne."

Edith stood up, but there was nowhere for her to back away; she was on the very edge of the cliff face. She began to beg, to plead. "Cerdic, you know that something is wrong with Father! You know he has changed in this past year. You know his edicts and commands have made less and less sense. You know he speaks madness!"

Cerdic appeared dazed, pale, and reluctant, but he was nothing if not a man of duty, beholden to the laws of Ahorne, beholden to the bonds of allegiance—and it seemed to him there was no bond of allegiance to him greater than that of the hold-lord, not even the bonds of blood.

"I am sorry, my sister. You know that I love you. You know what I must do."

Edith was crying, weeping, hysterical. Fortunato rose up, preparing to mount one last hopeless defense, not just for himself now, but for Edith as well.

And horns began to blow—countless horns.

Fortunato turned back to look at the great valley before Aerie Hold. From the mountain, dark shapes were pouring, filling the valley, countless battalions of rokahn, thousands in number. Such a force seemed impossible for all the might of the Vale of Ahorne to quell.

Cerdic took off at a sprint down the staircase, and his men followed after him. Edith fell upon Fortunato, hanging on his shoulders, weeping with relief, but Fortunato knew that there was no relief to be seen. Such a force of rokahn would be impossible for Aerie Hold's garrison to overcome. He turned and watched, with Edith still hanging on him, the force of rokahn making a rapid approach.

And under his breath, as his dread grew, he began to pray.

Chapter Thirty-Three: The Iron Crown

Here was the moment—and it was a terrible thing.

As the thousands of rokahn poured into the valley like a black tide, riding on black wolves or running at full speed, all the forces of Aerie Hold were going forth to meet them.

Every rider was galloping and every man-at-arms was running at the rokahn, and as Reev and Wrinn stamped out the fire, Gastreel hurried to Ivy and mounted her.

"Reev on Cobalt! Wrinn on Noble!" Gastreel said. "We abandon our camp! We ride now to Aerie Hold!"

Reev hesitated as Wrinn stamped out the last bits of the fire. Then he gathered his strength and launched himself onto Cobalt. By the time the two armies met in the valley, crashing into each other as two opposing forces, Wrinn had mounted Noble and the three of them were galloping with all due speed for Aerie Hold.

They descended into the valley, rapidly plunging toward the Matinberg. The sound of the rokahn army echoed as Aerie Hold drew closer. The fortress, of awesome size, was built on a high cliff, and it loomed above them, even at a distance.

And with each pounding of Cobalt's hooves, they drew nearer and nearer to their destination.

~

Up switchbacks they galloped, rapidly ascending from the ground to the height of the cliffs on which Aerie Hold was built. Fortress servants shouted at them as they made their approach, and as the cacophony of shouts and horns and steel against steel filled the valley with noise. More human riders were approaching from the west and the east. It did not seem enough to prevail against the large force of rokahn, but their victory or loss was not what concerned Reev; what concerned Reev was Fortunato above all.

They galloped through the portcullis as it was grinding shut, and the three of them broached the castle yard. Before them was a great door of wood, with iron hinges. Men-at-arms, about a dozen in number, charged them with swords drawn.

Gastreel cast a man-at-arms aside with magic force, as others retreated and disappeared into the dark corners of the castle yard. Reev drew Doomblade and Wrinn drew his quarterstaff, as amid the noise and confusion, the sun glittered upon iron—cages being opened, followed by loud barks and bays. A dozen hungry dogs being loosed from their prison—mastiffs with wet jowls and hungry yellow eyes, eager for the fight.

A mastiff lunged at Noble and Wrinn speared it in the head with his quarterstaff. The dog whimpered and withdrew, then growled, preparing to lunge again.

Cobalt hoofed a mastiff as it charged him, as in the distance more cages were opened, and a hundred war-dogs sprinted at them. Panic was overcoming Reev at the impossibility of the situation, at the sight of the swift and agile dogs with their yellow fangs, eager for blood, now charging at them with all due speed.

Reev watched as Gastreel raised his hand and summoned down a spear of blue lightning worthy of the storm god, a spear of lightning that crackled and sizzled and opened a hole in the cobblestones. The dogs yelped and scattered, buying enough time for Gastreel to fix his attention on the great wooden door that led into the castle proper.

Gastreel lifted his staff—the white Staff of the Archwizard— and thrust forth his left hand. He was calling up force, shooting forth energy that pushed the door back, and then pulling forward. Thrice he did this, until the door burst apart with a deafening crack of wood and metal.

The dogs had by now recovered from their fright, and were preparing to charge again, as Gastreel and Wrinn, followed by Reev, galloped for the castle proper.

A man-at-arms rushed to the parapets above the door, heaving a ram catcher in his hands. He hooked Gastreel with the ram catcher and sent him flying from Ivy, back toward the center of the yard.

Easy prey for the dogs.

Reev fought panic again, mad terror, as Gastreel scrambled to his feet alone, the dogs taking notice of him and beginning to charge. In the span of a moment, Gastreel summoned a dozen more bolts of lightning, and the dogs yelped and retreated.

"Reev! Wrinn!" he said. "Enter!"

On horse Reev and Wrinn galloped forward. They were passing under the gate when murder holes opened and molten lead fell red-hot from above.

But it fell about them and not on them, sizzling to the ground. Reev looked back and saw Gastreel mounted again on Ivy, hand raised, diverting the attack that surely would have killed them without his help.

And they were amid the warmth and splendor of Aerie Hold's great hall—Gastreel, Reev, and Wrinn—as the dogs growled helplessly outside, trained not to enter.

The scullions and the kitchen crew, the guards and the serving maids, and even the jester shouted inordinate curses at them, wagging their weapons and implements.

But Gastreel again called forth the weave, and infusing his words with power, shouted, *"Where is the Hold-lord Maerrick? I bring to him a message from his liege, Eventide, Chancellor of the Gallian League!"*

Men-at-arms drew swords and guards drew daggers, but Gastreel cast magic on them and caused them to blaze red and burn with heat. A set of doors opened and a man-at-arms charged forth, wheeling out a ballista, but Gastreel raised his hand and the ballista crumbled into a pile of wood. The people of the great hall fell backward, and it seemed it was dawning on them that they did not have the power to contend with a wizard.

"Where is the Hold-lord Maerrick?" Gastreel shouted.

A man in purple finery ran forward, a man who now seemed to be aware that he had been beaten. "What message will you have me bring him, Wizard?"

"I must deliver him, personally, a message," said Gastreel. "I come by the authority of Eventide, Chancellor of the Gallian League."

"I am the steward, Eodgar. I will go fetch him," said the man in finery.

Gastreel's face seemed disbelieving of Eodgar, but when Eodgar disappeared down a hallway, Gastreel did not follow, perhaps intending to catch his breath.

Reev looked about, also distrusting of Eodgar, fearful the castle servants would have something new up their sleeves. Wrinn's eyes darted about, eyeing the walls for arrow slits, or perhaps hidden traps set in the floor. All of them were shaken, including the castle servants standing there. All of them save Gastreel.

Outside, they could all hear the battle between humans and rokahn raging. As Gastreel, Reev, and Wrinn waited for Eodgar, rokahn war-horns were blowing increasing frequency, and at times, there were audible death cries from the humans. The sounds of battle were drawing closer—a sign perhaps of an imminent rokahn victory.

Amid the chaos, a door opened and a woman in a houppelande rushed out, followed by Fortunato.

"Fortunato!" Reev cried. Relief washed over him like a river, but he knew they were still in danger, and he wondered when Eodgar would return. But there was hope—Fortunato was standing before him, still breathing. Though their peril was great, Fortunato had been rescued, and Reev uttered a prayer of thanks under his breath.

"Fortunato!" Gastreel cried in turn. "You are safe!"

Perhaps, the gods were not totally against them.

"Who is this?" the woman said. "Your friend? What rudeness to ride your horses into the hold-lord's hall!"

"Fortunato," Gastreel said. "Remember our purpose; remember why we came."

Fortunato was dressed in a strange sackcloth robe. At Gastreel's words, the woman bristled. At the way she was hovering over Fortunato, Reev wondered if there was something more to their relationship than casual acquaintance.

"This is Edith… Maerrick's daughter," Fortunato said.

"Edith," Gastreel said, "your father is a madman. You must know this."

"Why have you brought your horses into the great hall?" Edith appeared beside herself, surveying the damage. "And you have broken down the door, and shattered the urns. Those pots you bowled over are worth ten marks each!"

"Edith, daughter of Maerrick!" Gastreel activated the starstone on his staff, and blue light poured forth, blue light that evoked lightning and storm. "Take me to your father."

"Go," Fortunato said. "Do it."

Edith fell back a step. "Off your horses!" she said. "Off your horses, and I will take you to him, you vagabonds."

Gastreel dismounted, followed by Reev and Wrinn.

"Take their horses to the stable!" Edith cried at the stunned and bewildered castle servants. And then, gathering the edges of the houppelande, she left through a great doorway, and the four of them—Reev, Wrinn, Fortunato, and Gastreel—followed after her down a stone corridor in view of many paintings of the Matinberg and tapestries that depicted battles between mankind and rokahn, they arrived at a massive iron door.

"Where is the steward?" Gastreel said to Edith. "He said he was summoning Maerrick."

"He lied to you," Edith said. "For my father goes not in or out. He has not been seen in months. It is his command that we slip our questions through this door, and at morning, noon, and night, the scullions take him his food."

"And this did not raise alarms, or questions of legitimacy? What if some bandit or traitor has taken up Maerrick's quarters, and is imitating him?" Gastreel said.

She sneered and twisted a lever. An iron slot opened up. She began to shout, and a scribe hurried over from one of the hallways, carrying in his hands a stylus and a wax tablet.

"What will you ask my father?" Edith said.

"I will ask him to his face," Gastreel said.

"This is what he demands—to remain hidden behind this iron door," Edith said.

"Madness," Gastreel said, and he eyed the door. "I sense magic at work. Is your father a sorcerer?"

"Of course not," Edith said.

"Open the door, then," Gastreel said.

"I do not have the key… only my brother does."

There were loud noises, metal against stone, as through the hallway large forms appeared, men in full plate armor, followed by Eodgar. Eodgar now had a crossbow in his hands.

"Eodgar! Stop this!" Edith cried.

But Eodgar loosed his crossbow.

Gastreel raised his fist and the bolt disintegrated on a shield unseen.

Reev and Wrinn scrambled away as with his staff Gastreel fired bolts of lightning at the armored men. With his other hand he began to work his magic on the door—clenching his fist, summoning the door forward, causing it to collapse on its hinges.

It fell with a deafening crash.

And there, Reev saw, in the dim stone chamber, piles of rotting food, and beyond, sitting on a chair, a corpse on whose head was the Iron Crown of Ahorne. The body was mummified and wretched, drained of liquid, shriveled and shrunken.

And Edith wailed, and began to weep.

The armored men ceased their running. Eodgar cried out in horror.

And the mummified corpse stood up, and drew from its side a sword.

It was now Gastreel's turn to flee, and he sprinted away as the corpse shambled out of the room. Its movements seemed rigid and unnatural, its limbs shifting suddenly in the manner of a puppet, as it engaged the men in armor. It struck with its sword, and Eodgar drew his dagger.

In the span of moments three men in armor fell, beheaded and impaled, by the precise strokes of the mummified hold-lord's sword, working through weaknesses in the armor that only a supernatural intelligence would know.

It struck at Eodgar, and Eodgar dived to the ground as an eldritch gleam appeared in Gastreel's eyes, the gleam of magic. Gastreel summoned within himself all his arcane strength.

Edith wailed as Fortunato approached, drawing Danenhir. Fortunato struck, and with a perfect stroke of its sword the mummified hold-lord disarmed him. Danenhir fell clattering to the ground.

Wrinn came barreling at the hold-lord as its body dripped a foul liquid and a horrid stench at last enveloped the hall.

Reev began to charge, but Gastreel restrained him with a mighty hand.

"Back away," Gastreel said, and Wrinn slipped to the ground by a force unseen. "It is not undeath we are dealing with. It is not necromancy at work here, but the magic of raw force. Someone is controlling this monstrous thing from afar."

Eodgar had backed away.

Wrinn was pinned to the ground.

Fortunato began to take steps backward as Edith wailed and wept.

And the mummified hold-lord's soulless eyes fixed at last on Gastreel.

The dispelling was like a wrestling of the arms, and only one could prevail, and one would lose at great cost. Gastreel raised his staff with a loud cry, then raised his free hand as a battle took place in another plane, wizard against wizard and mage against mage.

As Reev watched the unseen struggle, he could only imagine what Gastreel was enduring. At last, Gastreel fell backward with a cry as the magical contest ended. "Malison!" he shouted.

A vision flashed in Reev's mind: two brilliant brown eyes Reev thought he recognized, a wild shriek, and a dark form falling backward onto ice-slicked stone…

And an iron mask clattering uselessly to the ground.

The mummified corpse fell lifeless to the floor. All trace of the magic was gone.

Maerrick, Hold-lord of the Vale of Ahorne, had been dead for many months, and it was some vile sorcerer who had been giving those mad and reckless edicts.

Edith, in her weeping, rushed to Fortunato and clutched at his neck, confirming something was at work between the two of them; and what would Ambrass think if she saw the sight?

"So ends the reign of Maerrick, of the House of Atheling," Gastreel said. "In truth, his reign ended long ago."

Gastreel strode forward and removed from the corpse's head the Iron Crown of Ahorne, and ripped away the sword clutched in its desiccated claws.

"A new hold-lord now will reign."

~

It was twilight when the noise of the battle faced, and the sound of the castle yard's portcullis grinding open echoed through Aerie Hold's great hall.

In the dim light a figure was approaching, first on horse, and then on foot, walking from the castle yard through the broken-down doors of the hall.

It was Cerdic, son of Maerrick, of the House of Atheling. His armor was covered in blood, the dark blood of rokahn, so much blood it dripped from the plates of his armor.

And hoisted in his arms was a pike on which a head was mounted, mottled brown, with eyes of differing colors—green and blue—and two giant horns, the largest horns Reev had ever seen on a rokahn.

Reev thought he had seen that hideous face before.

"So ends the terror of Barka Bone-Crusher…" Cerdic announced, and whether out of exhaustion or resignation he made no demands of Gastreel or the others to leave. He planted the butt-end of the pike on the ground. "And the lives of two-thirds of our men."

"Two-thirds…" Edith breathed.

"Two thousand men have fallen in the Valley of Raehir," Cerdic said. "The dead rokahn number some five thousand."

"A black day," said Edith.

"And a good day," said Gastreel. He held up the Iron Crown of Ahorne to the light. "For today, a new hold-lord reigns."

~

"What devilry is this?" said Cerdic before the withered body of his father. "What happened? What became of him?"

"We were deceived," said Edith from behind him. "A sorcerer was controlling him, preying on our beliefs of absolute obedience."

Cerdic turned.

"And will you kill me, brother?" said Edith. "Will you fling me from the high rock to the *blodgarth*?"

"Of course not," said Cerdic. "I take my orders from the hold-lord, not a demon corpse."

Reev saw Fortunato approaching from the corners of the room. "And do you still think me a blackguard?" Fortunato said.

"No," answered Cerdic. "You are no blackguard, but an honorable man."

He shouted to the castle servants, "Go fetch this man his tunic and his trousers, and bring to him his sword and knife.

"And prepare a bier for what is left of my father. We bury him tomorrow, at dawn."

Chapter Thirty-Four:
The Vision

That night, in the great hall of Aerie Hold, Cerdic, son of Maerrick, was crowned Hold-lord of Ahorne, and the Iron Crown of Ahorne was placed upon his head by the chief priest. His golden hair was sprinkled with oil, and blessings were said over him in the light of the hearth, which was the largest Reev had ever seen, taking up an entire wall.

Despite the celebration, and despite the fact that three days of rest and festivities were declared in the Vale, there were precious few smiles. The dead lay in the valley outside Aerie Hold, and as the servants had prepared the coronation, Reev had overheard Cerdic say to his steward, "Another victory like this, and we will be destroyed."

The pike on which the head of Barka Bone-Crusher had been fixed was mounted near the hearth, and it still dripped black blood—a disgusting sight to behold, but the people of Aerie Hold appeared delighted by the sight of it, delighted that their great enemy had been defeated and was being displayed in such a humiliating manner.

The hour was late when the crowned Cerdic announced a feast, and great tables were brought forth from hidden rooms, and on them trenchers of hardened bread, and tableware made from horn.

Wrinn took a seat beside Reev, Fortunato was with Gastreel, and on a high table looming above everyone else were Cerdic with his wife Mildred and his nine children and together with them Edith and relatives of varying age, whose names Reev did not know.

The sun had long set, and candles were placed on the tables. A trumpet blew, and castle servants emerged from a dark room, carrying in their hands great silvered platters on which food was displayed, cuts of beef seasoned with spice, baskets filled with bread, and even roast pheasant to which the feathers had been returned. There was wine cooked with cheese, into which diners would dip their breads, and also bowls of almond pudding topped with raspberries. Flagons filled to the brim with ale were brought to everyone, and as ale and food washed away all concern for the Vale of Ahorne's dire trouble, minstrels took to the stage singing of the mountains' ancient heroes and their battles with rokahn. They sung of a valor and bravery that lived on in people like Cerdic and his warriors, but they sung of a time when there was still strength in the humans of the mountains, strength that was now spent in the wake of the coming, certain doom. In ancient days, the humans were mighty and often victorious, but now it was the rokahn's victory that was at hand.

The night deepened, and there was no end of the ale. So many crumbs were left of the bread that the inebriated diners began throwing them to the castle dogs.

Wrinn had had too much to drink, but Reev had only finished one flagon.

As the Vale of Ahorne's dire danger faded from the minds of the revelers, as lips were loosened and lewd talk filled the great hall, a Wrinn got up and began to dance to the music, and was joined by a serving girl. Reev stood up from his seat, wanting no part of the revelry, no part of the scene he knew was about to unfold.

Through the doors of the castle he walked, which had been hastily repaired, opening them up just enough to walk through and out into the night.

The stars were out and the moon was brightly shining. The castle yard was empty, and the portcullis was closed. But beside the doorway into the great hall where the din of revelry rose, was another passageway, heading north—not a door but an opening in the wall—toward what looked like a garden.

Nestled between two rock faces was a spacious plot of ground in which mountain plants like raspberry bushes and yarrow and Sawyn's wort were planted. Against one of the rock faces was what looked like a doorway into the mountain, and beyond it black darkness. Above it was a lintel whose runes were faded and eroded by time, in a script Reev did not recognize, but that looked vaguely like Dweorg.

"The Dim Roads," said a woman's voice, pure and resonant, and Reev turned to see Edith, garbed in a light colored houppelande.

Reev's heart shuddered slightly at the sight of her, not least for her nobility and grace that was so lacking in lowland Gallia. Such a face was kind, but hid her intentions well.

"That passageway is the work of Ëarno. That is what you look upon, Simeon's son.

"The Dim Roads will take you under the mountain, to places you will dread seeing."

"Have you been down there?" Reev said.

"Never," Edith said. "I am not a fool.

"No one dares walk through the Door of Kazh'n—that is what it is called—and no one without a death wish dares take the Dim Roads. Ëarno fell for a reason. If you go into those underground tunnels, what promise is there that you can find a way out?"

"I don't intend to go," Reev said. "I was only curious."

"What do you wish of us, Simeon's son? Why did the four of you come?"

"To evacuate the Vale of Ahorne," he said. "To ensure its people leave. To carry out the will of Eventide… the will of the League you are by law a part of."

But the High Country was different, and everything here was as Reev would have imagined Galiope seven hundred years ago.

"We once answered to a king of high blood," said Edith. "Now we answer to a corrupt aristocracy, squabbling fools who have never seen war and have never known true danger… oath-breakers and violators of customs."

"That is what you think of the Gallian League?" Reev said.

"Why did you leave the party, Simeon's son?" Edith continued.

"When the ale begins to flow," Reev said, "I leave."

"And me, the same," Edith said. "My brother rarely tastes beer, but when he does, he is consumed by it; and he can become violent. Many are dead at his hand, when people begin to slight him and he challenges them to duels."

"That is unfortunate," Reev said.

"It is," Edith said.

There was a pause. The wind was beginning to pick up. The brilliance of the moon was shining, and the clouds were sparse and transparent—silver wisps.

"The people of the flatlands demand so much of us," said Edith. "To pick up and leave this land where we have dwelled more than a thousand years, to go down to a place where we cannot see the Matinberg, to hole up in cramped houses and inhale the stench of smoke and tanneries…

"It is an awful lot to ask of us. But maybe, if the son of Simeon Nax demands it of us, it is not an unreasonable request.

"That, after all, is why you have come."

Here in the mountains, the birdsong was faint. The nights were so silent, Reev would never get used to it.

"I will leave you now," Edith said. She turned and walked back to the din of the party.

And Reev was alone, the rows of yarrow and Sawyn's wort wafting in the wind. He thought of Edith, and of what happened to her father, and wondered if whatever sorcerer was responsible for Maerrick's fate could further work his destruction on the Vale of Ahorne.

And he thought he heard a voice he recognized, and in his mind's eye saw two green eyes, piercing and terrible, a beautiful face, gold hair, red lips—the Lady of Danyen.

"Maerrick is not why you have come, *Velati Sonoren*," the Lady of Danyen said in this vision of mind.

"*Telantari*… Winter Ridge."

Chapter Thirty-Five: Brightsömer

In the light of the morning pits were dug for the brave dead, and rokahn bodies were disposed of in the way the Mountain Folk knew how to best disrespect them—by cremation. Gastreel on Ivy and Fortunato on Tyra Jade—who had wandered to Aerie Hold that night—rode under the sun, in the warming air.

They were following Cerdic, Hold-lord of the Vale of Ahorne, down a well-worn path through the brown grass. A cart was being pulled, on which was the funeral bier of Maerrick. The funeral was to take place in the burial grounds of the House of Atheling, on a high hill overlooking the glittering snow of the Matinberg.

And Cerdic and Gastreel had not yet spoken alone. Gastreel hoped Cerdic was wise to his father's madness, of the utter danger and slaughter that would await them with the coming of winter. Aerie Hold would not thwart rokahn in the numbers now pouring from the spawning pits. The "victory" against Barka Bone-Crusher had destroyed the garrison at Aerie Hold, and the army of the Vale of Ahorne more broadly. So Gastreel hoped that Cerdic would listen to the wit and wisdom of a wizard.

The mausoleums were built in rows on a high, flat-topped hill, works of stone that displayed remarkable detail, depicting battles of long ago between mankind and rokahn—so many they stretched into the distance. Names were etched before the entries to the mausoleums, names such as Cuthbert and Elwine and "Chedd of Atheling, who slew Black Waurka."

At the far end of the rows of tombs was an empty mausoleum with no markings, and there the funeral party stopped their ride, and Cerdic on his armored horse and Edith on her white palfrey rode to the front.

"Friends," Cerdic said, "we remember Maerrick of Atheling not as he is, but as he was: brave, bold, honorable to his oaths, just in his dealings, an enemy of the rokahn, and a champion of his people. He was worthy of the name Atheling, and he is worthy to lie here in the presence of his fathers."

The priest walked forth as the bier was unloaded from its cart, and he threw wildflowers before the bier as servants carried it into the darkness of the mausoleum. The servants left, and the doors of the tomb were shut. The priest handed Cerdic a chisel, and Cerdic walked to the mausoleum's lintel. In the High Country's strange, almost runic style of script, he carved the words: Maerrick of Atheling.

And the funeral was over.

As the funeral party departed, and Edith and others were galloping away, Gastreel drew near Cerdic and said, "Hold-lord, a word?"

He and Cerdic rode off, away from the tombs and mausoleums, out of sight, as the remainder of the party returned to Aerie Hold.

"What is it, Wizard?" said Cerdic.

Gastreel, astride Ivy, hoped his talent at speechcraft would prove useful. "You consider yourself an independent state of sorts, here in the Vale of Ahorne. But by law you are part of the Gallian League, and Eventide, the League's chancellor, has demanded your people leave."

Cerdic stirred, and his horse snorted. "It was long ago prophesied by the mountain seers and sages that the people of the Vale of Ahorne would one day leave our homes and the sight of the Matinberg, and we would go into the lowlands to dwell. It was prophesied that one day, the dark forces in the mountain would prevail, and we would be forced to retreat. And on the day of that departure, the hold-lord of the Vale would take up Aylmer's Horn and blow it."

"Aylmer's Horn?" Gastreel said.

"The horn lies upon the altar in the castle chapel," Cerdic said. "For all our time in Aerie Hold, it has lain there.

"Our ancestor, Aylmer, led us here. His horn will call us away."

The air seemed to be warming. The sun was rising, and all trace of the snow was gone, revealing green grass and wildflowers wafting in a rising wind.

"When my father refused to leave, I was surprised," Cerdic said, "but I was obedient.

"Utter obedience to the hold-lord is how our people survived these dark centuries. If we were not utterly obedient, if we did not obey his commands, if soldier and peasant alike did not work in concert, like one entity, we who live in the High Country would have succumbed to the rokahn long ago. That is why our view of honor is so strong.

"But when my father refused, I thought he was refusing the call… the long, ancient, prophesied call. One day, we will leave, and the hold-lord of the Vale will blow Aylmer's Horn."

"And will you blow the horn?" Gastreel said. "Your father was not as he had been. He had long been gone."

The wind was picking up.

"The way is not snowbound," said Cerdic. "Do you feel the wind blowing, the good winds, the southeasterlies? A Brightsömer is upon us, a few days of warmth before the first great blizzard and certain death."

Gastreel recalled a recent blizzard that had seemed terrible and great to him. But he supposed it was not on par with what the mountain was used to in the winter months.

"A Brightsömer, and a chance to speak, and deliberate," Cerdic said. "To leave the Vale of Ahorne, I must be sure. To blow Aylmer's Horn, and depart forever, I must be certain that now is the time.

"I will convene a Wismoot, and all our soothspeakers and wise folk will determine what we shall do."

"We may not have the time," Gastreel said. "The winds are capricious. They can turn in an instant."

"I and my blood have dwelt here since Gallia's waning days as a kingdom, when the city you call the Queen of the North was just a few villages in the shadow of a mysterious tower."

"I will not leave before a Wismoot is convened, and the soothspeakers tell me if now is the time."

But Gastreel, stirring there, could feel the southeasterlies already waning, and in his imagination could see snow drifting down, and the Vale buried in white. He could hear the howl of a blizzard wind, and rokahn horns sounding off in every direction, and dark shapes in dark armor everywhere amid the falling snow.

A Wismoot… there was no time for it. But Cerdic was not one to be easily persuaded.

"Cerdic, son of Maerrick," said Gastreel, "a sorcerer is at work in this valley. Your father's state proved that beyond doubt."

"And what sort of sorcery turns a man, healthy and wise, into such a thing?" Cerdic asked. "What sorcery causes him to change, and his body to become rotted and dried, and him to betray kith and kin?"

For a moment, Gastreel detected emotion in Cerdic's voice. He thought tears might be welling in his eyes, but on closer inspection it was a trick of the shifting sunlight.

"Not necromancy," Gastreel said. "A darker and deadlier magic, one I am not familiar with."

"And who did it to him? Who had a hand in it?" said Cerdic. "Could someone I trust be in league with this sorcerer? And why would this sorcerer so wish us all to perish? The time when my father fell ill, I had been away fighting rokahn. Edith had been drawn away to the Valley of Aíl. But perhaps, someone else would remember…"

"Perhaps you should abandon the Wismoot and sound Aylmer's Horn at once," Gastreel said. "Perhaps such a situation demands you refuse to honor your ancient customs."

"Our people have survived here for some thousand years because of the customs of our ancestors," Cerdic said. "No decision will be made without a Wismoot, whether the sorcerer is still at work or not."

And Cerdic turned, and he began to gallop away, back to the death trap that was Aerie Hold.

How long would Gastreel put up with Cerdic's obstinance? How long before Gastreel abandoned these people to the sorcerer Malison? How long would Gastreel wait before it was too late for he and Fortunato and Wrinn to depart? How long before he was risking even the life of the Sage—Reev Nax?

He was risking it now.

Chapter Thirty-Six: Edith's Gift

Reev and Wrinn were in the great hall, in the morning light, eating a breakfast of barley-bread dipped in ale. The castle servants had given them tall cups of milk, which they had both finished. They were talking idly about the dangers in the Vale when the great doors opened just slightly, and through the light Edith appeared, wearing a green gown embroidered in gold thread.

Coming back from her father's funeral, she did not seem burdened by grief. Her eyes brightened at the sight of them. Her father had been bewitched, and the perpetrator had yet to be uncovered, but Edith had said nothing about it. Perhaps she was unbothered, but Reev thought her nobility might prevent her from making complaint.

She smiled. "Simeon's son," she called out, "it is a good day, and do you know why? It is Brightsömer, and the good winds are blowing, and so a few days of warmth are here. It is the mountain way to give a gift on such a happy occasion. I am the hold-lord's sister. I have access to the treasury. Ask me for a gift, Simeon's son, on this Brightsömer, and I will give you anything—up to half the Vale."

Reev was tempted to ask for half the Vale, just to see the look on her face. But instead, he recalled what had happened to him last night, and the memory of what had happened just a short while ago.

Winter Ridge... *telantari*.

"I wish to go to my father's hometown," he said. "I wish to find my grandfather, Kal Nax. He's in danger, staying here."

"Can I come with you?" Wrinn said.

Adari. Helper. "Of course," Reev replied.

"Winter Ridge," Edith said. "That was your father's hometown, a village in the northeast of the Vale, in the northwestern Low Valleys, on the banks of Pymm Creek.

"It is near rokahn territory, and so you will need an escort. I think I can spare a hundred horse, if you promise to come back."

"I just want to see my grandfather," Reev said. "Ask him a few questions… tell him to head down to Galiope where he belongs, before it's too late."

"A doting grandson," said Edith. "You are like your father, Simeon.

"Hurry! Go gather your things. If you leave now, you can get there by nightfall. I will tell your friends, the wizard and that Fortunato fellow, where you have gone."

Reev got up, and hurried to the stairs and the room he'd slept in last night, to gather his belongings.

And before the morning he was on Cobalt, and Wrinn on Noble, and together with a hundred horsemen they had ridden off on the mountain road, under the custody of one Godwin of Atheling, who had been named Master of Horse.

Chapter Thirty-Seven: Gone

"What do you mean Reev *left?*" Gastreel howled.

As Edith backed away in Aerie Hold's great hall, he realized he was uncharacteristically rattled, uncharacteristically flustered. He was showing his emotions in a way he hadn't shown in decades.

He had considered his task done, that Cerdic would more likely than not order his people to evacuate. He had hoped to be making his way back down into Galiope tonight.

But no, he had been thwarted in the most unexpected of ways.

"Reev went where?" Gastreel asked.

"To Winter Ridge," Edith said, eyes flashing with indignation. "To his father's old hometown. He intended to see his grandfather."

"His grandfather…" Gastreel said. "Good gods, I believe I might faint."

"He will be back tomorrow, I am sure," Edith said.

"He had better be," Gastreel said. "I would bet a hundred marks that his grandfather is dead. How old would his grandfather be? And the mountains are not conducive to long lives."

"My grandfather Eadmund lived to ninety-nine," Edith said.

"Yes," Gastreel said, "fattened by oats and cuts of beef and rich bread and game—all that was available to him in Aerie Hold's larder. The Nax family was not rich. Kal Nax is dead… I am sure of it. Look at what you've done, Edith."

A door of the great hall opened and Fortunato walked out. He seemed more confident now in his tunic and trousers, and with Danenhir and Glyrnslayer clipped to his side. "Don't worry, Gastreel. Reev will be back in just a short while. Wrinn will look out for him."

"Wrinn…" Gastreel felt ill. "There is not enough common sense between the two of them to fill a puck's noggin."

"They are with a good man, my cousin Godwin," Edith said. "And a hundred horse. They are well protected."

"We're in danger of more than just rokahn," Gastreel said. "Time is our enemy. Time…"

Chapter Thirty-Eight: The Tavern Singer

The sun was growing low in the sky, the light shifting to shades of bronze and red, when Reev, accompanied by Wrinn and a hundred horsemen, found himself at a fork in the road. Godwin, leading the party, led them left, and soon, as the path descended, trees began to surround them, great junipers and spruces and mountain pines, and a novel sound began to echo: the babbling of a brook.

"Winter Ridge," said Godwin. "We are about there."

"And do you know where my grandfather lives?" Reev said.

"No," said Godwin.

Reev would have to find Kal Nax himself.

The dirt road took twists and turns before the forest, in view of peaks, beside cottages and stone huts where people were out working—people, Reev realized, that his father or aunt might have known, and alongside whom they might have grown up. Wonder filled him, and he felt a strange sense of kinship to this place as the road went on, and signs of the approaching village appeared everywhere.

At another fork in the road, Godwin stopped and told Reev he was at the threshold of the village, and that he should make his own way.

And Reev obeyed, riding down the road ahead on Cobalt, with Wrinn following him, and the village of Winter Ridge opened up before him.

The homes and workshops seemed to have a similar style, constructed sturdily of stone, with roofs that had tiles of wood. There were about a hundred buildings in the village center, and the people that wandered among them were Mountain Folk full and true, bearing swords and axes and fearsome daggers at their sides—men, women, and children.

And as Reev and Wrinn rode on in view of the mountain peaks, the road opened up to a square of cobblestone surrounded by buildings on all sides, the greatest of all being Winter Ridge Town Hall, and the second, not far behind, an inn of three stories with a great yard and a stable, and in front of it a sign that read: The Inn of Good Hope.

What better place was there to uncover the location of Reev's grandfather's house?

Night was setting in as they rode into the inn's yard, and servants ran out, shouting, "Let me take those horses off your hands, good sirs!" and "Welcome to Winter Ridge!"

~

The main hall of the Inn of Good Hope was dim and dark, and the hearth burned softly, shedding faint light. A few scattered people sat in booths, eating the night's meal—flat-cakes drizzled in gravy—and with it, ale. The innkeeper was approaching, but as Reev stood there, he couldn't help but notice the singer on the lonely stage, sitting on a chair, accompanied by a man with a fiddle. Soft, slow was the tune.

> *She's called Green Stockings*
> *Green as emeralds were her eyes*
> *Bright as emeralds was her smile*
> *Bright as sunshine was her gaze*
> *Green Stockings…*

And despite himself, the first question Reev asked was, "Who is that?"

"Dolley Wulfrun, our singer tonight," the innkeeper said.

"Well, actually, it's most every night that she sings here, save for feast-days.

"How long will you be staying with us? I can see that you are not from the High Country. Flatlanders, I see. Sorry you came to this place when it is so troubled. And right before winter, what's more. You aren't staying with us all winter, are you? It would get awfully expensive. A shilling a night for how many nights? I'm sure some kindly family will put you up."

"No," Reev said, "I didn't even want to stay one night. My grandfather lives in Winter Ridge and I'm sure he'd be happy to have me. I'm not stingy, though. I'll pay you if you tell me where to find him. His name is Kal Nax."

"Don't know anyone by that name," the innkeeper said. "But if you waited till morning, I'm sure our mayor, Jack, will be happy to locate him for you. Jack is mayor and town watch captain and guild-master and chief importer and chief merchant, too. There's no one he doesn't know in Winter Ridge or in the northern parts of Ahorne."

A night—it seemed a grim delay, but what other choice did Reev have? And he would be on his way in a matter of hours, when the sun dawned.

"One night's stay," Reev said, "for the two of us."

"Two shillings," the innkeeper said.

It was terribly costly, but how else would an innkeeper make a living in such an isolated place except by thievery?

~

Their hot plates of buckwheat flat-cakes were drizzled in a gravy-like mixture. Their ale was refreshing, but tasted thin and watered down.

And as they sat in their booth, the voice of Dolley Wulfrun was all about them, tantalizing, as she sang love songs and then ballads and then music meant for dancing. And as they sat, Reev and Dolley exchanged glances on more than one occasion.

And Dolley kept singing, and something was keeping Reev in his seat. He knew he wasn't going to be able to sleep tonight.

At least Dolley's voice overpowered the strange song that continued under the wind, rising and falling like bird-song—the strange song that those of the High Country called Malison.

From mountains to valleys,
I'll follow you, my love,
To peaks high, to waters deep,
To where the wild beasts roam

Reev knew the night was growing late, and he could see Wrinn's eyes growing weary and glazed. He was about to get up out of the booth when the music stopped and a shape was approaching: Dolley Wulfrun, her hair tied up in a great bun, her lips painted red, her cheeks dusted with makeup. Her gown was formfitting, and as she drew nearer, Reev could see all the things she had done to hide her age: wrinkles disguised with powder, hair dyed—hair that beneath the bright coloring was surely gray.

"You look familiar, boy," Dolley Wulfrun said. "You aren't a stranger in these parts, are you?"

"It's my first time here," Reev said.

"And do you like Winter Ridge, boy?" she continued. "Do you like this inn? Did you like my singin'?"

"I did," Reev said.

What could he say—no?

"What brings you here to Winter Ridge?" Dolley said. "A flatlander like you must have a good reason to be here when winter is about ready to start. And with all the trouble o' these damnable rokahn."

Now Dolley was prying a little too much, but Reev had a

thought, about her age that she disguised, about the way he looked familiar to her—and how Gastreel had said long ago that Reev had his father's hair and eyes.

"Do you know Kal Nax?" Reev asked.

A stunned expression came to Dolley Wulfrun. "Why, boy, I do," she said. "He was an old flame. But I haven't heard that name in years. He still lives, as far as I know, on the old Nax stead. His son and his daughter used to play with my boys back in the good old days, back when things in the High Country were on the up and up."

So Reev's father and his aunt knew this tavern singer, and his grandfather, too.

"How do I get there?" Reev said. "Do you know the way to the Nax stead?"

"Well, o' course I do," Dolley replied. "It's awful hard to get there, though. I'll write you down some instructions."

Wrinn's eyes were winking shut. He looked ready to fall asleep. But finally there was a little luck, thanks to this Dolley, whom Aunt Ramona and Reev's father had known.

Finally, a little luck... and he would see his grandfather tomorrow.

"Thank you, Ms. Dolley," Reev said. "Thank you."

Chapter Thirty-Nine: Only Worried

The night was dark, and as Gastreel stared out his window, sitting in the chair of his guest room, all he could think of was that Reev was out in it, out in that night. Somewhere, in that dark night, Reev was alone with Wrinn on a fruitless quest—and why?

This time, unlike others, it had not been Gastreel's negligence that put the Sage in danger. This time, it had been Reev's own vain desire, fed and watered by his Aunt Ramona. And in the span of an hour, Gastreel's best plans had been foiled. They should have been descending the mountains right now, but Edith—curse her—had acquiesced to those naïve boys' wishes and sent them, with her approval, on their way.

Edith…

As Gastreel retired to bed, he had seen her sneakily walking down the corridor in the direction of Fortunato's bedchamber.

Edith…

She had done a great deal of damage this day.

There was a knock on Gastreel's door.

"Come in," Gastreel said.

The door opened to reveal Cerdic, the new Hold-lord of Ahorne, still at this late hour wearing armor, still at this late hour wearing the Iron Crown of Ahorne on his head, with a sword buckled to his side.

"Wizard," he said, "I have called the Wismoot. Our best soothspeakers and wise folk will determine the next path."

"Cerdic, have you heard of Malison?"

"Of course," Cerdic said.

"Have you heard the whispers on the wind? The song rising? The violent commands that the weak-willed might well not resist?

“Malison, the sorcerer… what if his work affects the Wismoot, and the Wismoot’s answer is folly? What if whoever is responsible for your father’s fate is still at work, and he has some dark intent that has not ceased?”

“The soothspeakers and the wise folk will not be deceived,” Cerdic answered.

It seemed that Cerdic was convinced of his words. But Gastreel was not.

Gastreel did not have much confidence in soothspeakers, or in those who claimed knowledge by the use of elemental spirits. Such people could be led astray, if their work was not false to begin with.

And again, Gastreel turned to the window, to the night, and thought of Reev out there alone with Wrinn, amid its dangers, in a Vale that was soon to be overrun by rokahn.

“Reev Nax is out there,” Gastreel said to Cerdic, “in the night.”

“He is well protected,” Cerdic said. “A hundred horse. Simeon’s son will come back to us.”

“Edith allowed this,” Gastreel said. “Edith caused this.”

“My sister often attracts trouble,” Cerdic said. “But her heart is, for the most part, good.”

“I am not angry,” Gastreel said, “only worried… only afraid.”

Chapter Forty:
New Telantis

It was still dark when Wrinn and Reev left the Inn of Good Hope. Yet they were not alone. Godwin and the hundred riders were massed in the town square, approaching them.

"Reev, Wrinn," said Godwin, garbed in armor. "We have a change of plans, a change I am not certain you will like. The rokahn threat has greatly increased and they are beginning to make incursions in this area. We must meet the threat head-on, as demands the House of Atheling. You must return to Aerie Hold at once. My lieutenant, Cenhelm, will be your guide."

Wrinn had a look of fear. But Reev thought of *telantari*, and of the vision of the Lady of Danyen, and he would not be dissuaded.

"Wherever you go is your choice," Reev said. "But I have a task to accomplish. I cannot abandon it."

Godwin stirred on his saddle. He regarded Reev with a look that seemed to say Reev was the world's biggest fool. But ultimately, it seemed, Godwin did not much care what happened to Reev or Wrinn. He turned and galloped away, and the hundred riders followed behind him.

~

By the time the sun dawned, Wrinn and Reev were already outside Winter Ridge's town limits. Using the instructions from Ms. Dolley, they left down Winter Ridge's High Street, which became the North Mountain Road.

For an hour they traveled, variously ascending and descending, but inevitably ascending, toward one of the high, snow-capped peaks. The forest was dense and thick, and the boughs of the spruces, pines, and firs were slick with ice.

The area through which they rode became more and more remote, and as they rode, clouds rolled in, obscuring the sun.

Following signs, they came to a road called Sprinkle, and then another road, following the contours of a hilly ridge. They turned right, then turned left, and left again, and they followed the road on the opposite end of the hilly ridge—and it was not lost on Reev that they could have just ridden over it, and that they could have been at the Nax stead in better time.

Amid the grass and mixed forest, pines and spruces and mountain alders, there were homes in the far distance that looked dilapidated, and wells and abandoned implements that were rusted over.

And as Reev and Wrinn continued down the road called Country Town Ride, they noticed the air had grown much colder since the morning, and when they reached what Ms. Dolley had called the Nax stead, snow had begun to drift down, white snowflakes drifting so slowly they seemed suspended in the air.

The Nax stead, as Ms. Dolley had called it, was overgrown, and plots where buckwheat or barley or tubers or carrots had been cultivated were now covered in weeds and the beginnings of new trees. But far in the distance, Reev could see a spacious house of stone, two stories, with a large roof of wooden tile, and windows of transparent glass—but as Reev's eyes adjusted, he could see through the slow-falling snow that those windows of transparent glass were shattered.

"I don't think anyone's lived here for ages," Wrinn said.

Reev was inclined to agree with him. The thought of it was staggering to Reev.

He hadn't seen any people on the road called Country Town Ride either, only wells and rusted-over farming implements that had been abandoned in the grass.

But he had come this far.

Winter Ridge. Telantari.

And Reev tied Cobalt to the trunk of a fir tree, and Wrinn did the same with Noble.

Uttering prayers under his breath, Reev approached with Doomblade's hilt in his hand.

Who knew what awaited him in his ancestral home, the Nax stead where his father Simeon had lived before becoming a hero?

The door to the Nax stead was of wood, but it looked in terrible shape, and as Reev walked on the great porch, the boards seemed to buckle and creak underneath his weight. Had they rotted away?

When Reev touched the nob to the Nax stead, the door opened up at the slightest pressure.

Indoors, there was no warmth, no sign of habitation. In the corridor ahead, the roots of a tree had broken through the floorboards. And the Nax stead was as cold as the air outside of it.

"Grandfather?" Reev said, though he knew now that calling out his grandfather's name would be in vain.

Reev continued to walk through the corridor beside walls whose paint was peeling. Winds gusting through the open doors made Reev feel no different than he had outside, in the cold.

The rotted corridor opened to a dining room whose chairs surrounded a snow-covered table. Mice scurried away at Reev's presence, and so too did a robin who had built a nest in one of the open cupboards.

"Reev! Look!" Wrinn said.

And Reev turned to look into the great hall, where there was a stone hearth with cold, ancient coals, and before the stone hearth a rocking chair, and in that rocking chair a skeleton.

"Grandfather!" Reev cried, running up to him, seeing white marbled bones, a human being whose flesh had wasted away, who had now gone on to see the gods.

"He looks like he died in peace," Wrinn said.

But Reev couldn't be sure of it. No one had checked on him.

No one had ever known he was dead, or cared to know. And it was left to his sixteen year old grandson, who knew how many years later, to treat his body with respect.

"We must bury him," Reev said.

"Yes," Wrinn said, "but we should do that last. Don't you want to take a look around?"

Reev supposed he did, but that seemed the least of his concerns. He had come to see his grandfather, and now, he knew his grandfather was dead.

Wrinn wandered upstairs, up the creaking, dilapidated steps, and Reev explored the main floor.

The Nax stead was being reclaimed by nature, and in every room it seemed, some variety of bird had built a nest, and flew away at Reev's presence.

There was a parlor whose floor was nearly gone, and a larder whose food had long ago been pilfered by animals. There was a bedroom whose bed had been torn apart by wild beasts—but Reev saw next to that destroyed bed what looked like a wooden chest.

Amid the wind in the windows, and the sounds of animals in what was left of the walls, Reev approached the wooden chest, and saw that it was locked with a heavy padlock.

But time and disuse had caused the padlock to loosen, and the wood of the chest to deteriorate. Reev took the padlock in his hands, and gave it a light shake, and the chain fell apart like it was made from string.

He opened the chest to the smell of must and mildew, and within he saw documents—at the top a property deed to the house, but beneath it, more…

And amid the gathered papers of varying materials and varying inks, some so old they crumbled at the moisture of Reev's fingertips, he saw the gleam of metal near the bottom of the chest.

It was a coin that had been fixed to a silver necklace, and on the front of that coin, which was made from a bright yellowish metal, was writing in a script Reev had never seen before, in Gastreel's lessons or elsewhere. In the middle of that writing was the image of a mountain, and at the base of that mountain a city.

He flipped the coin to the other side, and there, forged in the metal, was a striking face, and on its head a knotted headband. What was it called?

A diadem.

In wonder, Reev took the coin necklace, and laid it over his neck. His grandfather would surely want him to have it, now.

Then he continued filing through the papers, seeing documents related to his father Simeon's birth, and also his Aunt Ramona's. There were letters in an old dialect of the Imperial language, letters that crumbled at the touch, and scribbled drawings—had the toddling Simeon been an artist?

At the bottom of the pile of documents was what looked like a case for a scroll.

Reev took out the scroll's case and opened it, and out rolled a piece of parchment so fragile he feared unrolling it.

But carefully and patiently, he did just that, and though it crackled at Reev's touch, he managed to gently unroll it without damage.

There in ink on the ancient parchment was what looked like a map, a map of an island surrounded by sea, at the top of the page the words "New Telantis" and written in various places, names such as "Tribe Nax" and "Tribe Ajax" and "Tribe Gens."

Unsure of what it was, or what it meant, but remembering Glenda's words, *Telantas* and *Telantis,* and the words of the Lady of Danyen in his mind's eye, he carefully rolled the parchment back up, and managing not to damage it, placed it back in its scroll case and sealed it.

New Telantis… an island in the sea. If that was New Telantis, then what was the old Telantis?

And what was the coin that Kal, Reev's grandfather, or some

more ancient relative, had fashioned into a necklace? What kingdom had issued it? What king was depicted on the obverse?

Wrinn came storming down the stairs and into the room, holding a dusty book in his hands.

"What are you wearing?" Wrinn said.

"Something I found in this chest," Reev said. "A coin necklace… like an amulet. Something I hope my grandfather would want me to wear. And what are you holding?"

"A journal," Wrinn said. "I found it in the upstairs attic, above one of the bedrooms. Dare we?"

It seemed a violation, but his grandfather was dead, and so too was Reev's father—as far as he knew.

Reev took the journal and opened it, and began scanning through the entries lightly.

They were mundane, recording Kal's frustration of living alone, without the help of Simeon and Ramona and his deceased wife, Reev's grandmother, Trita.

The last entry was dated Sextil 23, 1136.

The year Reev was born.

I am worried they will get me, like they got my great-grandfather. I am worried I will have to up and move again.

Kal Nax was paranoid, maybe delusional, clearly driven mad by fear to the bitter end. And he had been lying dead for this long? More than sixteen years.

A terrible feeling dawned on Reev, an unshakeable sense of danger. Through the shattered window of the bedroom, the snow was falling in thicker and more numerous flakes, and what's more, he knew they were on the edge of rokahn territory.

"Let's bury him!" Reev said. "Hurry!"

~

The snow had accumulated on the ground by the time Wrinn and Reev found shovels, and together, began to dig. The wind was picking up pace, and the sense of danger in Reev was only building, and with each stroke of the shovel he looked to the dark woods in the distance, expecting to see the mottled face of a rokahn.

"Hurry!" Reev said, and the ground was rocky and tough, and difficult to displace, but he wouldn't leave until his grandfather's remains were treated with proper respect, and Kal Nax had had a proper burial.

Amid the building snow and the icy wind, a rokahn horn blew—no, it was Reev's imagination. Wrinn hadn't looked up from his work; he was still shoveling.

At last, when they were both exhausted and heaving in ragged breaths, and their hands both looked raw and sore, they had created a two-foot-deep pit in the poor soil.

They hurried indoors, and uttering prayers, took the bones from the house to the yard, to the pit, and dropped them in.

With a speed borne of the imminent danger they both now sensed, they heaved the dirt into the pit, and then covered up the bones. Reev hurried into the woods, grabbed a stick and returned, hammering it before his grandfather's grave to mark his resting place.

"Let's get out of here!" Wrinn said, and Reev agreed.

Reev shoved the scroll case into his pack and adjusted his coin necklace. A horn blew again—so he thought—but again Wrinn showed no sign of hearing it.

The horses seemed nervous as Reev and Wrinn sprinted toward them. Noble was nickering, and Cobalt stirred against the rope tying him to the fir tree.

They fled, and it was still morning.

The flurry of snow was quickly turning into a storm.

Chapter Forty-One: Watching, Waiting

Gastreel sat in a high room at Aerie Hold, having been offered a tea brewed of lemon balm. The Wismoot was meeting and their pronouncement would be made law, and Reev was gone…

Gone, on a vain quest with his fool of a friend.

Cerdic approached from the corner of the room. "Wizard," he said, "when the Wismoot acts, will you leave?"

"I would have left already if Reev Nax hadn't been taken from us," Gastreel said.

"Simeon's son," said Cerdic, who was also clutching a cup of tea, brewed of dried lemon balm leaves. To believe the people of Aerie Hold, it would ward off sickness. "He was not taken from us. He went himself, with my sister's permission. You say he is a boy of exceptional importance. Why then do you doubt his judgment? Why do you question his will?"

"This mountain valley will soon be filled with rokahn," Gastreel said. "The way down will be snowbound, impossible to traverse. What he wills is perhaps not mine to question, but I realize the danger we are all in… that *you* are in, Cerdic."

"He will be back soon," Cerdic said.

"Back soon…" Gastreel said. "Let us hope so."

Far below them was a makeshift garden of yarrow and Sawyn's wort and raspberry bushes, now withered and dead from the cold, and a doorway that looked like a *khameirrat*—an entry to the Dim Roads. In that garden was Fortunato and Edith, and even from this height, Gastreel could see her brushing his cheek with her hand.

"Oh, Fortunato…" Gastreel said.

And Cerdic drew nearer. "I do not know what to do about my sister. In her actions, she was discreet enough to avoid my father's notice. And no shire court would dare charge, let alone convict a member of the House of Atheling. She goes after flatlanders most of all, the more foreign, the better. A peddler from the western kingdoms had to push her away. A man of the village called Avebury took up with her last summer."

"Oh, dear," Gastreel said. "A shame."

But he turned away, his mind on other things.

Chapter Forty-Two: The White Cord

"What color was the elf-maid's hair?" Edith asked Fortunato as her hand went from his cheek to the white cord that had been tied around his left wrist.

"Red," he said.

"Red," Edith repeated. "And was she fair? Fairer than I?"

Fortunato would not tell her the truth.

"Maybe I will get a dyer from the flatlands, and have my hair red for you," Edith went on. "Tell me. What was her name?"

"Yanenré," Fortunato said.

"Yanenré," Edith said. "Well, that's a mouthful."

"We called her Nenré," Fortunato said.

"That isn't much easier to say," Edith replied. She continued stroking the precious fabric of the white cord. Though she jested and she joked, Fortunato thought her jealousy ran deep.

And yet Nenré was not the reason he had intended to leave Galiope, before he found himself on this star-crossed journey. No, the one he had truly loved had sent him away.

Winds were blowing from the northeast, and the skies had grown cloudy. As they stood there in the castle garden, snowflakes began to drift down, so slowly it seemed they were suspended in air.

"Not a Brightsömer," Edith said, "but a False Brightsömer. And that means we can expect terrible snows, and a harsh winter. Snowbound any hour now."

The silence that followed broke the spell of this silly love affair, and for a moment Edith's hot passions seemed dispelled by the more primal emotion of fear and the human need for safety. Danger lurked everywhere and doom was written for the Vale of Ahorne.

Cerdic had not given the command to leave. And why not?

Chapter Forty-Three: Cerdic of Atheling

Gastreel and Cerdic still drank their tea of lemon balm in the high room when through the door came a portly man, a scion of the House of Atheling called Auderick, who had been responsible for the Wismoot.

"What did the soothspeakers say?" Cerdic said.

Auderick seemed ashen, and his eyes appeared shallow, full of fear. "The soothspeakers have announced that now is not the time for us to depart. We must remain in the Vale through the winter."

"Madness!" Gastreel shouted.

"We will not disobey the words of sooth," Cerdic said, "lest we chance the wrath of the gods and our ancestors.

"We remain for the winter."

"And you will die!" cried Gastreel. "Look into your heart, Cerdic. You know those are not words of sooth, but instead the words of bewitchment, of Malison. Have you forgotten what happened to your father? Do you not know that the sorcerer is likely still at work?"

"Wizard," Cerdic said, "I think you and your party have overstayed your welcome, giving unwelcome counsel where it is not asked, despoiling my sister..."

"I don't think Fortunato was the driver of that affair," Gastreel said.

And an anger appeared in Cerdic's eyes that Gastreel had not seen since he first entered the Vale, when it was under the thrall of Maerrick. But now it seemed his son was just as taken with madness.

"In olden days," Cerdic said, "when a man said something that offended a member of the House of Atheling, his tongue was pulled out with piping-hot tongs, and molten lead was poured over his eyes. Shall we do the same to you, Wizard?"

"Listen to reason!" Gastreel said. "You know you sentence all who dwell in the Vale of Ahorne to death."

Cerdic's hard gaze softened. "You had best leave, as you said."

"I will not leave without Reev Nax," Gastreel replied.

"You will depart Aerie Hold, with your companions, tonight," Cerdic continued, "because the lord of Aerie Hold has said you will."

Cerdic's tone gave no space for a reply. His green eyes were filled with slow burning wrath.

So Gastreel and Fortunato would be forced out tonight, and Cerdic would do the will of the sorcerer who had bewitched his father.

But as Gastreel set down his half-finished tea on the window ledge and exited the room, he could not help but think of the fifteen thousand innocent souls still locked here, in this troubled vale, peasants and farmers, good folk of the soil. And he could not help but remember that Cerdic had told him where to find Aylmer's Horn... on the altar of the castle chapel.

~

The chapel was located on the first floor of Aerie Hold, on the ground level. Gastreel had only to search a few corridors before he found it. The door was unopened, unguarded, and as he entered, he could see a spacious chamber, lit by candles, with eagle motifs everywhere, and treasures of gold.

Eagles were painted in gold leaf on the blue walls, and on either side of the pews were reliquaries of gold also forged in the shape of eagles, holding the bones of the pious dead. The carpet leading up to the altar was blue, woven in gold thread, with eagle shapes and patterns. The ceiling was painted with pictures of eagles against a bright blue sky, and among them a mighty eagle with brown feathers, ten times the size of the others.

Beyond the pews was an altar, on which a candelabra still burned, and before that candelabra, as Cerdic said, lay a horn.

As Gastreel drew near he felt a presence behind him and turned, and there standing in the dim light was a priest in a brown frock, his dark hair cut in a tonsure.

"Have you come to make an offering to the castle chapel, Mr. Wizard?" said the priest.

Gastreel stood there a moment, uncertain of what to do, uncertain of what to say. Then a new strategy came to him—but would he lie to a priest and in the sanctity of a chapel?

"Your Lord Cerdic has told me to go fetch him Aylmer's Horn," Gastreel said.

The priest seemed to shrink back. "So it is time," he said. "I have long known it is time, time for Aylmer's descendants to leave. I know it. We all know it. I have long known it. But it will grieve me greatly to no longer see the Matinberg or drink fresh milk from the alpine pastures."

"But safety and security will follow," said Gastreel. "At least for a little while."

"A storm has begun," said the priest. "I fear it is already too late to depart."

"Let us pray not," Gastreel said. "For your sake, and for mine."

The priest walked down through the pews to the altar, and gingerly took Aylmer's Horn in his hand. The horn, forged from a goat's horn, looked in good repair, obsessively cleaned and kept. Then the priest crossed the room and handed to Gastreel Aylmer's Horn.

Gastreel took it, and disguised it in the folds of his green robe.

"It is time," said the priest. "I have long known it. Cerdic now knows it, too."

Cerdic did know it, Gastreel was sure, if he peered into his heart. But soothspeakers had convinced him to do folly.

~

From the ground level of Aerie Hold, up winding stairs, through the fortress's mounting levels, Gastreel traveled skywards, higher and higher, until he began to grow exhausted, sweat dripping from his brow. From Aerie Hold's ground level upon the cliffs up to a place of impossible height, to the highest tower, Gastreel traveled, until his heart burned in his chest and he heaved in painful breaths.

But as he broached the highest level and found himself on the roof of the tallest tower, there was a commotion behind him, the peal of a trumpet and scattered shouts.

Gastreel, his body bare to the icy air of the outdoors, placed the Horn of Aylmer to his lips just as Cerdic burst through the trapdoor and lurched forward, as if to wrestle him to the ground.

But Cerdic did not lay his hands on Gastreel, nor was the look in his green eyes violent or aggressive. Instead, Gastreel saw in those eyes a newly-confirmed respect.

"Wizard," he said, "do not blow Aylmer's Horn. For a flatlander to sound his horn, and not a man of Atheling, descended from him, would be a greater sacrilege than my ignoring the soothspeakers."

"So if I give it to you," Gastreel said, "will Cerdic, son of Maerrick of the House of Atheling, sound Aylmer's Horn?"

Amid the whipping wind and drifting snow, here on the highest tower of Aerie Hold, Cerdic's gaze softened and his presence seemed to shrivel. "It is time," he said. "I know it, in my mind. It is time to blow Aylmer's Horn."

Cerdic took the goat's horn in his right hand, and he steadied it in his left. He placed it to his mouth, and sounded the horn, first once, then twice, then a third time. And its tone was resounding and pure, deafening even, and in the darkening twilight, in the valleys beyond the Matinberg, horns of a similar sound one by one began to blow. For more than a millennium, the nobles of the villages had waited for that call, and now that call had been sounded.

From Aerie Hold to the farthest recesses of the Vale, the message to depart would be heeded.

"The Hold-lord of the Vale and all his family leave the last of all," Cerdic said, "and not until his people are safely on their way."

The last of all, he would leave, and with him Edith and the House of Atheling. Gastreel could not imagine this noble family from a bygone age, whose speech even seemed from a far-gone era, heading down to Galiope and holing up in a townhome in Greenwater. It was a topic fit for a comic actor, but there was nothing comedic about the situation they had found themselves in.

The Horn of Aylmer had been blown; the call for the people of the High Country to leave would be heard in the farthest recesses of the Vale.

And Reev was out there, somewhere in the coming night.

Chapter Forty-Four: Midnight Flight

Reev and Wrinn hurried out of their room in the Inn of Good Hope, heaving bags and saddlebags in their arms, dreaming of the relative warmth of the lowlands, tramping through the main hall in their muddy shoes. Dolley Wulfrun was on the stage, her hair tied in a bun, gently strumming the edges of a harp with her fingers, singing a song about two ill-fated lovers.

Reev, remembering she had known his father and his aunt, thought he might say goodbye to her.

He intended to ride as far as he could tonight to Aerie Hold.

But as Reev stood there, hesitating inexplicably, a new sound arose, a piercing and deafening peal of a horn, and time seemed to stop. Dolley fell silent, and everyone sitting in the booths ceased their eating. The innkeeper of the Inn of Good Hope, looked up, seemingly to the sky.

"Aylmer's Horn," said the innkeeper, his eyes touched by wonder.

"You all know what this means," he said to the patrons gathered in the booths.

" 'When you hear Aylmer's Horn,' " he recited, " 'flee your home and take nothing with you; look not back, not even to the Matinberg. Look back but once, delay but a moment, and disaster will fall upon you. Flee then to the lowlands, where, for a time, you will be safe.' "

Dolley said, "You heard the man, you all. Let's heed the warning o' those who came before us. That horn is our curtain call! The show is over. Grab your things and make a run for the lowlands. And don't stop for no night or no cold."

Not all in the booths reacted with urgency, or paid attention to those sagacious words. Some had looks of irritation or annoyance or disbelief. But others left their drinks and plates of food behind, and hurried to gather their things.

Reev and Wrinn scrambled out of the Inn of Good Hope into the piercing cold of the growing night. As servants furiously worked to procure Cobalt and Noble from the stables, other horns sounded from the faraway mountains, the harsh and unmusical sound of rokahn horns.

And as they departed Winter Ridge there was the sound of far-off battle, and Reev thought of Godwin, and the hundred horse.

Godwin and the hundred horse, who apparently wouldn't be leading Reev and Wrinn back to Aerie Hold.

~

They galloped down the road, Reev on Cobalt, Wrinn on Noble, as the night deepened, and the snow was growing. As they galloped, Mountain Folk were joining them on the way, Mountain Folk who had at last been given the command to leave, riding or walking, from alpine hamlets and high pastures, from villages great and small, those who heeded the call of "Aylmer's Horn," whatever that meant, and the words of sages who had spoken long ago.

The snow was building, and the winds were blowing, and the stars and the moon could not be seen. They rode at the fastest pace Noble could manage, though Cobalt was desperate to gallop away at an elvish horse's speed. The roads were becoming crowded with Mountain Folk families, and those lucky enough to have horses passed by those who walked. They held lanterns as they made their way down, those wise enough to listen to the blowing of the horn and the mountain sages' words.

But as Reev and Wrinn rode through the growing snow, into the dark of night, there were signs of trouble that these Mountain Folk families were ill prepared to face. Rokahn horns were blowing in the faraway hills, and in the mountains between the Vale of Ahorne the light of rokahn torches burned in the dark.

It had to be the witching hour, or past it, when they drew near the Matinberg, and the lights of Aerie Hold appeared in staggering height in the distance. Wrinn was almost asleep in the saddle. Reev could barely keep his eyes open.

But at the portcullis, after they had ascended the steep switchbacks, there were still guards posted on the battlements, and alert.

"Who goes there?" one cried.

"Simeon's son," Reev said.

And orders were given among the deepening dark night, and the portcullis opened, and in they rode, into the death trap that was Aerie Hold.

Chapter Forty-Five: Council Rock

"Simeon's son has returned!" a servant cried, waking Gastreel, and the morning of the twenty-fourth day of the month of Brightleaf, 1152, began to welcome news. The sun was shining in the windows, and the light was reflecting in his spare guest room.

As the servant left, Gastreel hurriedly donned his green robe, grabbed his white staff, and after a cursory look in the mirror, headed downstairs.

They would depart at once, without delay. The way could already be snowbound, but Gastreel would never have left without Reev or Wrinn.

~

Gastreel found the two of them in the great hall, eating a breakfast of bread dipped in ale.

"Reev Nax!" Gastreel said, walking up to him, he who had caused him great anxiety and a sleepless night, but who was now safely in his care.

And Reev was wearing something strange about his neck.

"What is that?"

"I found it in a chest in my grandfather's house," Reev replied. "I don't know what it is, but I thought my grandfather would want me to have it."

Gastreel took the coin in his hand, the coin to which the silver necklace was tied, and was baffled by the sight of it. "I am a man of words, Reev, a scholar of ancient things, a master of languages. Not only can I not read this writing I have never seen this script before, and certainly not a coin like this. It must be a thing of incredible antiquity, something even the wizard order does not know of. And it has something to do with your grandfather, Kal Nax?" Gastreel said.

"Maybe it has something to do with me, as well," Reev said. "Me and Fortunato."

"Fortunato?" Gastreel muttered in bafflement. But as if he had called up the name of a ghost or a spirit, Fortunato approached them, now wearing a jerkin of leather over his tunic and bearing his weapons Danenhir and Glyrnslayer at his side.

"Green Wizard," Fortunato said. "Time to leave?"

"The hour approaches," Gastreel said, and he wondered what Edith felt at Fortunato's hasty departure. "First, I must bid goodbye to the hold-lord. You, Fortunato… go ready the horses. We will head to the lowlands in a matter of moments."

~

Gastreel ventured up the stairs, past forgotten rooms and ancient passageways, to a room called the Starred Chamber, which of late had served as the place of the House of Atheling's deliberations. There, as he expected, was Cerdic and Auderick, but also Edith and a few trusted advisors, too.

As Gastreel stood there in the dark chamber, its walls painted with gilded stars, the air in the room seemed to swivel and change. Cerdic straightened up.

"Wizard," he said, "we are glad of your presence. A warband of ten thousand rokahn is marshalling to the west of the valley, and a warband of eight thousand to the east. As things stand, these forces will easily crush the paltry remnants of our forces."

"Cerdic," Gastreel said, "I only came to bid you goodbye, and give you my best wishes for the evacuation. But I suppose I can offer a bit of advice.

"Your thinking is stuck in the past. There is no victory against the rokahn. There is only retreat. You should ride tonight with all your family, down to the lowlands, before the Vale is swallowed whole."

"The hold-lord leaves last of all," Cerdic said. "His departure comes when the people he protects are safe, and no sooner."

"Some will delay," Gastreel said. "Some will refuse to leave. Some you cannot save."

"But within reason," Cerdic said. "When all of good character, who will leave at Aylmer's call, are departing the Vale, that is when the House of Atheling abandons its possessions."

"Mr. Wizard," Edith said, "your kind are known for their wisdom, and are consulted by great kings and emperors for advice, but you do not know the mountain way. To us, the nobly born, are given great privileges and comforts, but at a terrible cost. For it is we who are the sword to the peasant's plow and the shepherd's cane. We are the ones charged with the Vale's defense, and we will not depart until those in our custody are safe."

What a two-sided figure was Edith, for this noblewoman of blue blood uttering high-minded paeans to duty and honor had been seen falling all over Fortunato. And Gastreel thought she could put on this outward cloak of majesty or take it off like a mask. Gastreel felt that although Cerdic would not admit it, Fortunato had dealt a severe, maybe fatal wound to the House of Atheling, and that if the House of Atheling survived the rokahn crisis, it would collapse to pieces in a great crash. Already, tension was in the air.

The door to the Starred Chamber opened and a man of war strode in, garbed in a chainmail shirt with a blue cape, a sword dangling at his side. "Milord," said the man, "a report. And I fear it will trouble you.

"Evacuations were going well, and most in the valley—all with sense—were departing."

"Were?" said Cerdic.

The man of war continued, "But as they began down the road

one of the nobles of the town of Ethelwhite has turned rabble-rouser. He has begun to speak in grandiose notions and declared you, Cerdic, illegitimate and traitorous. And now a great many thousands of our people are refusing to leave, gathering in Ethelwhite, maybe even plotting a rebellion against you."

Gastreel felt he would be sick. "Malison. Malison!" he said. "It is the sorcerer Malison controlling that 'rabble-rouser.' "

And something else he recalled from the town of Ethelwhite, the rumors he had overheard, that the voice everyone had heard for months—the song under the wind, "Malison"—was coming from a place called Council Rock.

The innocents in the Vale of Ahorne deserved rescue. The evil power in the Vale had to be ended.

"Cerdic," Gastreel said. "Tell me… what do you know of Council Rock?"

"Council Rock?" said Cerdic. "It is a place in rokahn territory of great antiquity, where the rokahn war-chiefs would gather for their dark festivals. They would hold council there on that rock, and they would light ritual fires, and in the flame sacrifice their human captives.

"Why, wizard?"

It was a desperate gambit. It was mad, insane. But what other hope was there to end the evil in this Vale, and allow the people to leave?

"How many men can you spare?" Gastreel asked. "How many men can you spare for an old wizard?"

~

With Fortunato on Tyra Jade and Gastreel on Ivy, and five hundred men on horses, they left that morning for Council Rock. But on all of them was an eye that had watched their every move since the flatlanders entered the Vale. On all of them was fixed a power half of magic and half of darkest hell.

Chapter Forty-Six: Rabble-Rouser

Fortunato and Gastreel had left swiftly and suddenly, bolting out of Aerie Hold's great hall, and as Reev finished his breakfast, warriors were donning armor and tabards, and fixing swords to their belts. Outside the doors of Aerie Hold's great hall, there was the sound of thundering hooves, and the first thought Reev had was that the rokahn had laid siege to the castle itself—but he had heard no rokahn horns.

Wrinn seemed just as confused, just as worried. But when the warriors had at last left, leaving the great hall behind them, a door opened, and Edith walked out, dressed in a green gown with gold thread.

"My children," she said, "how are you holding up?"

"Where have Fortunato and Gastreel gone?" Reev asked.

Reev would say it wasn't like Gastreel not to tell him where he was going—but that was not altogether true.

"They ride to Council Rock," Edith said, "a place in rokahn territory. Why, I do not know… but I will not question the will of a wizard."

She crossed the room into the light of the gently burning hearth, whose size Reev still marveled at. "Have you made your preparations to leave?" she asked.

"Haven't you?" Reev said.

"Last of all leaves the House of Atheling," Edith said. "At the blowing of Aylmer's Horn, when the people are safely on their way, then I and the rest of my family will go by the old road… to the flatlands."

"The people are on their way, Lady Edith," Wrinn said. "Aren't they?"

"No, our plans have been upended," Edith said. "A notable of the town of Ethelwhite has turned rabble-rouser, and he is inciting the people to rebellion. The wizard claims it is the work of Malison, a sorcerer—the same sorcerer that bewitched my father."

Council Rock… Malison… "Controlling others' minds, inciting mobs," Reev said, "that doesn't sound like sorcery."

"Then what does it sound like to you?" Edith said.

Reev recalled the vision he had when he first entered the Vale, the man in the strange robe, the iron mask that had belonged to Gogg, the chief of the Six Servants. And he recalled the dark whispers that had afflicted the minds of Gastreel and others, the dark whispers he had heard as well. And he wondered what would have happened if he or Wrinn or Gastreel had succumbed to those whispers instead of resisting.

"Not the power of magic," Reev said. "The power of the Dark One."

The lightness and grace in Edith's demeanor seemed to evaporate at his words, and she even appeared offended that Reev would say those words aloud.

"That sounds like something for the Sage, not Gastreel or Fortunato," Wrinn said.

And though it would put them at great risk, Reev was inclined to agree. But his power appeared at unexpected times, and he could not tame it or harness it, nor could he ever gain control of it.

"Where is this rabble-rouser?" Reev said. "Where did he come from?"

~

The ride from the Matinberg to Ethelwhite was swift without the threat of Cerdic's men hunting them down, though now in the distance in places there were rising tendrils of smoke, signs of either the disposal of rokahn corpses or the burning of villages.

The snow was building, and showed no sign of slowing down as Wrinn and Reev galloped until the glistening white snow approached Cobalt's hocks. If the way was not snowbound already, if leaving the Vale was not already impossible, it would be so in a manner of hours.

They began to ascend a steep hill, and when they reached the apex, Reev could see the scattered homes of Ethelwhite. But there among them was a crowd thousands strong, stretching from Ethelwhite to Drury Village, packed together—Mountain Folk all. The children sat on others' shoulders, and from a raised platform in the distance a man was shouting.

Reev rode nearer, and Wrinn, too, and there far away was a man who looked vaguely familiar, portly, in overalls, and as he shouted and raised his fist, twisting this way and that, Reev noticed something strange about his eyes. They were white, featureless, and yet this rabble did not seem to notice. In a voice that seemed to carry unnaturally far, he was impugning the honor of the House of Atheling.

"Cerdic is not half what his father was!" the man was shouting. "He is not even a tenth of Maerrick! He does not measure up!"

The rabble cheered in reply.

"He wants you to leave the High Country because he is in league with the wicked Eventide!" shouted the rabble-rouser. "And when you reach the flatlands, they'll make you forget the mountain way! They will bind you in chains and force you to work in the fields of some lord! Cerdic wants to sell you into bondage!"

Reev felt the situation was untenable, the tension in the air so great that one stray spark would send this mob storming down to Aerie Hold to murder Cerdic in cold blood. Reev wondered what he could do, how he could stop this, how he could free the people of Ethelwhite from this grave delusion.

"What shall we do, Wrinn?" Reev said.

But Reev looked to Wrinn, and Wrinn appeared fixated on the

rabble-rouser.

"What of the rokahn?" the man continued to shout. "The rokahn may be your enemies, but they never asked you to leave your homes. Cerdic did that!"

Wrinn lifted a balled fist, and he cheered.

Reev was the only person, it seemed, not blinded by the rabble-rouser's words. He did not know what to do. He did not know how to stop this. So under his breath, he began to pray.

Chapter Forty-Seven: Fire and Steel

With his cloak flapping in the wind, with his knees clutched to Tyra Jade's saddle, with Danenhir firmly in hand, Fortunato followed Gastreel through rokahn territory. Rokahn chased after them as they deftly wove through the snow-covered valleys, underneath the light of the sun, amid the growing snow. But the horsemen of the Vale of Ahorne were too swift, and they were entering so suddenly and so unexpectedly that the rokahn were unprepared.

The snow was drifting down, and the snowflakes were getting thicker, and as Fortunato rode he knew the taste on the wind, the taste of a coming storm. It began to dawn on him that the way was snowbound—if not now, then they had at best an hour.

And if he and Gastreel were stuck in the Vale of Ahorne, then as the winter set in and the spawning pits spewed their vile treasures, a sentence of death was proclaimed for them all.

He tried not to think of it, tried not to belabor it in his mind as he rode, for the danger he was in now was more immediate.

Through the snow he and Gastreel traveled, followed by five hundred men on horse. At times, the Green Wizard would summon up a bolt of lightning to scare off the rokahn that drew too close, and at times, the riders would engage rokahn with their swords, but their strategy—as outnumbered humans—was surprise and speed, to catch their enemy off-guard and bowl their way deep into enemy territory before there was a chance to retaliate.

Fortunato had followed Gastreel into many dangerous situations, but none seemed quite so reckless as this. The talk of Council Rock from that parish priest of Ethelwhite could be just that, idle talk and rumor. And if they did find this Malison, this sorcerer, what promise was there that he could be defeated? Fortunato knew of no wizard as mighty as Gastreel, but that did not mean he did not have an equal.

Up ahead, on a snowy ridge, were the crude piled-stone walls of a dark-hold, and from that dark-hold rokahn poured out, some—toltar—short and weak, bore slings. But a tall, lanky red rokahn—a kehrad—had a bow, and was fitting arrows to the string.

Other dark-holds were ahead as Fortunato and Gastreel and the five hundred others followed their guide, a man of Atheling named Oswald. Rokahn horns were beginning to blow, and the rokahn were becoming aware of the intruders in their territory.

But something did not sit right with Fortunato—for though the rokahn were numerous, they seemed too few in number for the cataclysmic spawning crisis that had been reported.

He thought too at that moment of the Vale of Ahorne, of the mighty walls of Aerie Hold, and wondered at the Mountain Folk who had survived in such a dangerous situation for more than a millennium. And he said a prayer for Edith, who had remained behind.

Rokahn appeared ahead, a line hundreds strong, in dark armor and dark helms, bearing dark swords, and in the drifting snow and icy gales, Fortunato and Gastreel and the five hundred met them head on.

The force of their charge bowled over the rokahn lines, but as Fortunato and the others stabbed and parried and overcame them, Fortunato knew their position was precarious, that this reckless incursion into rokahn territory was being met at last with resistance.

Fortunato hewed down a kehrad at the cost of a buffeting of a war club. He slaked the thirst of Danenhir on a rokahn warrior, but nearly lost his grip on Tyra Jade's saddle.

And more were appearing in the distance—hundreds. More than Fortunato and Gastreel and their force of Vale riders could overcome. They crawled down from high dark-holds; they emerged from canyons and caves.

The riders of the Vale of Ahorne were faltering before the rokahn, and with each passing moment rokahn were overcoming the riders, piercing them with their crude swords and hewing them down with their axes, toppling horses with their war clubs and driving them down on their black wolves.

At last Gastreel raised his hand and his staff, and summoned down a spear of lightning, so bright and so pure, so immense, that for a moment Fortunato could not see, and his eyes had to adjust to the light.

Oswald of Atheling, their leader and guide, took out his horn and blew it and shouted, *"Ride!"*

The rokahn, stunned but for a moment by Gastreel's magic, were distracted enough that Gastreel and Fortunato and the Vale riders could break free of them.

And again they and the Vale Riders galloped, deeper into rokahn territory, as the snow picked up in great flurries, falling in blankets, and had reached in depth Tyra Jade's knees.

At last, hours after this journey began, amid the drifting snow and icy wind, after many Vale riders had been slain and the rest had been exhausted or injured, in the distance appeared what looked like a table of black rock, and on that black rock, a boulder over which appeared a burning fire.

The song, once gentle on the wind, was now deafening, audible, louder than the gale that blew and louder than the rokahn horns that echoed in every direction.

Fortunato could make out two figures near the fire, one short, one tall, and they were not rokahn. They were too lithe, too shapely. As the gales howled and the song entered Fortunato's mind, he felt a strange compulsion to turn back and flee. Tyra Jade resisted him and he rode her forward. Gastreel followed, toward that black stone table and that ritual fire.

Council Rock.

~

When Fortunato on Tyra Jade and Gastreel on Ivy reached the top of Council Rock, rokahn were everywhere below, pouring in from canyons and valleys, and the Vale riders struggled to fight them off .

The fire was an inferno, towering above the mountain ridges, and what was burning was not clear.

But those figures he had seen became clear, one a man stunted and pale, thin and gaunt, in a black robe, with thinning hair—one hand clutching a staff, the other hand summoning up the ritual fire.

The other figure was tall, slender, wearing a white robe and also an iron mask—the iron mask of a Servant of Seymus.

But this, Fortunato knew, was no Servant.

Chapter Forty-Eight:
The Confrontation

"Ariya, White Wizard!" Gastreel shouted. "How low you have come! What depths you have plumbed, wearing the iron mask of a fiend. And why? What power is worth becoming a tool of the Dark One?

"And Durgo… Durgo… Always the apprentice, never the master. When your former master died you slinked away, but like a pestilence you always seem to reemerge."

The song emitting from Ariya's mouth, the contours of the words, were becoming clear, and from her mouth came the language of Doomsday, the language of Seymus's Servants.

Execrable Durgo ceased his summoning of the ritual fire, and summoning up a sphere of flame in his left hand, cast it at Fortunato. But Gastreel, summoning up the weave, caused it to sizzle up in smoke.

Fortunato charged him. Staff met sword.

And Gastreel struck at Ariya with the power of the weave, and the iron mask she had worn fell, clattering, to the ground.

"Gastreel! Fool!" cried the White Wizard, she who had betrayed him long ago, and who now betrayed all light and all goodness— the very gods. And Gastreel knew in that moment that it was she who had cast her dark spell over Maerrick, and tried mightily to bring death to the Vale of Ahorne.

"Do not think I act alone, impostor!" Ariya shouted. "You are not the true archwizard. You will be laid low."

Fortunato was battling Durgo, sword against staff and gouts of flame.

And Ariya was growing in size. A wizard she was, an accromancer, with power over speed and increase. Her veins bulged, her muscles radiating outward. The white fabric of her robe grew, stretching at the seams. Strength was filling her, the strength that the heroes of old were said to have.

But her foul song had ceased, the utterances were gone, and now there was only the sound of the icy gale, the far-off clang of steel against steel, and the shouts of rokahn and the shouts of the riders of the Vale.

Hideous, Ariya now was, putrid, half again Fortunato's height and twice his width. In her state she could break down doors and tear down walls.

She charged him, but Gastreel knew how to deal with accromancers. Deftly and with the aid of the weave he jerked Ivy to the right, and he dodged out of her way.

In the distance, Durgo had summoned another fireball, a blazing sphere of fire smoking in his hands. He was ready to cast it at Fortunato when Fortunato tackled him to the icy ground and sent the blaze uselessly up into the air and away, dissipating into smoke.

Fortunato stabbed at Durgo, but Durgo rolled out of the blade's path.

Fortunato slashed at Durgo, but Durgo dodged and shot a jet of flame from his fingers, singeing Fortunato's hair.

The ceasing of the ritual fire had caused the rokahn to take notice, and when Gastreel looked down on the battle taking place below, he could see the rokahn eyeing the four fighting figures. Now, without the ritual fire, they no longer viewed Ariya or Durgo as their allies, no longer as masters ruling over them. If Gastreel and Fortunato were to vanish by some miracle of the gods, Durgo and Ariya would be the rokahn's prey.

Durgo thrust his hand forward and sent Fortunato flying, yards, to the ice-covered ground. Fortunato slipped as he returned to his feet, as the pain-maddened Durgo drew up another fireball, and at last, successfully, cast it at his foe.

But Fortunato slashed with Danenhir, and the letters the elves had written on the blade seemed to glow. The blade cut the fireball, and the fireball sizzled and flew back, directly at its creator.

The fireball exploded and opened a blackened hole in Durgo's chest. As Durgo fell, Fortunato rushed forward and took Danenhir in both hands. He pierced Durgo straight through, into the heart, and stood over him in victory. So fell Durgo, Jerek's apprentice, and then Ariya's apprentice after him.

Gastreel wheeled around Ivy to face Ariya, who was now a hulking monster of flesh, her white robe beginning to tear, her staff no longer fitting in her lumpy ball of a hand, and clattering to the ground.

Fortunato charged her, but she struck him with her hand and he fell sharply to the ground.

To Gastreel's right, the iron mask that had belonged to Gogg was smoking. And snow began to fall so heavily that Gastreel could barely see Ariya.

He could barely see a foot ahead of him.

Rokahn horns were sounding in every direction. The sound of the distant battle was fading as the Vale riders succumbed to the rokahn.

But Gastreel could sense Ariya's presence from afar; he could feel her weave strengthening her body yet weakening it, causing it to contort and develop in ways that should never be.

Tyra charged at her and Ariya swiped her away. Fortunato came running and slashed at her with Danenhir, but her flesh was so distended and swollen it made little difference.

At last Ariya gave a deep bellowing cry, and rushed away from both Fortunato and Gastreel. As Gastreel sat astride Ivy in horror, she laid hold of the boulder on which the ritual fire had been burning with her massive, swelling hands and with a guttural cry lifted it up, breaking it free of its place. Gastreel could do nothing as she pitched it back, and hurled it in the direction of Fortunato.

Fortunato dived away, Tyra Jade scrambled out of the boulder's path in the nick of time, and the stone shelf called Council Rock shuddered and cracked in two.

Gastreel was helpless to slay her. But Gastreel knew that Ariya was vulnerable. The ritual fire, tricking the rokahn into believing they were allies, was beyond her ken to recreate—an accromancer she was, not a pyromancer like Durgo. Yet the iron mask would give her power.

He scrambled astride Ivy to the smoking iron mask and summoned it into his hands, deftly tucking it into the folds of his robe.

"Fortunato! We flee! We leave her to die!" Gastreel shouted.

Fortunato rushed to a frightened Tyra and mounted her, and Gastreel galloped away as Ariya gave chase. He plunged off the ruined Council Rock on Ivy, landing with a harsh thud, and Fortunato followed a moment later.

Ariya came charging at them, but her swollen, monstrous legs were clumsy, and as her white robe began to burst, she leapt off Council Rock in their direction and fell to the ground, failing to catch them as they rode away.

The bodies of the Vale riders were all about them, but the remnant of them that survived, one of whom was Oswald, began to gallop for home, for Aerie Hold, amid the deepening storm.

Snow fell in sheets, blanketing the ground, blinding all view, and Gastreel knew the way was snowbound now. And where did that leave them? As the snow reached Ivy's hocks and was building toward her withers, she was more hopping than galloping. Gastreel had saved many lives in the Vale of Ahorne, but at the cost of Reev.

Reev, still at Aerie Hold.

Reev, on whom the hope of the world rested.

Chapter Forty-Nine:
Into the Depths

At Ethelwhite, the rabble-rouser's speech had ended as soon as it had begun, and mid-speech the pupils and irises had returned to his once-white eyes, and he had fallen back in confusion. And then, as a blizzard began, the thousands gathered at Ethelwhite had come to their senses all at once, and with the rabble-rouser among them, had turned and fled in a stampede for the roads that would take them to the lowlands.

Reev was left alone with Wrinn among the building snow, the cutting gale, and the snowbound death trap that was the Vale of Ahorne. The town of Ethelwhite had been abandoned. And they were alone, with a choice to make.

"Do we flee?" Wrinn said. "Will we leave Gastreel and Fortunato behind?"

"No," Reev said, and his conviction was resolute. "We return to Aerie Hold."

"We'll be trapped there," Wrinn said.

But Reev could not leave Fortunato and Gastreel behind, and moreover, he did not know how to travel in such difficult weather, or how to descend the mountain passes.

Snow was falling heavier and heavier, covering Cobalt's mane, and Reev was shivering—but he knew not what else to do. He knew Gastreel and Fortunato had departed on some reckless quest, but that if they were to return, they would surely meet Reev and Wrinn at Aerie Hold.

"Come on, Wrinn!" he said.

Reev yanked Cobalt's reins and wheeled him around. He galloped off down the road in the direction of the Matinberg, which he could no longer see, and heard Wrinn join him a moment later.

As snow fell, blinding him and clinging to his brow, and as the day's light began to wane, rokahn horns began to blow to his left and to his right and behind him, growing closer and closer and more numerous in every direction.

As the temperatures dropped, plunging every moment, and as the snow flurries became a blinding wall of white, Reev coaxed Cobalt on, no longer trusting his own navigation but trusting instead in Cobalt, the hopes that his own horse would lead him to Aerie Hold.

He felt the road begin to descend, and the rokahn horns were now sounding hundreds at once, closer than a mile away. He felt Cobalt begin to ascend a high ground—the switchbacks of Aerie Hold—and as the sun began to set and twilight was falling, Reev realized he was at the portcullis and loudly began to shout, "Let me in!"

The rokahn horns approached and he even began to hear their far off voices and the stamping of their iron shod feet.

"Let me *in*!"

"Aerie Hold is shut," a voice echoed just faintly above the raging wind.

"It is Simeon's son… Simeon's son, and *adari*—his helper."

The portcullis began to grind open, just enough for Reev and Wrinn—whom he could now see—to pass through. The portcullis began to grind shut then, and Reev realized at that moment that their worst fears had been realized, that they were now snowbound in the Vale of Ahorne, that rokahn had assumed control of the High Country, and they were trapped in a castle that was fated to fall.

~

In the great hall, a fire was burning in the hearth, and near the fire was Fortunato, sitting in a chair, while Edith cleaned a bloodied wound on his head and was beginning to mend it shut.

Gastreel approached from the room's dark corners. "Where have you two been?"

He was taking out his anger and fear on Reev and Wrinn, though now it was all of them who were doomed to die.

Cerdic was in armor, approaching, his sword dangling from his side. "We will fetch the two of you armor—armor, and a shield, and a tabard. The rokahn are already massing outside."

But it was no use. At the rate the rokahn were emerging, the fall of the castle was inevitable. Reev began to think, and try to imagine his way out of the death trap, to dream up of some plan or some possible way to escape. But they were trapped within Aerie Hold, high in the mountains, with rokahn armies between them and the downward-leading road and impassible snow and the threat of avalanches between that road and Galiope.

The castle shuddered, and there was the sound of masonry cracking and crumbling and falling to the ground.

"To the walls!" Cerdic said. "We defend our hold. We drive them off."

But they were doomed and even Cerdic knew it. If his mouth did not say it, then his face revealed it.

What warriors they had were pouring out of the great hall. The steward Eodgar came running up to Reev and Wrinn, and offered to them what was bundled in his hands—two cuirasses of mail, tabards of night blue with eagle marks upon them, and daggers as weapons of last resort.

But Reev ignored him and turned to Gastreel. "Gastreel, we will die."

"We will fight as long as we can," Gastreel said.

The castle shuddered again, straining at the blow of the catapult.

"Eodgar, forget them," Edith said, "they are cowards, refusing to fight. Go get bowls of water and set them on the ground, so that we may detect miners."

"Gastreel," said Reev, as Eodgar glared and turned away.

"The Dim Roads…"

Gastreel looked at him aghast.

Edith scowled. "No one has used the Dim Roads for hundreds of years."

"And yet," Fortunato said, his head wound now sealed, "I think the son of Simeon has a point. This castle *will* fall. And in the garden there is a way under the mountain."

"A *khameirrat*," Gastreel said. "But if we journey into the depths, do we know there is a way out? Can we be sure?"

"No," said Edith. "No, and what madness it is to speak of it."

"A *khameirrat*," Gastreel said. "A way below, that those of Ëarno made… Dweorg of the ancient world."

"Didn't they fall?" Wrinn said.

"They fell," Edith said, "for they were greedy and covetous. They fell long before humans claimed the High Country."

"I say we go," Fortunato said. "The way… under the mountain, the road carved by Ëarno."

"Madness!" said Edith.

"Edith, you must come with us," Fortunato said. "Aerie Hold is a death trap."

"Never," Edith hissed. "A woman of Atheling will not travel into those demon-haunted halls."

But it seemed to Reev that a woman of Atheling would take up with a foreigner, with an Imperial, in the most unbecoming of ways.

"We go!" said Gastreel. "Swiftly gather your things."

"What of the horses?" Reev asked.

"We take them to the postern gate," Gastreel said. "Set them free… and pray that their abhorrence of rokahn will lead them home."

It seemed a poor bet to make, but on deeper thought Reev considered it the best option for Ivy, for Noble and Cobalt. Lightless subterranean tunnels were no place for creatures of the forest and plain.

"What of Tyra?" Reev asked.

And Fortunato smiled. "She will take care of herself, I am sure," he said. "And she will take care of others, maybe, too. The snow and mountains are where she thrives. But I am sure she will make it safe to Galiope."

That could be said of Tyra and no one else.

"Hurry!" Gastreel said. "*Ananda!* We go!"

~

Carrying everything with them, leaving behind what they did not need, the four of them—Gastreel, Reev, Wrinn, and Fortunato—fled into the castle yard as the castle itself shuddered under the weight of more catapult strikes.

And there, beyond the walls, was a sight Reev could not believe, a sight that made him wonder if he had left the real world and entered into nightmare. Amid the darkness of the Vale, the rokahn were like a sea, filling every inch of the landscape beyond Aerie Hold, their harsh horns blowing so often and so numerously it was a cacophony.

Cerdic and his men were battling vainly on the outer walls. And as Reev and Wrinn, Fortunato and Gastreel, hesitated in the castle yard, it began to hail…

No, it was not hail. Large dark objects were being flung from the sea of rokahn, some bursting like melons on impact.

They were the severed frozen heads of Mountain Folk, of they who had not heeded Aylmer's Horn.

"Go! Go! *Ananda!*" Gastreel cried, and with Reev and Wrinn and Fortunato, he sprinted into the garden as more severed heads fell like a rain.

More stones struck Aerie Hold in the darkness and terrible doom was written for those that stayed behind.

Amid shriveled garden plants and snow-covered bushes they fled to the dark door into the mountain, which Gastreel had called a *khameirrat*. And as another volley of heads began to fall like rain, there was a scream, and from the doorway in the garden Edith came running, weeping.

"Fortunato, love!" she said, and met him in an embrace. "Do not do this! Do not take the Dim Roads—it is death!"

"Aerie Hold is death," Fortunato said. "Come with us!"

"No, no," Edith said, falling back, weeping. "I cannot... I cannot!"

And she kissed Fortunato, and staggered back.

"If I make it to Galiope, where shall I meet you?" she asked.

"The Dragonpaw Inn," Fortunato said.

But the House of Atheling would not be surviving this black night—Reev knew it in his heart.

Edith turned and fled back toward Aerie Hold's doors, and screamed in disgust and fear when another volley of heads landed on the ground, some bursting on impact.

Reev, Wrinn, Fortunato, and Gastreel at that moment fled into the *khameirrat*, into the darkness, as more stones fell and seemed to shake the ground.

~

In the darkness of the mountain, it was still.

But blue light appeared on the tip of Gastreel's staff and the stone chamber was illumined.

The cavernous room was covered in cobwebs, and contained ruined stone slabs and debris, crumbled masonry and the faded remains of writing on the walls.

"There is no way down," Reev said, and like that he knew they were trapped in Aerie Hold like the others.

"There is a way," Gastreel said. "That is the point of a

khameirrat. Look!"

And they began to search the broken pieces of stone and crumbled remnants of what had once been a stone-carved chamber.

The ground shook. Reev fell, and the darkness seemed to deepen. "What's that?" he began to say but then saw the stone of a catapult had struck the doorway of the *khameirrat,* forming a mound of debris, trapping them inside.

"No way out," Gastreel said.

"And no way in," Fortunato said. "A pity for the House of Atheling."

Reev had expected a bit more emotion in Fortunato for Edith, to whom he had allegedly made love.

"Look!" Wrinn cried, and as he stood in one of the chamber's dark corners, began to push away a broken bit of stone.

Reev ran to him and saw that beneath that stone was a hole, and the remnants of a foothold.

Gastreel approached. "Into the depths we go "

The sound of battle raged outside.

"Into the depths… let us pray for our good fortune."

Gastreel entered first, climbing into darkness. Wrinn was next, then Fortunato, and Reev was alone.

The sound of battle and the deafening thunder of the stones of the catapults echoed. An unfathomable host of rokahn was massing in the Vale of Ahorne, but it was not a tenth what Galiope would face.

That, however, was not Reev's immediate concern.

He wedged his shoe into the foothold and climbed downward into the darkness, into the Dim Roads, into the deep chasms of the earth, as outside the sound of the hordes and legions of rokahn was like the raging of the sea.

Chapter Fifty: Balor

As a rain lightly drizzled down, and the hearth of the Dragonpaw Inn glowed brightly, Ambrass was enjoying her first restful night in days. She was still a serving maid, still on duty, technically, but the crowded main hall of the Dragonpaw Inn had been turned into a makeshift theater. In every booth, on every table, was enough food to satisfy the hungriest belly—mushroom pies, crispy bread, beer-basted chicken, and more. Ambrass now could recline, sit back, and enjoy the performance on this St. Wolfrick's Night. The juggler was up, and as the brightly-clothed entertainer threw the knives and balls, and the children gasped in wonder, a figure walked through the inn's doors.

He was brushing the rain off his cloak. Pale was he, dark-haired—Nocturne, her love. And Ambrass sat up just a bit from the booth she'd been sitting in, and called him over.

He smiled and her heart raced at seeing him, not just for love of him but also those white fangs that, at the right angle, were noticeably different from human teeth. He walked over and sat down, and Ambrass wriggled her way into Nocturne's lap. She did not care if she was publicly seen with him, though it was a mark against her reputation in the eyes of the haughty and the proud.

The Mountain Folk children, who with their parents had been growing more and more civilized and who along with them no longer wore their weapons openly, had taken seats on mats on the floor. The festival of St. Wolfrick's Night, on the twenty-fourth of Brightleaf, was celebrated differently in different towns and villages, but in the Dragonpaw there was always a performance to keep people off the streets, to keep children from the practice of mumming and guising. Glenda considered going door-to-door begging for sweet treats risky.

"What do we have here?" Nocturne said. "A juggler?"

"A juggler," Ambrass replied. "Now, two."

A female juggler in bright pink and purple clothing had joined the other, and in her hands began to toss a set of keys and trinkets. The little children sitting on the floor, a mixed population of Mountain Folk and native Galiopeans, clapped their hands and gasped in wonder.

The performers juggled standing on one leg, and then blindfolded, and then while standing on one leg and blindfolded. The wonder of the little children seemed to grow, and by the end of it, even their parents seemed impressed.

And then, as the jugglers exited through a set of doors, Glenda walked out. She was the makeshift mistress of ceremonies for the evening. "And now, friends of the Dragonpaw," Glenda said, "a pantomime in Imperial style, the one and only Dioneo."

A swarthy man strutted out dressed in an outrageous costume, a billowing thing with colorful patches up and down the side. On his head was a conical cap, and at once Dioneo began to prance on his feet.

"The story of Brecko and the Nine Nymphs."

Elaborately he danced, playing the part of the nymphs, and he twisted and bent his body like it was made of gelatin, as if he had no bones at all. He played the part of the female nymphs well, in a way that would shame most prideful men, and at the last moment he assumed the part of the god Brecko, and the front of his pantaloons swelled up.

There was scattered laughter among the adults who understood it, but Ambrass didn't think it was funny, nor appropriate for the city's children.

"Remind you of anything?" Nocturne said softly, and she groaned and lightly struck him.

Dioneo left, and when Glenda returned as mistress of

ceremonies, she was blushing bright red. "Well, well. That's that.

"And now, our last performance, two dancers telling the story of a dark chapter in our city's history."

Drums and stringed instruments began to play—performers on the corner stage, well hidden—and a singer began to chant nonsensical words that sounded like incantation.

A dancer twirled out of the door, and in his hand was a knife, his lips were painted bright red and his face a bright white. Another dancer twirled out, dressed in rich robes of fustian, his fingers covered in rings. As the haunting, rhythmic music played, the dancer with the knife pursued the other as he tapped his feet, circling around the room. The children appeared to be scared, and between this performance and Dioneo's, Ambrass was wondering about Glenda's judgment.

At last the dancer with the knife touched the dancer in fustian with his weapon, and the music stopped.

When the dancers left and Glenda walked out, she seemed even more embarrassed than by Dioneo. She cleared her throat and said softly, "Whoever guesses the event gets a year-long supply of cottage pies at the Dragonpaw.

"So what was it, do you think?"

There was uncomfortable silence for a while, and the bewildered and offended Mountain Folk families said nothing. But an elf at a table ventured a guess: "The Wars of '41 and '42?"

Glenda sheepishly shook her head.

A woman in a booth, a Galiopean, shouted: "The murder of Emperor Marcus!"

Again Glenda shook her head.

"The High Street Slasher!" Nocturne shouted just behind Ambrass.

And a nervous smile grew on Glenda's face as she awaited any more guesses. But no more guesses came. "It was the assassination of Lord Mayor Percival."

A little Mountain Folk girl looked to her parents and said, "Mother, what's assassination?"

And Glenda's humiliation was complete.

~

Through the streets Ambrass and Nocturne walked, and it was after dark. When she was with him, she did not fear for her safety, but in the dim light she remembered Nocturne's own words, his guess that those dancers depicted the High Street Slasher. And why—why would that come to Nocturne's mind? Some claimed he was that murderer from a forgotten age, that mortal fiend who had taken those innocent lives. Ambrass knew that Nocturne wasn't the High Street Slasher, that if he wasn't good in a high-minded sense, then he wasn't evil. But Nocturne's words had reopened a matter that she had tried so mightily to keep closed, hidden away, and forgotten. And as they crossed the Bridge-O'er-Galios in the growing night, Ambrass began to have a sense of dread she had not felt in months, and she wondered if she was walking hand-in-hand with a murderer.

They ate a light supper in Nocturne's house, had two glasses of wine, and talked quietly for an hour amid the ambient night noises and a gently burning fire. That night they retired to bed, and when they made love, something seemed different, something seemed changed. Nocturne fell asleep on her chest, and when he was still and beginning to snore, she carefully crept out of bed and in her smock, descended the stairs into the living quarters.

Where would she find evidence? She grabbed a candle from the mantelpiece and in the hearth, set the wick alight.

Where would she find evidence? A blooded knife from all those decades ago, now crusted over in dried blood? A fingerprint? A memoir penned in a codex—*Blood and Terror: My Life as the High Street Slasher?*"

But she did find herself walking over to Nocturne's bookshelf, whose selections were few and did not even fill the entire space. There was a book of rules and etiquette, *The History of the Druen Race*, *Quartillo: Selected Plays*—how strange!—and a manual on lovemaking. What a scandal. But there was also a copy of the priest's book, thick and unwieldy, bound in leather, and Ambrass thought it strange a man such as Nocturne would be interested in religion.

And she took the bulky tome in one hand, and walked to the divan, and began to page through it and its entries, one by one.

One line toward the beginning was underlined in red ink: "I am the avenger, the enemy of the gods' enemies."

The rest of the book was unmarked, she saw, until the very end.

He had circled the passage in red: "The world will not end until the son of Gilden and Ivé sits on the throne of Solendir; and he will be called Balor."

"Ambrass!" Nocturne snapped, and Ambrass nearly screamed. She closed the book.

He was in his nightclothes, and in the light of the candle he looked like a phantom.

"Why are you up?" he asked.

"I could ask the same of you," Ambrass replied.

"You know I'm a light sleeper at night," Nocturne said. "This daytime schedule we've been keeping is no good for me.

"And why are you holding the Book?"

"Why did you circle that passage," Ambrass said, "about Ivé… Balor…?"

Nocturne drew near, no longer having that sense of smugness and self-satisfaction that seemed ever present on his face.

"It might seem strange for a man like me to have a copy. I guess it seems strange to me, too. And I don't know if I believe it all… but that passage says the world won't end until the son of Gilden— the first vampire—and Ivé, the first human woman, sits on

Solendir's throne. That's the throne of the elves.

"The world won't end until a boy, half-human and half-vampire, sits on the elvenking's throne. And so I thought I had a chance at being the father of a king."

"Is that why you went after me?" Ambrass asked.

"Of course not," Nocturne said.

" 'Bala' sounds an awful lot like Balor," Ambrass said.

"Do you think a seven-year-old would be able to pronounce Balor?" Nocturne said.

And a terrible chill crept up Ambrass's spine.

Chapter Fifty-One:
Mama

Bala was stumbling in the dark, thinking of going back to the Dragonpaw Inn, thinking of even returning to Dada Nocturne's house. Ever since Mr. Aleksander said his training would be "delayed" and sent him away, he had struggled to find something to do, some way to spend his time. During the day, he'd go to sleep in an alley, and at night he would go search for coins and shiny trinkets and things to collect. And like Mr. Aleksander asked, he never used his magic in public, because it was "illegal," he said, and wrong.

He headed down the Bridge-O'er-Galios, northward toward Middletown, in the direction of the Dragonpaw. In the distance, shapes appeared—his size, one for every finger he had. Bala froze up, getting a terrible sinking feeling, as those little shapes began moving toward him.

Up close, they became visible to Bala: children about his age, dressed in those funny clothes the Mountain Folk wore. Most terrible of all, the biggest and meanest of them carried a knife in his hand, and not the kind of knife used to cut butter but instead a knife used to poke people.

Bala screamed, knowing he couldn't use his magic because it was "illegal" and, Aleksander said, wrong.

"You, pointy-ear," the biggest and meanest of them said. "Give us all your candy!"

"I don't have any candy," Bala said. "Who are you?"

"We're the Big Bad Wolves," the boy continued. "And we're going to teach you a lesson!"

But a light was shining on them now, suddenly, the bright and focused light of a bull's-eye lantern, followed by the galloping of hooves.

The gang of children, the "Big Bad Wolves," turned back to look.

And there, on a horse, with a nightstick at his side, was a town watchman in armor, a blue tabard over his breastplate.

"You children," he said, "vagrants. There's a curfew ever since the mountain crisis began. Where are your parents? Oh, bother, forget it! I'll take you right to them, with or without your help."

~

In Middletown High Court, the "Big Bad Wolves" were escorted to their parents one by one. When it came time for Bala's turn, the watchman asked him, "Where do your parents live?"

"My parents don't live together," Bala said.

"Where does your father live?" the watchman said.

Bala didn't want to go near his Dada Nocturne, at least not now. "He… he… he's dead."

"And your mother?" the watchman asked. "Where does she live?"

Bala paused, hesitating. Mama… when was the last time he had seen her?

"You have a mother, don't you?" said the watchman.

Bala didn't know what to say.

"Oh, bother it all," the watchman grumbled. "We have his name, Bala Rabaam. Look it up in the registry books."

~

Through the dark streets Bala was led, in the moonlight, as a misting rain fell. He walked down side streets through the lights of Middletown, and the farther he walked, the dingier and more dilapidated the houses became. Some houses had windows that were shattered and had been boarded up. More and more, trash was left in the open, on the streets, and the cobblestones were stained with the remains of chamber pots—something even Bala knew was against the law.

The people in this part of town were sitting on their doorsteps this late at night, gawking at Bala as he walked by. Their clothing was dull and ratty, in faded brown or gray or black colors. Bala began to wish he had told the town watchman the truth, that his Dada Nocturne was alive and well. At least then he would have a familiar bed, and he would have been among his own kind.

"Lucy Cotter," one of the watchmen said. They had stopped at the doorstep of a brick townhome, a tenement overlooking the shores of the River Galios. "We're at 11 Crinkle Way, Greenwater. This is it." And the watchman walked up the steps, and knocked on the door.

The door opened, and to Bala's surprise, there were candles burning, and the fireplace blazed brightly. A slender woman appeared in her nightclothes, to Bala's mixed wonder and apprehension. He realized he knew that face, a face like a half remembered dream, her hair a bright blond, her eyes a brilliant blue. The chemise she wore was colored a bright pink, and in the distance, Bala could hear the far-off sound of murmuring and talking.

Mama had company.

"Bala!" Mama said, but it had been so long, and he barely remembered anything about her.

"This is your child?" the town watchman said.

"Why, of course," Mama said. "Come inside."

Coals were burning in the fireplace, and in the living quarters, a set of couches and divans faced the fire. On those furnishings was a motley crowd, a man of bucked teeth, and two women in drab gowns.

"Bala, it's been so long," Mama said. "Ever since Eventide's men took you from me."

The buck-toothed man had a lute in his hands, and he was chewing something.

Mama turned to that motley crowd, and said, "This is Bala, my son."

The buck-toothed man waved lightly. Bala wondered who he was, and who Mama's two friends were.

"Oh, Bala," Mama said, "I've missed you so."

And she leaned down, and she kissed him on the cheek. He could feel the lipstick mark on his skin.

The buck-toothed man was playing songs on his lute, and in one of the women's hands was a bowl with a black drink she would occasionally sip. A pot boiled over the coals, unattended, and Bala was about to say something to Mama, but Mama took him by the hand, and led him through a side room.

The room was filled with scattered forgotten objects that had been heaped up in piles, clothing and cooking implements, and in the far corner, a mattress of straw that Bala supposed Mama slept in.

"Oh, Bala," she said. "I had you for only a year, and then Eventide's men came and took you from me, and gave you to your father."

Bala had begun to think that that had been for the best.

"Oh, Bala," she said, "when you were in my belly, I went to Selwyn's Parish and had a gypsy woman read my fortune. And she said you were going to be a girl, and I had a name picked out— Elly—and I bought dresses and dolls and little toys fit for a girl."

She began to rummage through some of the old clothing and forgotten objects. She pulled out a little dress made from cotton, brown with gold thread.

"Why don't you try it on, Bala, and make your mama happy?"

"But... but..." Bala said.

He didn't want to do it, he rather liked his ash gray robe and his top hat, and what's more, he wasn't a girl, but a boy.

"Come on," Mama said. "Come on, Bala, won't you do it, just for me?"

~

He walked out into the living quarters in the dress, blushing. Mama had smeared lipstick on his lips and now she was lurking over him.

The buck-toothed man laughed and the two women chortled.

"Garrick, play the Greenwater Soft-shoe," Mama said, and the buck-toothed man began to strum his lute.

"Dance, Bala! Dance!" Mama said, and Bala, after a nervous giggle, began to prance his feet and tap his toes, to an enthused reaction from Mama's friends.

~

Mama at last fell asleep, and as she was snoring, Bala hurried out of the dress she had given him, and pulled his ash gray robe over his head. He set his top hat over his hair. And he realized, for all Dada Nocturne's faults, he was glad to have lived with him for those years.

He crept outside into the hallway. Mama's friends had collapsed and were sleeping on the floor. The pot that had boiled over was now smoking and burning. And through the windows filtered the happy light of dawn.

Bala did not know where he would spend the day, or on what bed or under which roof he would sleep, but he didn't want to stay with Mama anymore. And he was glad that Gastreel had made him into a wizard, and he hoped and prayed he could return to his training soon, and that Aleksander would know where to find him.

Where would Aleksander be able to find him? He would have

to choose a public and well-known place.

Chapter Fifty-Two:
The Dim Roads

How many days had they spent under the ground?

There were no days. There were no nights.

There was only the light of Gastreel's staff, and the ever present sense that they were in danger.

Reev was following Gastreel through a tunnel, and he could tell it was descending, that they were headed downward, into the mountain's heart.

The tunnels, carved with exact precision, perfectly squared, and decorated on the top and bottom with lifelike floral reliefs, had been their ever present companion since they had descended into the darkness of the hole beyond the *khameirrat*. Reev would think from time to time of the House of Atheling, and when he dreamt he would dream about Cerdic, stoic and stone-faced, and of Edith, alternatively dispassionate and full of passion. But other dreams he would have, too, in these dark tunnels, when Fortunato set out their bedrolls, and the dayless and nightless hours of traveling came to an end. Those dreams Reev barely remembered, but he would wake up cold and breathless, with a sense of raging chaos and the memory of a bottomless pit. And though there was only the light cast by Gastreel's staff, and the forms of Fortunato and Gastreel and Wrinn traveling alongside him, he had an ever present feeling they were being watched, and an inexplicable conviction that they were not alone.

Days or nights or hours, months or weeks or minutes after they had descended the dark hole into these Dim Roads, after three bouts of sleeping—he had counted—the tunnel abruptly fell away, and he saw a great bridge across the cavernous depths, with bits of the masonry having fallen away, and beneath that bridge pitch blackness, something like the bottomless pit he thought he had seen in his dream.

And that cold, terrible, reeling feeling he had when he awoke from his dayless, nightless slumbers assailed him at that moment, when he considered how perilous and how far was that drop, and when he wondered what slept at the bottom of that black pit.

"A Dweorg bridge," Gastreel said.

He did not know its name or its type. They had come to a place, the Dim Roads, of which there was no mortal living memory, and not even wizards or scholars of the ancient world knew much of Ëarno, the kingdom of Dweorg who made these roads. Amid the chaos of the passing of one age to another, books and scrolls and knowledge are lost, and entire peoples fall out of memory.

"Guard yourselves!" Gastreel said. "Watch your step, and do not look down."

Taking the Dim Roads had been Reev's idea, and he was sure that Aerie Hold would fall, but was this a worse fate? At last running out of food or coming to a waterless place or being hunted by something that no one knew of, of which nothing was recorded?

But Reev knew in his mind that nothing was hunting them. They were alone, and not even the rokahn were foolish enough to do what they now did, travel the Dim Roads.

He followed Gastreel across the bridge of stone, over the bottomless chasm, and felt his breath quicken and his heart begin to beat faster, so hard he could feel it in his chest.

Under the mountain, across the bridge, they walked, and the bridge despite the damage it had sustained was broad enough for an ox cart to travel through.

Before the awesomeness of the cavern, the impossible size, Reev felt he was a mite or something smaller, something infinitesimal. But at long last the bridge was behind him.

"This way must take us somewhere," Fortunato said. "It's a highway of sorts, under the mountain. It must have a destination."

"It has many destinations," Gastreel said, "but some ways have been shut and sealed off. Others are to cities underground that have been abandoned."

They had reached a large stone chamber, and amid that chamber were three doorways, two of which had writing above them and one of which, to the right, was so damaged and crumbled no writing remained.

"Can you read the writing?" Fortunato said.

Gastreel stood before the doorways, staff in hand, and began to sound out the words.

"To the left, *nirzun*… treasury. Ahead, *kharzun*."

Some things, it appeared, Gastreel did not know, some words and some dialects of Dweorg were ineffable to him. There were enigmas that the Green Wizard—no wizard—could solve, or so it would appear.

"What path shall we take?" Fortunato said.

"Perhaps," Gastreel said, "we should ask the Sage."

They turned to Reev—Gastreel, Fortunato, and Wrinn—as if his guess was better than theirs, as if somehow he would hold the key to avoiding death amid these subterranean caverns, when it was not so. But Reev did have a feeling, one he could not explain, an inkling toward the right, toward the ruined unmarked tunnel, and he began to walk toward it.

"A strange choice," Gastreel said, but they all followed him anyway.

~

Through nightless and dayless slumbers, past tunnels and beyond forgotten rooms, the dreams Reev had were growing in intensity.

The four of them were growing gaunt, and hunger was their constant companion. When they had finished off their waybread,

Fortunato began to gather the mushrooms that grew along the edges of the Dim Roads, and to catch slinking subterranean creatures, maybe rodents, that, with salt and a little heat, were edible.

How many miles had they traveled? How many times had the sun risen and fallen? Time seemed to blend all in one, and every hour and every inch of the tunnel was the same.

Chapter Fifty-Three: Memories of Love

Outside the frosted windows of the Dragonpaw, snow was drifting down, the first snow of the coming winter. It was the month of Candlebright, and Glenda wanted Ambrass to put up the Yule decorations, and make certain there was a festive atmosphere. On the front door she had placed a wreath. On the doors of the rooms that Mountain Folk families still occupied, she had fixed holly and berries. But it didn't seem enough for Glenda, and lately, with the coming winter, she had seemed on edge.

The Gallian League expected a war in the coming spring, when the rokahn would venture to the lowlands. And underneath the jollity and gift-giving of Yule, a sense of doom seemed to underlie every comment, every remark.

Glenda was walking down from the main corridor. "Ambrass!" she said. "We've gotten a little sloppy, haven't we?"

She walked up and adjusted the holly wreath, which to Ambrass's eyes had looked perfect but to Glenda had appeared ajar.

Glenda's curt comments seemed to be growing in sharpness, but Ambrass wouldn't let them bother her. She was due on this Candlebright night to see her love, Nocturne, and in his presence all this tension in the air would be a memory, and nothing more.

But something was wrong with Glenda, and Ambrass knew it. Something was bothering her.

~

Afternoon turned to night, and the Mountain Folk families were given their meals. After all patrons had retired to bed, Ambrass swept and gave the main hall a thorough clean.

Then she went to fetch her cloak from her bedchamber.

There, in the darkness, was her garden of Grayman's beard, and she approached it, and took just a bit of the green moss, which when boiled into a tea was much easier to consume, especially with honey. It was the reason she was not with child. The priests condemned it, so her little garden was a secret. What would the Vidowa and Bruno think? It did not matter.

"Ambrass." Glenda had appeared in the doorway.

Ambrass slipped the Grayman's beard in her mouth and began to chew and pucker at the bitter taste.

"I'm sorry for my cutting comments," she said. "You know I'm worried about…"

"We all are," Ambrass said, "even if we won't admit it."

"It's not really me I'm worried about," Glenda said, "or us…

"You know, Gastreel the Green Wizard and Fortunato went to the mountain valleys. They haven't been seen. They are presumed dead…"

But Fortunato had been presumed dead before and had reemerged, and he was a master of the wilds, a master of nature.

"Fortunato," Ambrass said under her breath, and at the sound of his name, the way the words flowed off the tongue, she felt her eyes water and her vision dim.

She imagined him in the icy snows, amid the raging wind, at the heart of this crisis that the Gallian people had found themselves in.

It had not been so long ago that she had sent him away. To her he had been gentle. Her sojourn with Nocturne had been all passion, all fire and no warmth.

And at the thought of Fortunato, at the sound of his name, Ambrass felt herself fall backwards slightly, at last sitting on the bed.

"That is terrible news," Ambrass said. "But it's strange, Glenda, all these years later, long after our story was ended, I feel I would know if he lived or died. And I sense in my heart that he is alive.

"He's gotten out of terrible situations. He is eminently

capable."

At the thought of him, at her own words and pronouncements, Ambrass felt some of the icy shell she had developed melt away. "I think... I think I'll stay at home tonight."

And perhaps, for his safety, she would pray.

"I think that's a good idea," Glenda said. Glenda had warned her away from Nocturne, told her to stay away.

"How long have Fortunato and the others been gone?" Ambrass said.

"They left in Brightleaf," Glenda said. "There was an early snow. The ways became impassible. I... I... I did not want to alarm you, Ambrass. I didn't... I only wanted to explain why I snapped at you, and now, maybe, I've made things worse."

"It's quite all right," Ambrass said. "Quite all right."

But now she could think of Fortunato and little else, and she cursed the day she had sent him away. What a fool she had been... in her hands she had had a priceless treasure, and now it was forever gone.

What was her sojourn with Nocturne? Where was it headed? Where indeed was her life going, and what was the destination?

Glenda turned and left, shutting the door behind her.

On Ambrass's windowsill was a piece of Fortunato's cloak, and she took it in her little fingers, and she put it to her chest.

Where was her destination? There was a way of knowing, one that was normally asked of her by the patrons at the Dragonpaw Inn.

Still clutching the piece of Fortunato's cloak, she walked to her closet and found her cards of *tabbac*.

"What," she said, flipping the cards over one by one, "is Fortunato's past, present, future?"

Past, *The Lovers*.

The past—not the future, and Ambrass softly moaned.

Present, *Judgment*.

But who and what was being judged? It was not, necessarily, him.

Future. *Varda.*

The world, which could indicate many things, but most often indicated a great journey.

"And what of me, Kama?" she said to the god of the gypsies.

And she shuffled her deck and laid them out one by one: past, present, future.

Past, *The Lovers.*

And at the sight of it, the confirmation that Ambrass and Fortunato's love was in the past, not the future, she felt herself tear up, though she knew she had pledged herself to Nocturne Rabaam.

Present, *Night.*

Surely, that meant Nocturne. And she hesitated just a moment before revealing the future.

Her finger lingered on the card, tattered and worn from years of use. But she took a deep breath, and flipped it over.

There on the card was the painted figure of a skeleton with a scythe in its hands. In bold letters, the card read *Death.*

But Ambrass had a sense, from years of such readings, that it was not the death of her physical life, but the death of something else, the death of something that was nonetheless good.

Her breath had grown shallow. Hurriedly, she took the cards and shuffled them, wondering just what part of her would die, and what the reading truly meant.

Chapter Fifty-Four: Motion

Reev had lost count of how many dayless and nightless slumbers he had taken, but spending so long in darkness, through subterranean tunnels and the remains of abandoned underground cities, having not bathed in surely weeks, he wondered if he was physically changing, that if he by the gods' luck saw the sun again, if he would melt and wither, and his skin burn away.

Reev's stomach was turning as they walked down yet another tunnel, whose slope was noticeably and visibly downward. He had just forced down a meal Fortunato had made from one of those creeping underground creatures whose bodies offered barely more than a thimble-full of meat. Cooked in the open in a coal fire, he had for the first time seen what he had been eating all these dayless and nightless hours, a rodent-like face, sightless white eyes, and white fur that lacked color. He had for the first time watched Fortunato dress and prepare it, and then roast it in the coals, and now he wondered if he'd be able to eat it again, or if he would decide that hunger was better.

The tunnel opened up into a great vault, and in the ceiling up above was glittering silver-work, reflecting on the light of Gastreel's staff. The stars, of a silvery material, corresponded perfectly to the night sky, and the vault even had a waning crescent moon.

"Oh," Reev said, "to see that sky again."

And in the vault were towering statues of stone the height of towers, carved in the shape of Dweorg kings, short and squat yet large, with great beards and with axes in their hands, and on their heads the shapes of crowns.

Reev saw motion in the great cavern, and he screamed at the sinuous movement—in breadth and width thicker than a tree. The shape vanished into a hole that had fallen away from the stone floor.

"What is it?" Fortunato said.

"I saw something move," Reev answered him.

"These halls are abandoned," Gastreel said, "not even rokahn use them."

"And why don't rokahn use them?" Reev said.

Silence followed his question, and they had no good answer. Fortunato seemed to draw back. When he spoke, his voice crackled slightly: "Let's get on the move," he said.

"We must be getting close to a portal or a door," he said. "There is a way out… that is the point of the Dim Roads."

Past the starred vault and the chamber of statues of kings, Reev and Wrinn and Fortunato and Gastreel continued through yet another tunnel.

The slinking subterranean creatures weren't sustaining them, nor the mushrooms that grew in the dark, and Fortunato and the rest of them were growing pale and thin, unhealthy. Yet to stop moving, to succumb to the lack of sustenance and the fatigue, was to welcome death. And so they continued on through the Dim Roads, but Reev never forgot that motion that he saw, and in his dayless and nightless slumbers his dark dreams grew more potent, and his terrible suspicion that they were not alone became a conviction and a belief.

Chapter Fifty-Five:
The High Street Slasher

Yule went by, and the blizzards fell upon the city of Galiope, raging torrents of white and blistering icy winds. Snow piled up everywhere, faster than the boots of the people of the city could tread it down. But in City Square outside the Dragonpaw, the young men of the city were training, running back and forth and practicing with swords and spears, readying themselves for war. In the afternoons, Ambrass would peek outside through the frosted windows and gawk at them, handsome and hale and full of life. They had been joined by the men of the Mountain Folk families, ages sixteen and older, and the smithies of the city blazed all day as swords and axes and shields and armor were produced.

One winter morning, Ambrass was observing the young trainees, a broom clutched in her hand, as they ran to and fro with packs filled with stones on their backs. And it struck her at that moment that winter would soon come to an end, the snows would begin to melt, and then the long-feared rokahn invasion would meet them head on.

And then what? What if Gallia failed? What if Ambrass died? What then would have been the purpose of her life? What would she have left behind... a stash of coins, a well swept floor, a few broken hearts—including her own? She wanted to think everyone had some sort of purpose, some sort of calling, some story the gods would tell. If disaster fell, and Ambrass died, and Galiope was put to the flames, what then would her purpose have been? She couldn't think of one, now.

There was a knock on the Dragonpaw's door, and that surprised Ambrass, because now Galiope was little more than a military camp, and the people of the city had little time for eating or drinking or gaiety. Nonetheless, she walked up to the door and opened it—and saw no one. But then she looked down, and there was the diminutive form of Bala, dressed in an ash gray robe, with a top hat on his head.

He was crying. He said, "Ambrass, I'm cold."

"Oh, sweet Bala," Ambrass said, "come inside, and we'll get you some bread and some milk—your favorite."

Bala stamped his feet on the rug. Ambrass could see that he was blue and shivering.

Glenda hurried out one of the doors and shouted, "I'll draw a bath. Poor thing!"

Ambrass had him sit down in one of the booths, and hurried to the pantry, from which she grabbed a loaf of bread, and then to the larder, from which she fetched a bowl of milk.

Bala was sobbing.

Ambrass draped a blanket over him and took a seat across from him. He began to dip his hunk of bread into the milk and take bites—a good sign, from her perspective.

"Tell me what's wrong, Bala," she said.

"Mr. Aleksander said my training was 'delayed,' " he said, "and so I was outside for a little while and then it got cold and so I went to Dada's house this morning and he said… he said… I wasn't welcome and I should come back tonight."

"Well, you're always welcome here, Bala," Ambrass said. "You know that, right?"

Bala nodded.

"And your father should always welcome you," she said. "If you don't mind, I'll go have a word with him."

Nocturne had never been the best of fathers, but this seemed outrageous—on a cold winter's day, with snow and icy weather and all the accompanying dangers, to forbid your own child from entering your house—it bordered on criminal to Ambrass and she wondered if Nocturne was no good for her after all. She would definitely have a word for him, and if he did not listen to his poor, shivering son, maybe he would listen to his love.

~

They drew Bala a bath and helped him scrub down, then they washed his clothes and hung them out to dry. And though it was noon and the lunch crowd was about to arrive, Ambrass felt this burden had been placed on her heart, and she had to confront her love—for now, at least, her love.

"All right," Glenda said after she asked permission. "Hurry back. Don't dally. We haven't even begun to make the tuber cakes."

Ambrass recalled the menu, borne of the city's rationing. She pitied anyone who would have to bite into those meager, grainy cakes made not from wheat but from milled tubers.

She hurried to her room, grabbed her cloak, and rushed outside into the military camp that was City Square, down snowy streets that were patrolled by soldiers, past High Street and its stately homes, from Middletown to Lonen Town.

~

Ambrass began to get a terrible feeling as she entered Lonen Town, a feeling she could not explain, a wind of change, the card— *Death.*

The Lonen women in their *sarés* and their aloof children and insulated grandchildren seemed to scowl and glare at her more openly than before. Nevertheless, she pushed on, down the streets that seemed better shoveled than any other part of town—and which in the summer were always the cleanest.

And she wondered as she walked, as she dreamed up the scolding she would give her love, why he had sent Bala away this morning, and told him to come back at night.

The Bloodmoon Inn appeared, the inn owned solely by vampires, and she turned then down Night Owl Way, and saw up ahead the balcony of Nocturne's flat, the porch, and the blue door.

And something seemed different, something seemed changed—not the house itself, not the fabric of the upper story drapes, and certainly not the blue door.

She approached, prepared to knock.

And she heard a woman moan, "Nocturne," and the sounds of lovemaking followed.

She grabbed the doorknob, twisted, and to her surprise, the door fell open. She rushed upstairs and burst through the door.

And there in the bed was Nocturne, and with him a woman Ambrass thought she recognized, dark-haired and dark-eyed, an actress she had seen in mystery plays, whose face she thought she knew.

And what came over Ambrass was not anger, not wrath, but a gutting feeling, and the deep knowledge that she had been a fool.

She had been a fool for years.

~

The harlot had fled; Nocturne had dressed. Ambrass was leaving, walking toward the door.

"I am sorry, Ambrass," Nocturne said.

"It's too late," Ambrass said, and turned to face him. "Far too late… and I was a fool from the very beginning. I was a fool to have left Selwyn's Parish. I was a fool to want to join this society… this society that has people like you."

Nocturne's outer shell seemed to have crumbled, and the grief in his eyes appeared genuine—but Ambrass didn't care. She despised him, and now she always would.

"What can I do?" Nocturne said. "How can I earn your forgiveness?"

"You can't," Ambrass said. "You and I... oh, what a fool I was."

"I am sorry," Nocturne said. "I was wrong... I... I... the prophecies..."

"You won't be the father of a king, Nocturne," Ambrass said. "But you are the father of Bala, or should I say, Balor. That's why I came here, your negligence... And what a fool I was. What a fool. You are everything your enemies say you are."

She looked at him, standing in the distance, his black hair tousled, his undershirt ruffled—and she thought of something.

"You've betrayed me, Nocturne," Ambrass said. "But maybe I deserve some truth."

~

At the door-side table, Nocturne poured Ambrass a glass of wine, and then himself a glass. He took a seat across from her.

And in dull tones he began to tell a story, one Ambrass didn't think he had ever told anyone before.

"It was the '20s," he said, "and the crime in Galiope was at a level never before or since equaled. The woman I had married had just died. Not Lucy Cotter, but my first love. And I had begun to give in to my worst inclinations. At one time, I was carrying on a dalliance with a married noblewoman, the wife of the Baron Ackley. One day, Baron Ackley left on a business errand in the Lune Valley, and I spent the week with her.

"And that week, as she slept I was awake, at night, and I stumbled upon a Black Book, a register of people who had pledged themselves to the Dark One. Their names were written in blood, and among them was the Baron Ackley. They were names I recognized, men of nobility, men of wealth and refinement—all pledging themselves in evil. And for some reason, I—no moral man—was filled with anger.

"I took the Black Book with me. I memorized the names. I took matters into my own hands."

"So you are… You are what they claimed you were," Ambrass said, and she was never more glad to be leaving this place, never more glad to put a romance behind her.

She would never fall back into Nocturne's nets, but something dawned on her—that she no longer wanted to be a part of this society, that she no longer wanted to consider herself a Galiopean.

What was she, then? What else was she, except a gypsy?

Ambrass left hurriedly, fleeing the sight of the blue door, fleeing Lonen Town and the memory of her sordid love affair. She felt betrayed, but she felt she had escaped danger, and what's more, she had come to a realization.

How long would she remain at the Dragonpaw Inn? How long would she pretend to be something she wasn't? How long would she avoid the inevitable, and resist going back to her people, where she belonged?

Chapter Fifty-Six: Hope and Fear

Reev, Wrinn, and Fortunato were following Gastreel underneath the tunnels, following the light of his staff as if they were moths and his staff was a flame.

Reev didn't know if it was day or night, if it was winter or fall or spring, but he thought—though the Dim Roads kept a constant temperature—that it might be summer or even the winter of 1153, they had been traveling so long.

He'd grown bone thin, and his shivering had become constant, and even when they found a stash of coals the Dweorg had left behind and Fortunato fashioned a fire, he couldn't get warm. He was racked with a headache, and to his chills had been added dull pains, and struggles with digestion. He wondered if they had entered the underworld, and there was no Varda left.

But as he half walked and half stumbled, there was a fluttering sound, and from the recesses of the cave a swarm of bats began to fly, disturbed from their nests.

"Bats," Fortunato said. "We are close, so close."

"Close to what?" Wrinn asked, and he too sounded wearied and injured.

"Close," Gastreel said, "to another *khameirrat*. A way out."

Reev would believe it when he saw it, when the sun's rays kissed his skin and birdsong filled his ears, when the warm wind blew and there was food besides mushrooms and slinking skinny creatures.

"Come on!" Fortunato said. "Let's hurry."

And they did quicken their pace, but only a little while. The tunnel turned into yet another Dweorg bridge, but Reev could see it was a bridge over another tunnel, two intersecting highways of Ëarno.

"Look!" Wrinn said, and they all stopped.

Wrinn was pointing to the Dim Roads highway beneath them, which appeared covered in black silt.

But that silt had hardened—it was excreta—and amid that black, putrid soil were mangled bones, each individual bone the size of a horse or larger, and the skull the size of an oxcart.

"The remains of a silver drake," Fortunato said.

"What monster could swallow a silver drake whole?" Reev asked.

"Hurry!" Fortunato said. "Hurry! Run!"

And they took off at a sprint.

Chapter Fifty-Seven: Memories of Life

The rain was washing away the winter's snows, patting gently on the Dragonpaw Inn's thatched roof. Ambrass's cases of luggage were filled with all her belongings for the short trip to Selwyn's Parish, and Glenda stood at the doorway of her bedchamber with a tear running down her cheek.

"Ambrass, don't do this," Glenda said. "Don't leave me. Don't regress."

"Regress," Ambrass said. "I'm not some sort of clay pot you can mold and mend. And this isn't regression—it's a return to where I belong."

"You belong here—with me," Glenda said.

"I don't belong with the *kallowen*," Ambrass said. "I've seen you all up close. I know what's in your hearts."

"What's wrong with what's in *my* heart?" Glenda said.

Ambrass didn't have an answer.

"You're marrying Gaius? Really?" Glenda asked.

It had been decided—in exchange for the lifting of charges by the Vidowa, she would return to her betrothed. They would marry in a matter of months.

"Remember how he cursed you?" Glenda said. "Remember how he treated you? The way he shouted at you and controlled you?"

"But he didn't betray me," Ambrass said.

Nor had he been a killer.

It was now early spring. There was no joy in what Ambrass was doing, no joy at all, but she knew it was necessary, and she was convinced it was the right path to take.

"I didn't betray you," Glenda said. "Fortunato didn't betray you."

Fortunato… She dared not utter his name, lest her mind be filled with idle fancies, and she be dissuaded from this task.

She grabbed the bags, which were tightly packed, and slung them over her shoulder.

"Ambrass, please," Glenda said.

"Glenda," Ambrass said, "have you ever known love?"

And Glenda's eyes seemed to water all the more, and her lips slightly trembled. "Not the kind of love you're thinking of. Not the love of a man.

"It was a different sort of love.

"Her name was Rose, and she was my close confidante, a serving girl like you at first, and then a co-owner…

"A co-owner, and then a friend."

Glenda seemed to be looking away from Ambrass, now, looking past her, consumed with thought and memory.

"She was thin," Glenda said. "Her hair was a bright auburn. She was thin, but she was strong. She did whatever I asked; she was a hard worker.

"Thin but strong… She was a warrior of a kind, not a soldier, though she was good with the sword. Hardships did not seem to bother that Rose, and during the Great Scare, when everything seemed to be falling apart in Galiope, she was like an anchor that the people at the Dragonpaw clung on to."

"She was a warrior?" Ambrass asked.

"A warrior in her heart," Glenda said, "but she could fight, too, and in the west she fought in the Pit. A swordswoman, a rare thing, and if you needed someone to change a wagon wheel, you could do a lot worse."

"And what happened to her?" Ambrass asked.

"Oh, Rose," Glenda replied. "If only I knew. Toward the end of her time at the Dragonpaw, her eyesight began to worsen, and soon she couldn't cook or even clean. I hired the best doctors, the best leeches, and the best pharmacists. No salves, no ointments, no herbal cures could stop her from going blind.

"And though she was useless to the Dragonpaw at that time, I insisted she stay. But old Rose had too much pride. One morning I found a letter she dictated to her brother, which he had written… she was leaving the Dragonpaw, and Galiope, for good, in search of a miracle cure.

"I hope she found that cure, Ambrass. I never saw her again."

"That's too bad," Ambrass replied. "A sad thing."

"Terrible," Glenda said, "and now, it looks like it's happening again."

But Ambrass could not, and would not, be Glenda's new Rose.

And for some reason, as she readied to leave, though it was not spurred by Glenda's words or anything—perhaps only the bittersweet feelings of sadness and duty—her mind was drifting off to that night on the battlements, when she had sent Fortunato away.

How would her life have been different if she had not made that choice?

Would it have been worse?

No. No, if she had not sent him away, it would have been better… infinitely better.

Chapter Fifty-Eight: Judgment

The tunnels' rapid descent opened into a massive chamber lined by columns, and Fortunato ran ahead of the group. There was a rushing sound up ahead, and in the distance a doorway, beyond which was the blinding light of the sun.

"We made it!" Fortunato said.

But Reev, ever dour, replied, "Not yet!"

Fortunato's run morphed into a sprint, and he was at the threshold of the doorway, and at the cusp of the brilliant light of the sun, when that light was swallowed whole, and before him slithered a thing of nightmare.

Its body was the thickness of tree trunks, segmented and ridged, pale and colorless—it knew not the light of day. It stank of death and of putrefying flesh, and at the top of its body, facing down toward them, was a head that looked almost human, but with a great maw of a mouth and jutting fangs—like the mouth of a lamprey.

Not a worm it was, but a wurm, a creature from a forgotten age, that there was no record of. And it had been hunting the four of them all this time. No—it had been playing with them, allowing them to travel, allowing them to get to this doorway, maybe even leading them here, and now snatching that hope away.

"Back!" Gastreel cried. "Back, son of Lindorm!"

The wurm hissed and sputum sprayed them all as it gathered its body about itself and prepared to strike.

It dived at Wrinn but Wrinn leapt back. It turned to strike Reev but Reev cut the lips of its hideous maw with Doomblade. Black blood began to drip from that wound.

The wurm turned to Fortunato and fixed on him with an eyeless gaze. It adjusted its quivering white lips and then, according to its primordial mind's calculations, acted in one swift motion.

Fortunato was in darkness—he couldn't breathe. Covered in slime that was beginning to burn his skin, he heard the panicked screams of Reev and Wrinn outside the fleshy prison. He twisted and shifted across the chamber with the wurm's body in utter darkness. He slashed with Danenhir amid the darkness, but the skin was iron hard. He stretched and struggled and tried to force the wurm to vomit, as he continued to slide deeper and deeper into the wurm's segments toward the monster's stomach.

He uttered a prayer. He thought—panicked—of Glyrnslayer, his adamant knife, as the burning sensation began to truly scald, as the digestive acids began to envelop him. He reached for what he thought was his leg—no, it was his arm. He reached for his head but felt some slimy digit. At last he reached again, and grasped hold of the slime-covered hilt of Glyrnslayer. He took it and began to cut wildly, and then to saw, as the wurm's ancient primordial hide began to at last give way to the sharpest type of blade ever invented.

There was a rush of liquid, and like rain expelled through a chimney chute he was vomited out of the hole he had cut, covered in acid and sputum and a black slime that smelled of rotting flesh.

Reev howled in relief.

Fortunato landed hard on the stone floor and shook off the slime, drawing first Danenhir in his right and then Glyrnslayer in his left.

Gastreel called down lightning, but the energy did not so much as burn or injure the monster's stinking white hide.

The wurm, now driven mad with pain, began to dart erratically around the room, knocking down pillars and ancient stonework. The tiles above, on the ceiling, began to fall, letting loose dirt, threatening collapse at any moment.

At last, the floor gave way, sending up a cloud of dust. The pillared chamber became a narrow bridge with Gastreel alone facing the primordial wurm.

Gastreel called up another lightning bolt, another useless blow of energy that only seemed to anger it.

The wurm drew back its hideous head and bowled Gastreel over. Gastreel slid across the newfound bridge and grasped hold of the edge, dangling over inestimable darkness.

The wurm had taken Gastreel out of its way, intending to settle scores with the only creature who had ever threatened it before.

Fortunato stood before the wurm as it pitched back its head, intending again to swallow Fortunato whole, and this time not give him up.

Reev wailed in the distance.

Wrinn shouted threats uselessly.

And Fortunato, acting half out of senseless fear and half out of unconscious memory, took Glyrnslayer and hurled the blue blade into the wurm's maw as the maw swelled in size.

The wurm swallowed, then began to cough and then to choke. It writhed and wriggled in pain until it at last spat up the blade. A river of blood began to pour from the wurm's maw as Fortunato grasped hold of Glyrnslayer.

Gastreel set his staff back on the bridge and pulled himself to safety behind Fortunato. The wurm swung its head like a hammer at Fortunato, but it was missing now, dazed and confused by pain, taking wild miscalculations as its bodily chambers emptied. It began to lunge at foes that weren't there, sliding toward the chamber's now-bottomless floor.

It drew near at last once again, and Fortunato slashed at its lips with Danenhir, now opening up a small wound.

The wurm whined as it slipped away, hemorrhaging blood, slinking off to die in humiliation, at last shrinking its body through some narrow crack in the wall and disappearing completely.

The makeshift bridge began to collapse behind Gastreel, Reev, Wrinn, and Fortunato, forming a bottomless chasm that could not be spanned.

"Run!" Fortunato called. *"Run!"*

And the four of them bolted through the doorway ahead, into the blinding light of the sun, and were spattered with water from a flowing waterfall.

Chapter Fifty-Nine:
The Eagle Rising

Below Reev was a sight he never thought he'd see again, the green earth and the sun's light—but he supposed, in all his life, he had never quite beheld something so beautiful.

Below them were green descending valleys in view of snowcapped peaks, a land well-watered and lush, and beyond the waterfall and the descending stream, green pines of all sizes and shapes, stalwart cedars and brilliant purple wildflowers, and the scent of rosemary and water-mint. The sky, a brilliant blue, was crossed by sparse clouds, and the sun was at its apex—it was midday.

"What time of year is it?" Reev said.

"Spring," Fortunato said as he washed off his adamant knife and his slime-covered clothing in the waterfall. "Look! Over there! Can't you see the plum berries?"

On a rugged incline was a green bush bursting with blueberries, and at the sight of them, at the sight of something humans *should* eat rather than mushrooms and cave creatures, Reev hurried to the precarious slope and began to devour them off the branch. Succulent, sweet they were, and their seeds had a delightful crunch. Wrinn joined him, then Gastreel, and after they'd eaten their fill, they took some the berries in their hands for later.

"Where are we?" Reev said, his mouth still full of tangy berry flavor.

"The southern slopes of the Dragonteeth," Fortunato said, "somewhere."

"I feel like I've seen this place before," Wrinn said.

Reev doubted that, but he was grateful to the gods that his long journey was over, that for the first time in surely months, what was over his head was the celestial vault, and not the ceilings of dark tunnels no human should traverse.

Popping berries in their mouths, they descended down into the green valleys, and forests of pine and cedar and juniper surrounded them. Streams were flowing everywhere, bubbling down from the mountains, and the farther they walked, the stronger the scent of mint and rosemary and garden herbs grew.

But the berries seemed to only have stimulated Reev's hunger.

They built their camp in a clearing, and off they went, searching for food.

~

At dusk, when they returned, Fortunato had in his hands three rabbits and a grouse, and Wrinn a bundle of leafy green vegetables, mushrooms (though Reev retched at the sight of them) and fruits and starchy tubers. Reev, who had not drifted far from camp, was empty-handed—but Gastreel had managed to find something, a sprig of rosemary and a white flower—*sindomas*—that would keep them healthy.

That night, by the fire, the rabbit and the roast grouse restored Reev's spirits, and he thought he might live again. For the first time in surely months, his stomach was full, and now, his energy felt boundless. Where they were, it seemed no one knew, but it was a place of plenty, where game and fruits and leafy greens could be found with little effort, where water was never far away.

As the fire burned, they looked to the stars, and saw the constellation of the Eagle was rising. "I wonder," Reev said, "if the rokahn have already struck Galiope."

And he couldn't understand why there were no rokahn in this lush land, why they avoided this place of peace and plenty.

"A dark thought," Gastreel said, "one we should not dwell on.

"We should be glad we ended the evil that was in the Vale of

Ahorne. All they who heeded Aylmer's Horn have surely left."

"And what evil was in the Vale?" Wrinn asked.

Gastreel's eyes glinted, and it seemed that Wrinn's words had brought to mind something that lurked just in the background, buried just beneath. And he went to his pack and began to rummage through it, at last seizing upon something—a hideous iron mask— from which was emitting heatless black smoke.

A thought came to Reev, powerful, a thought audible like a shout: *You will die here.*

And under his breath, Reev said, "*Illuné vadila,*" and the whispers lessened.

"The mask of a fiend," Gastreel said. "The mask of Gogg.

"A wizard wore it upon her face, and through it gained but a little of Gogg's true power—the powers of accusation and suggestion, and of influence over the weather."

"Why did you take it with you?" Wrinn said, sounding almost angry, and he edged away from it.

"See it smoke?" Gastreel said. "See the ectoplasmic issuance on the back of the mask?"

There were faint drippings of white where the wearer's face would be.

"Jerek's spell of reanimation remains," Gastreel said. "Gogg will return in his weakened state unless it is dispelled. That is a task for Bala Rabaam."

Bala—Reev wondered how the little child was doing.

And he looked at the mask, and thought he heard another whisper, vile and violent, *Nicollo—I will send him after you.*

"Put it away," Reev said. "Don't let us see it."

"Does it talk to you, Reev?" Gastreel said.

"Put it away!" Reev said. "I mean it."

And Gastreel, with a bit of mischief in his eyes, did just that.

~

That morning they arose and began to travel, hoping to find a road or a village or some way back to Galiope. How far could the city be?

They filled their stomachs with water in a babbling stream, and through the forests of cedars and pines they made their trek, underneath the blue sky, in the sunshine.

At noon, they set up camp again, and decided to forage, and Reev set off with a basket, vowing not to go too far.

At the edge of the clearing, he found more mushrooms, dense brown mushrooms he did not know were good to eat or not, and then, following the contours of the ravine, was stunned to see the sight of a doe bounding away—which Fortunato, with his bow, would surely have quickly shot. He stumbled through the dark woods, and found yet another bush of plum berries, juicy and crunchy, and placed as many as could fit in his basket.

He ventured on through a meadow, and searched through the grass for any edible fruit or fungus. He scoured the edge of a pond, and searched the shores of a creek.

Through the sunlight he saw the gold grass of another clearing, and hoping for *sindomas* or mushrooms or starchy root, he walked out into the middle of it, and as he stood there, there were footsteps and a shouted word, "*Io!*"

It was the Imperial language.

And from the eaves of the trees came soldiers in glossy metal breastplates and red half-capes, helmets crowned with horsehair crests and at their sides a shortsword and a dagger each—all of the same size and look, and of the same high quality.

Imperial soldiers—what were they doing here? And what land had Reev ventured into?

"Hands up!" one of the soldiers shouted, and Reev lifted his hands as they requested, dropping his basket of food.

They removed his belt and Doomblade with it. They took his

hands and bound them behind his back. And then they pushed him on, leading him forward. Like a lamb to be slaughtered, he followed the soldiers' commands unquestioningly, and wondered if he would ever see his friends again.

Chapter Sixty:
In the Sacred Grove

Fortunato and Gastreel were hunting together—a strange thing, but they had done so before.

Gastreel followed Fortunato a step behind through the dark woods, past bushes, along the shores of a creek. Here the foliage was dense, and thorn bushes brushed up against Fortunato's trousers.

Gastreel began to shout—against Fortunato's instruction.

"Look!" he said. "Apples!"

In the sunlight, Fortunato could see apple trees, a grove beyond the creek. But there was no fruit in their branches; they were out of season. Instead, their leaves were crowned in white flowers, and in the bright sunlight it seemed they were evenly placed, a sign of habitation. If a farmer lived here, he could tell them where they were, and how to get back to Galiope.

And so he crossed the creek and walked into the grove, bow at the ready though he knew not why. He kept an eye open for a house, for any sign of habitation—a sign of smoke wafting up from a chimney, a dog's bark, a child's cry.

But it seemed to Fortunato they were alone, and so this orchard was a natural occurrence somehow, evenly placed and set in square rows.

"Drop your weapons!" someone shouted. "Hands up!"

And from the darkness of the woods, figures were approaching garbed in green, several and then dozens, with bows and swords in their hands.

Fortunato looked to Gastreel, hoping for some gout of lightning or celestial flame, but the wizard had staggered back and obeyed, dropping his staff.

Fortunato followed a moment afterward, dropping his bow, and the green-garbed figures rushed them, tackling Fortunato to the ground and then knocking him with a sap.

~

When Fortunato came to, he was in a place he did not recognize, in view of snowy peaks, and the wound from the sap ached in his skull. He had been tied, hand and foot, and a fire was burning in view of low walls. The figures in green were rifling through his belongings, some of which he had left behind in camp. Beyond the fire, Wrinn was there, tied up and being questioned by a man in green.

Others of these bandits were patting down Gastreel in the distance and searching him for anything of value.

One bandit began to walk toward Fortunato. He lowered his green hood. He was blond, fair-eyed, young, with suntanned skin, and a keen light to his gaze.

"You," he said, "their leader. What were you doing in the sacred grove?"

"I consider no grove more sacred than another," Fortunato said. "We were searching for food."

"You consider no grove more sacred than another," said the bandit. "Not even that of Dodoena?"

Dodoena—a god favored by those who lived in the Lune Valley.

They were in the Lune Valley, that's where they had emerged. The topography, the mountains, the south-facing slopes—it all made sense. What didn't make sense was that they had traveled hundreds of miles underground. How skilled at stonework had been the kingdom of Ëarno?

"What will you do to us, bandit?" Fortunato said.

"I am Anthanlas," said the young man. "You will address me

as Anthanlas, or better, 'milord.' What will we do to you? We will do to you what is required to the uninitiated who lay their eyes on the sacred grove—we will, at dusk, take knives, and put you to death."

"You will not!" a voice rang out, clean and pure, and by the fire was a woman, blindfolded, her hair some shade between red and brown, at her side a silvery sword. "These are good men, sent to us by Dodoena; that is why they found themselves in her sacred grove.

"You will unbind them, Anthanlas, and you will feed them."

"So be it, Sister," Anthanlas said, and from his belt he took a knife and cut away Fortunato's binds.

~

As clouds began to roll in, the air took on a chill. Gastreel, Fortunato, and Wrinn sat down beside the blazing fire, and to them were given dried venison and berries, and a drink made from berries in clay cups.

Anthanlas took a seat by the fire.

"What brings you here?" he said.

"If we told you," Gastreel said, "you wouldn't believe us."

"Perhaps, it is best if it is not uttered," said Anthanlas.

"And what of you?" asked Fortunato. "Bandits, of the Lune Valley?"

"Once bandits of a kind," said Anthanlas, "now rebels. According to the law, traitors."

"Traitors," Gastreel said. "Traitors to what?"

Anthanlas smiled, and took a stick from the ground and poked the fire. It seemed to Fortunato that the story he was about to tell was one he had told many times before.

"A few weeks ago, St. Alan's Day…" late winter, early spring— the third of Primrane… "the Empire, triumphant from its victories in the west, came to the Lune Valley and asked of our Lord

Protector obscene demands, namely, that we would stop our banditry and raiding, which has been the Lune Valley's livelihood for all its history. "When our lord protector refused, the Empire declared war. In the span of three days, they built a bridge across the River Lune... a feat no one in history had thought possible, let alone in seventy-two hours. And when the legions crossed over, our lord protector was so frightened he surrendered, and asked all the 'bandits' who had given him protection to turn themselves in.

"Ha! What a laugh.

"We did not relent. The Empire is rampaging through our land. And here we are."

"So the Lune Valley is under invasion," Gastreel replied.

"Yes. The Empire claimed it for themselves, like they claimed the west," said Anthanlas.

"The west has fallen, then," Gastreel said.

"The throne of Zarubain is no more." Anthanlas poked at the fire with his stick again. "County Cambion to our west has surrendered to the Empire. The count has agreed to become the emperor's puppet."

These bandits of the Lune Valley considered themselves freedom fighters, resisting the Empire's power. But it was a dangerous gambit, and Fortunato questioned whether he too would be considered an enemy of the Empire now—a traitor to the country of his birth—just by virtue of sitting among them.

"In your camp, we found four beds," said Anthanlas, leader of the bandits. "But the three of you were unaccompanied."

"Reev Nax," Gastreel said softly. "Our most important companion."

Yes, Reev was important—but Fortunato thought Gastreel should not talk about him like that.

"I saw him," said Anthanlas's sister, sitting by the fire, blindfolded. "I saw him in a vision. Dark of hair, with a coin necklace about his neck."

Only a true seer could have witnessed that.

"He was taken by the Imperials. He is in Nicollo's custody."

"Who is Nicollo?" Gastreel said.

Chapter Sixty-One: Nicollo

The Imperial soldiers led Reev through woods and fields, past ponds and rivers and small lakes. The forests of pine that filled the Lune Valley were all about him, and the darkness between the trees seemed deep.

The soldiers had said little since his capture, only prodded him and nudged him along. The sun was high in the sky, and the eerie light of afternoon was falling when through the trees appeared towering walls of wood, and voluminous smoke wafting up.

It was a military camp, hastily yet masterfully constructed.

Reev was led through the gate, and beyond, hundreds of red tents had been erected in perfectly placed rows. Hundreds and hundreds of soldiers, their breastplates glossy and perfectly forged, the red of their half-capes and helmet crests contrasting strikingly with the dark color of steel, went about their business.

To their number were added staff, garbed in red and gold—cooks, perhaps, or maybe cleaners, squires, shield-boys, or servants. And there were prostitutes, too, mixed among the masses, offering their services—natives of the Lune Valley likely, taking advantage of an opportunity where they saw one.

Reev walked down the row of tents to the northern edge of the camp, and there, up against the palisades of the wooden wall, was a high seat that almost looked like a throne.

The man who sat upon that seat wore a breastplate embossed in gold, and from his belt dangled many medals of service. If Imperials were thought to be uniformly dark and swarthy, this man was proof against it. He was fairer than anyone Reev had seen in Galiope, his hair a bright blond and his eyes a ghostly blue. By his side was a giant bulldog, white of fur.

The Imperial soldiers who had captured Reev cast him before the man's feet.

"Nicollo," said one of them, "we found this boy wandering the woods near where Anthanlas has been operating."

Nicollo looked down upon Reev, and his pale eyes seemed strangely dark, wolflike in the pupils. It seemed he was the battalion commander, and fancied himself a judge over others.

"What is your name, boy?" Nicollo's voice was as cold as his eyes.

"Reev," he replied.

"Reev," Nicollo said. "A strange name—and he bears bound around his neck a coin of Telantis, the True Empire."

What was he talking about?

"He must have a high opinion of himself to wear such a thing as a talisman."

"I don't," Reev said, "and I just want to be taken back to my friends."

"Your friends…" Nicollo said. "So you are not alone. How many others, how many with you?"

"There are four of us," Reev said, "and we want no trouble with you, only to be on our way—to return to Galiope."

"Galiope," said Nicollo, and for the first time, a bit of emotion appeared on his face—the faintest curl of a smile. "A city that has declared war on us. Ten thousand were sent to fight against us."

Reev remembered seeing off those soldiers, and he girded himself and vowed not to speak to this self-styled judge again without thinking.

"What happened to the soldiers?" Reev said, and he had a terrible feeling that Nicollo knew.

"Dead, or scattered," he replied, "the fifth of Anthanos—the Second Megaran Legion met them in battle in the fields outside Carribor. They were crushed without much resistance."

The news was gutting. Reev didn't want to believe it—that the

Gallian League's efforts to rescue the west had been in vain. And that they had been defeated only a short while after they had disembarked.

"Pity, pity," said Nicollo. "Tell me, Reev, if you are a Galiopean, why, then, were you wandering around in the woods of the Lune Valley?"

"My business is my own," Reev said.

"Not true," Nicollo said. "I am proconsul of Cambionia. It is my business if bandits harass and steal from those in my custody."

"I am no bandit," Reev said.

He had a sinking feeling that this Nicollo, these Imperials, would refuse to allow him to leave. There was no easy way out of this situation, no path of escape that Reev could think of—only courtesy and deference, what some would call blind obedience.

"No bandit," Nicollo said. "That is what you say. I repeat my question: what is a Galiopean doing in the Lune Valley?"

And Reev struggled to think of an honest answer that would end this line of inquiry. At last, he settled on the truth. "We were sent on a mission to the Vale of Ahorne, to see it evacuated from the rokahn threat."

"The Vale of Ahorne," said Nicollo, and it seemed he was well acquainted with the Northern World's geography. "That is far from here."

"There is a way," Reev said, "under the mountain. The Dim Roads."

Nicollo straightened up in his seat. That curl of a smile became more noticeable. "Fanciful stories you tell, boy."

"Will you let me go?" Reev said.

"I am afraid not," Nicollo said. "A boy, bearing about his neck a coin of the True Empire, claiming to have traveled under the mountain. It is awfully portentous."

Portentous… like a portent.

"Further questioning is needed, and I and this camp are ill

prepared to find the truth." He looked to the soldiers, and the faint curl of his lip vanished. Resounding was the sound of his voice: "Prepare a cart and four horse. Take him to Fort Midean."

Fort Midean... Reev thought he had heard the name, maybe in idle talk from a Galiopean or chatter from an itinerant merchant. "Nicollo, please! I mean the Empire no harm. And I... I... I am an Imperial citizen."

Nicollo's eyes widened, and he pursed his lips. "An Imperial citizen, you say. Fort Midean might feel familiar to you, then. Take him away!"

The soldiers seized him by the arms, and he knew better than to resist. He was led through to a cart yoked with four horses.

What would they do to him? What did they intend? Reev knew he had committed no crimes, not against the Empire or anyone.

He clutched the coin of the "True Empire" in his hand, and wondered what his grandfather, with the gods, was thinking now.

Chapter Sixty-Two:
The Blackmoor Bog

The long shadows of afternoon were stretching lazily across the bandit camp. The fire was burning and Fortunato took stock of his surroundings, tents and makeshift wooden structures, an outdoor smithy, a storage barn perhaps for loot, an outhouse, and a mill. The bandits seemed to live surprisingly well, but Fortunato's head still throbbed, and he wasn't sure if he'd ever forgive them for striking his head with that sap.

"What of you?" said Gastreel to Anthanlas's sister, blindfolded and still like a statue. "How did you get into banditry?"

"We in the Lune Valley for the most part come from somewhere else," she said. "We are all running from something; some of us find each other here, in this place. My roots are in the west, in the heartlands, but as youths my brother and I sought our fortunes in Gallia. Now we are here, in this blessed valley."

"And what happened to your eyes?" Wrinn asked—a point of rudeness but something that was on everyone's mind.

"I was blind," said Anthanlas's sister, "and that is why my brother and I came here, for physicians. The best doctors failed us, but the priest of Dodoena here in the Lune Valley, on the slopes of Caravail Peak, offered a miracle cure.

"And I went there, and donned the robes of an initiate, and I swam in the Pool of Ecko, and I breathed deep the vapors of the cave. And the priest of Dodoena came to me, and said, 'Dodoena has blinded you so that you may truly see.'

"There was no cure according to what I had selfishly desired. There was no physical healing of my eyes, but there was an awakening in my heart and my mind, and I did begin to see things others couldn't, in colors and detail more vivid than anything I had witnessed previously.

"Dodoena has shown me what she wishes me to see. And she has told me that the four of you are special—especially the fourth of you, who, now, is in grave danger."

"What has happened?" Gastreel asked.

Anthanlas's sister, bound in a blindfold, pursed her lips. "The vision I see is of a boy loaded in a cart, and that cart is being escorted by soldiers. They are taking him down the westward leading road."

"County Cambion," said Anthanlas.

"Fort Midean," said his sister.

To take Reev from the cart, to waylay those soldiers, would be a crime. And if Fortunato harmed any of them, it would be treason. But some things were more important than the ties of nation and of family—some things, like the cause against Seymus and his servants in the mortal world. To that cause, Reev held the key.

"We must rescue him," said Fortunato. "At once! Do you have horses?"

"Their carts are swift, and they are masters of roads," said Anthanlas's sister. "You will not be able to catch them. Only pray that Emperor Khandaraeus has mercy."

Khandaraeus—a new emperor reigned, and Fortunato had not known about it. Sometimes, in the span of a year, the White Throne would pass between multiple people.

"There is a way… dangerous," said Anthanlas, "a shortcut by which we can intercept them. We will be able to cut them off at the western leading road, long before they reach Fort Midean. The Blackmoor Bog—"

"That way is haunted," said Anthanlas's sister. "It is the abode of hags and wild beasts. A graveyard of mankind, where heathens would sacrifice their kin in the ages of darkness. To disturb that ground, where so much evil occurred, is to invite evil."

"But you said, Sister," Anthanlas began, "that the one these folk called Reev Nax is important."

"Important," she said, "in ways that we of Lune Valley do not understand."

She stood up, and she drew her sword.

~

Quietly, Anthanlas, his sister, and about two dozen of the bandits armed with swords and bows left the camp, and with them Fortunato, Gastreel, and Wrinn.

The afternoon shadows were falling, and the sun was low in the sky, when they began their trek through the woods, swift yet silent. The pines and cedars covered them and Fortunato expected an Imperial soldier in steel armor and a red cape to come bounding through the trees at any moment, for he knew his nation well—that when they intended to conquer a new land, they did not rest until the task was finished.

When it was approaching dusk, the ground began to grow damp, and the quality and size of the trees began to lessen, scrub pines and thorns and thistles growing closer together, until at last the sky opened up, and before them stretched a flat bog as far as he could see. The bog waters were covered in blue scum, and at the shores of the bog were dozens of canoes, of wood, that appeared little used and old.

Nevertheless they hopped inside the canoes. Fortunato was given a pair of oars, and they set out through the Blackmoor Bog, which Anthanlas had claimed was haunted.

~

The air rising above the bog was cold, and had the smell of metal and of rot. The sun was beginning to set in brilliant red colors, a staggering light show across the sky, when they drew near the bog's center, and Fortunato thought he heard something.

Up ahead was a fire, and then another, flames seemingly suspended in air above the water. Fortunato looked into the water next to him as he rowed, and just underneath, beneath the surface of the water, was a face—blackened and withered, wilted, with leathery skin, a hood of poor material over its dead face.

Fortunato swallowed a scream and struggled to remain calm for the sake of the rest of the party, and for the sake of Wrinn, who was riding in the canoe in front of him.

Fortunato looked ahead, and there amid the fires was an island in the bog, and on the island a series of stone menhirs—heathen works of a forgotten civilization—and there among them what appeared to be a woman, so wrinkled her skin was like rawhide, and only sparse strands of white clinging to her scalp.

Fortunato looked down again at the water and saw more faces: a man and a woman, a child too—blackened and leathery… bog bodies, mummified by the peat. Then their lips twitched.

Fortunato screamed and fell off the canoe, plunging into the icy cold water, as up above he heard the sounds of the bandits screaming, doing battle with the bog bodies. He felt something touch his foot as he swam and writhed helplessly in the water. He looked up and saw the bog bodies had arisen to the lake's surface and were striking at the bandits on canoes with rusted-over swords of a primitive make.

Fortunato tried to scramble to shore as the wizened woman on the island began to dance, and far-off began to utter curses in a foreign tongue. More bog bodies were rising. Fortunato knew they were also below, and would drag him down to the depths and not let him go.

But Anthanlas's sister rose up from her canoe as her brethren battled. "Friends," she said, "fellow fighters. Nothing you are seeing is real! The dark spirits in this lake that led our ancestors astray, feed on fear. Fear is what they want. Stop fearing them, and they will cease. They cannot truly hurt you.”

Fortunato spat up water and tried to follow her words. The bandits on boats were continuing to battle, ignoring her command. But Fortunato attempted to listen. He tried to see things as they were. He tried not to fear. He exhaled, and thought of the gods, and goodness, and light.

The waters became still. The foul hand grasping at Fortunato’s foot disappeared. And Fortunato looked anew at the island, and saw that the woman he had witnessed was a gnarled dead tree, gray in color. And the bog bodies were long gone.

“She is right!” Fortunato cried out. “She is right! And as she said, she is blind, but she can see by a greater sight than any of us. None of this is real…”

The bandits, fighting imaginary enemies, began to strike weaker and weaker. Then they began to cease one by one amid cries of, “He is right!”

And Blackmoor Bog was still.

“Dodoena forfend,” said Anthanlas’s sister. “I can hear their voices… sacrificial victims in a watery grave.”

A tribe of humans had once lived here, the people of the Northern World’s ancestors, and they would perform rituals, and along the shores of these dark peat bogs make their sacrifices. But the spirits who received the sacrifices could not ultimately hurt anyone who did not allow them power.

“Illunaddori vadila!” Gastreel cried, as the feeling of oppressive darkness seemed to wither away, and Fortunato was helped back into his canoe.

They drew to shore as the sun sank beneath the horizon. No hag had bewitched them, nor had imagined bog bodies forced them underwater.

Now, their enemy was time… time, and the nation of Fortunato’s birth.

Chapter Sixty-Three:
Enough

In the cart as it rattled down the road, Reev imagined what he would say to the judge or the prefect or whatever official would question him in the fort called Midean, how he would defend himself, and what words he would say. He knew not of any crime he had committed. He had only traversed the Dim Roads and emerged in a land the Empire had claimed, but which wasn't theirs.

And he realized as the cart rattled and shuddered and shook, that in the soldiers' presence he did not feel afraid or in danger, but instead bothered, and eager to make his way back home.

He peeked out the window and saw through the pines that the sun had set, and the sky was a flaming red, as if it had caught fire.

Soldiers were flanking him, a dozen, six on each side, riding briskly on horses. He wondered at their breastplates, steel strips tied with leather that covered their chests, each suit identical to the other, and higher in quality than anything Gallian soldiers wore. Their helmets too were identical, and fine, and over their horses were cloths of red and gold: the Empire's colors.

He did not know how far off Fort Midean was, or even where it was, in what county or town, or if it had been recently built in the Lune Valley. He did not know why Nicollo had sent him there. And he had reason to be suspicious, and feel in danger, but the Imperials were a legitimate authority, and had customs of fair trials and equality under law. What's more, Reev's Imperial citizenship forbade them from killing him extrajudicially, for in theory he was as free and as valued as these soldiers riding alongside him.

The sun's red color had dissipated, and the darkness was spreading. They had entered a part of the woods that was overgrown with brambles and stunted scrub pines. The road was growing rough and covered in pools, and sharply the cart would shake, bumping up and down, left and right.

The air seemed to change. The night—in the span of moments—seemed filled with danger, and the Imperial soldiers' horses began to nicker. The cart stopped, and the soldiers began to shout.

He heard one say "*Io…* what's that?"

There was rustling in the bushes, and one of the horses pulling the cart reared up and then bucked, attempting to free itself from the restraints. The driver began to shout, and arrows began to fly. Most bounced uselessly off the Imperial soldiers' armor, but one stuck in a soldier's chest and he fell from his horse.

Reev grabbed hold of the cart's door, and amid the dark woods green-garbed figures appeared, charging the Imperial soldiers—and there was Fortunato, Gastreel, Wrinn.

Reev yanked at the door but it wouldn't budge. It was locked. He yanked again, and then harder, all the more.

At last he kicked, and the door burst open, and he stumbled out of the cart. The Imperial soldiers had dismounted; some were engaged with the green-garbed figures. The sounds of shouting and the clang of steel against steel rang out.

The Imperial soldiers would be overcome. There were too many of these green-garbed figures; their swords and bows were inferior to the Imperials', but they had the advantage of numbers.

Among those green-garbed figures was a woman clothed differently from the others, not in a green cloak but in a gold robe, and over her eyes was a white blindfold. She held in her hands a sword, and even without the sight of her eyes, she was engaging one of the soldiers, fighting better than one who could see.

She parried and struck, twirled and slashed. She took off a soldier's nose, and cut again, and sliced off one of his fingers.

"Enough!" Reev cried. "Enough!"

And he felt something fill him—light, peace.

Chapter Sixty-Four: Transformed

When Reev spoke, the battle stopped, and Gastreel wondered at the sight of it. Five Imperial soldiers lay on the ground, dying or bleeding, but Anthanlas's men had ceased fighting, and the remaining Imperials were backing away.

Reev stooped down and knelt next to the Imperial who had been felled by an arrow.

He placed his hand on the soldier's chest, and there was the flicker of light, and his wound sealed. He raised his other hand, and light swirled about him in a tongue, and the other soldiers bleeding on the ground had their wounds suddenly mended.

He walked to the Imperial whose nose Anthanlas's sister had sliced off and took his nose and his severed finger from the muddy ground. His nose and his finger reappeared on his body in a burst of light, and amid the silence of the damp wood, there was quiet, and there was tranquility.

"Do not harm these men," Reev said. "Servants of their nation—not our enemy."

The soldiers fell back toward the cart, and Reev turned to them. They had anew drawn their swords.

"If we let a prisoner escape," said one of them, "we will be put to death."

"Better that," Gastreel said to them from afar, "than to bring harm to the Sage, *velati sonoren,* the Prince of the Dawn."

"I have it on high authority," Reev said, "that the gods will guide your words. And you will not be punished for allowing our escape."

The light and grandeur about Reev faded, and he seemed to almost shrink.

Gastreel wondered if he'd have any memory of what he had done.

The soldiers, after a moment of silence, began to mount their horses. They were skeptical of Reev's words, but they feared him now. They brought his sword and his pack to him from a sealed case. Then into the distance they traveled, leaving Fortunato, Wrinn, Gastreel, Reev, and all of Anthanlas's men alone.

In the Lune Valley, at night, frogs trilled in the distance.

On the face of Anthanlas's sister was a smile. "A blessing to be with you, Sage."

"We must get back to Galiope," Gastreel said, "as swiftly as possible. Though I fear we will not be long for that city, and refuge must be sought elsewhere."

"There is a ferry to our southeast," Anthanlas said. "Well hidden—the Imperials do not yet know of it. The ferrymen is in league with those the Imperials call 'bandits,' and he will be glad to aid you."

He turned to Reev. "Of your importance… I believed my sister, but the Prince of the Dawn? I am honored to be in your presence. We will guide you to the ferryman. He is three days' hike away, and he can take you across the River Lune."

Quietly, swiftly, under cover of the darkness, they began their journey.

~

Through the woods they traveled, through lush greenery. They had brought little food, but the Lune Valley in its abundance provided it for them, berries and roots and fruit-bearing vines, wild grapes and the mushrooms that grew in every dark hollow. Game was so abundant that they almost seemed to walk up to Anthanlas's and Fortunato's outstretched bows.

Occasional showers of snow did not hinder them, and

Anthanlas led them swiftly on their way.

Imperial soldiers they did not see, but as the days wore on, it became clear that they were being hunted, and occasionally through the tree cover, they would see signal fires being lit, a reminder of the search parties that now pursued them.

They followed no road or path, trusting solely in Anthanlas's sense of direction. And at noon on the third day of travel, the vast waters of the River Lune appeared. At its banks were flowering apple trees and tresses of grapes, and near the banks a shanty house hidden in foliage, and beside it a dock with a mighty canoe tied to the wood.

Anthanlas and Anthanlas's sister explained to the ferryman their peril, and the ferryman agreed to provide his service with no pay.

Reev and Wrinn, Fortunato and Gastreel, and the ferryman, hopped in the canoe with their packs and all their belongings, and then set off across the water's expanse to the well wishes from Anthanlas, and from Anthanlas's sister, the blessing of Dodoena.

Chapter Sixty-Five: Whispers

Beyond the River Lune, Reev, Fortunato, Wrinn, and Gastreel found themselves in a barren heathland, which no nation claimed. Weeds and flowering bushes, thorns and tendrils grew on the poison earth, but nothing that would be of benefit to agriculture. The skies were a dark gray as they set out, and they traveled swiftly, walking all day, headed due east.

That night, they built a fire, and as they sat there talking dully, Reev thought he heard a whisper—*"Turn back! Back to the Lune Valley."*

Rain began to drift down, turning to snow. The mask's powers were going stronger, and even tucked in Gastreel's pack, it spoke.

Reev recalled the night in the temple of doom, when Gogg—whose mask that was—had been destroyed by supernal power. Yet his mask had remained in the care of the wizards—and why? His mask had remained in the care of the wizards—and a wizard had taken it for herself.

"Turn back! Fling yourself in the river!"

And the compulsion was growing stronger, the uttered command so powerful his first inclination was to obey.

"Gastreel," Reev said in the light of the fire. "We must leave the mask here. We must leave it behind."

Gastreel's tone gave no space for disagreement: "Its magic must be dispelled."

"Turn back! Run to Nicollo, you lawbreaker!"

Reev's body jerked in that direction, toward the river, and he thought of Nicollo's ghostly blue eyes, his striking countenance.

So under his breath, Reev uttered, *"Illunaddori vadila."*

But each minute, each hour, each passing moment, the mask

was growing stronger—a sign, perhaps, of the Servants' imminent return.

Reev recalled Gastreel's statement that the Servants had been in a weakened, undead state, reanimated by magic, and he shuddered at the thought of what they would have been if they had possessed their ancient power.

In the tent he hardly slept, tormented by whispers issuing from the mask. From the netherworld, Gogg's power radiated outwards, and it was a terrible thing.

Chapter Sixty-Six: Warzone

From the barren wilderness, toward their destination, Galiope, they continued to make progress. Through chilly nights and damp days, they made their way across the Northern World, and those days turned to a week, and the week a fortnight. The wilderness became a land of agriculture, farms, and sprawling estates. At last, they reached the Royal Road that would take them to Galiope, and there as towns and villages passed by, Imperial soldiers were mixed into the crowd, but took no notice of them.

Some thirteen days after they departed the Lune Valley they came to a great walled town called Terrence, and on the towers of its walls, Imperial flags flew—red and gold. The walls of the town showed no sign of damage. They had surrendered without a fight.

Accordingly, seeing how far the Empire had advanced, Gastreel and Fortunato, Reev and Wrinn, began to keep a good distance from the road, but as the days wore on, they began to see that even the wilderness could not hide them.

The fifteenth day since they had left the River Lune, Fortunato called out, "Stop!"

And there ahead, down a hill, in Gastreel's view, was a sight he never thought he would behold.

It was a rokahn war band, hundreds strong, who had ventured down from the mountains, with dark helms and dark spears, bearing serpentine standards. Facing them was a century of Imperial soldiers.

The Imperials had locked shields, with swords at the ready. Far away, on a hill, were wooden machines that had the look of giant crossbows, and men behind them fixing javelins to them. The machines began to launch those javelins, piercing multiple rokahn with each ballast, and when the weakened rokahn reached the Imperial lines, they were cut down with ruthless efficiency.

"The rokahn threat is solved," Gastreel said softly, "but I don't like the solution."

"We must travel even farther from the roads," Fortunato said. "If the Imperials can even be avoided."

Through the farmland they traveled, through farms and smallholdings, and the rumor began to reach their ears—the three Great Towns, Terrence, Dunway, and Hammond, had all surrendered to the Imperial forces of Nicollo.

The country west of Galiope had since become a warzone of Imperials versus rokahn, and in every skirmish Gastreel and the others witnessed, the Imperials were the resounding victor.

The machines from which they launched javelins were called "scorpions," Gastreel learned, and to these technologies were added ballistae and onagers, fearsome torsion catapults and compact stone-throwers. The disorganized rokahn were slaughtered like pigs whenever they fell upon the Imperial line.

Galiope was now surrounded, but sneaking through the farmland, Gastreel and the others managed to avoid the Imperials' detection, and on the eighteenth day since they departed the River Lune, they reached the border of Gallia—the Galios River.

It was late afternoon and the sun was shining, the heat building to a summerlike warmth, when at the shores of the river Gastreel and Fortunato, Reev and Wrinn, were treated to a stunning surprise.

It was Tyra Jade, and following a moment later, Cobalt, then Ivy and Noble—all looking gaunt and not well fed.

Tyra had led the beasts out of the mountain passes, and by the gods' favor they had survived.

"Tyra!" Fortunato shouted, and knelt down.

Tyra sprinted to him and jumped at him, licking at his mouth with her tongue.

"Tyra!" Fortunato said, and a tear came to his eye.

"Tyra!" He began to scratch her vigorously.

In the struggle down the mountain, the horses had lost their saddles. Gastreel and Fortunato, Wrinn and Reev would have to ride bareback. But it was just as well. Their animals had survived.

On the nineteenth day since they departed the banks of the River Lune, the walls of Galiope appeared before them, and mighty Godsgate. The Tower of Pythor stretched into the sky like a dark pillar, a monolith. The river ran through the city... the city that welcomed exiles, the city they loved.

At the threshold of Godsgate, Gastreel called after Fortunato, and Fortunato halted Tyra's stride and turned to face him.

"What is it, Green Wizard?" he said.

"I told you when we left for the Vale," Gastreel said, "that if we came back, and you wished to return to the Empire, then you would go with my blessing."

Fortunato smiled, in view of Godsgate, and the light bathed his dark hair and young face. "Not I... Not I... A traitor to my country, according to some.

"I belong with all of you... and you belong with me."

They entered the city that morning. A city in crisis, under the shadow of war.

Chapter Sixty-Seven:
The Ship of Burial

War had not yet been declared, but the city was a cesspit of rumor. As Gastreel returned to his home in Wodenscross Court, he heard from some that three legions were already on their way to besiege Galiope, and from his neighbor that the Lord Eventide had already preemptively surrendered.

But as a member of both the Council of Wizards and the Council of Galiope, it was Gastreel's task to sort fact from falsity, to uncover the truth and act rationally.

Now, though, he had a duty that was far more important than the coming war. As soon as he had set down his pack in the vestibule of Rosetree Manor he began to go about it, taking from among his belongings the iron mask, and vowing to promptly locate the wizard Aleksander and also Bala Rabaam.

Gastreel knew that Aleksander and Bala had not yet disrupted the five other masks, for only all at once could the spell be removed. The hideous mask was still smoking, and as he peered into its hollow eyes he saw in his mind's eye a striking face, red-haired and unkempt, with terrible blue eyes. A thought came to his mind: *"You will soon see him."*

And Gastreel fell back, his breath stolen. He shouted, *"Illuné vadila!"* but he knew to cure this dark power required Bala Rabaam—it required magic. And he let the mask fall to the ground, smoking heatlessly, and before he could gain his bearings, there was a thunderous knock on the front door.

He rushed to the front door and pried it open.

Standing there in the sun's light was a person he did not expect: Bartholem, the rector of St. Sigmund's Cathedral, a member of the Council of Galiope, who, paradoxically, had been instrumental in the decision to fight the Empire. There were tears in Bartholem's eyes.

"Gastreel," he said. "I beg of your help."

"What is it?" Gastreel asked. "I hate to say it but I am terribly occupied."

Could he say no to those tears, tears in a man who rarely showed emotion?

"It is Eventide," said Bartholem, "our lord mayor. He has turned to heathenry. Maybe you can stop him!"

~

Outside Godsgate, on a hill called Hollowen, the Lord Mayor Eventide had constructed what looked like a ship. On the deck of that ship, the rotted body of his son Ethelbert lay on a bier, and piled about him were objects of gold and silver, items of ivory, and porcelain cups and bowls—Ethelbert's possessions in life.

Eventide stood there without tears in his eyes, what was almost a scowl on his face, and his wife Fiona was nowhere in sight.

Around him were gathered nobles Gastreel recognized, barons and marquises—members even of the Council of Galiope, including most prominently the Lord Alden.

A boy in front of them carried a torch, and the burial ship, Gastreel could see, was dripping with oil.

"Eventide! Fool..." Gastreel said. "Do you intend to dispose of your son like this—like a pagan king, before we knew of the gods?"

Eventide turned to Gastreel with a scowl. "And so you at last appear, after all this trouble, Green Wizard, and heap on your condemnation. I shall not relent. You say I know not the gods. What have the gods done for me? They took Ethelbert from me."

Behind Gastreel, Bartholem was weeping—but what did he expect Gastreel to do?

"Don't do this," Gastreel said, "this is a sacril—"

"As my ancestors did, so I will do," said Eventide. "Toss it!"

The boy threw the torch before Gastreel could snatch it away, and the ship became a blazing inferno, sending up black smoke and burning up the grass around it.

"Eventide!" Gastreel shouted at the sacrilege.

"Maybe," Eventide said, his eyes dead and emotionless, glinting in the light of the fire, "the spirits our ancestors honored before the gods will aid us in the coming war."

"Gods save us!" cried Bartholem, and he turned and fled.

Gastreel beheld Eventide amid the fire's heat, and never before had he been so convinced of Galiope's coming defeat, and the Empire's inevitable victory.

As the fire raged he turned and walked back to Galiope, trying to gain control of his emotions, and to remember his chief task— the iron mask.

But as he walked the streets he heard that the priests who lived in Cathedral District had already excommunicated the lord mayor, and that some, the devout of the city, were speaking of open revolt.

Chapter Sixty-Eight: The Realization

Gastreel hurried from Godsgate to the Dragonpaw and there found Bala, and from Bala he learned that Aleksander was to be found at the Tower of Pythor.

With the mask concealed in a dark bag, he followed Bala, and, using the portal, they made their way to Aleksander's living quarters. At the door, he knocked.

The door opened, and the sight of Aleksander was never kind, thin and yet so tall he would have to stoop down to leave the room, pale and white and bloodless, almost bald. He was said to be a master of the undead, yet he looked like one of them.

"Gastreel," he said. His voice was trembling, filled with fear. "I… I… You have come. And you have brought Bala."

"What troubles you?" Gastreel asked.

Aleksander looked at Gastreel, then eyed Bala as if he didn't want the child to hear what he was about to say. "That mask… it was stolen… stolen from a secret room. Where did you get it? How have you found it?"

"Let me worry about that," Gastreel said.

Aleksander seemed to twitch at the sight of the iron mask. "Whoever took that mask from our safekeeping is highly ranking… a wizard of importance."

"Let me worry about that as well," Gastreel said. "What we do now matters not just to the future of the wizard order, but the future of the world. Come with us. Aid Bala."

And Aleksander weakly nodded.

~

Beyond the guarded chamber, with the six iron masks set on the table, Bala—using his training—lifted his hands, and set about his work.

But then he drew back with a cry.

"What's wrong?" Gastreel said.

"I... I... There is no spell. There is no spell." Bala looked up at Gastreel, and a terrible realization settled over the Green Wizard.

If what Bala said was true, the black smoke wafting up from the masks, the ectoplasmic fluid that dripped—it was not the power of magic, but the power of the Dark One.

And it meant the prophetic times were almost here, when the Six Servants of Seymus would not wander in undeath but at their full strength.

Their time, then, was almost at hand, their time when they would not be restrained by the power of the gods.

"Come with me!" Gastreel shouted to Bala and Aleksander. "Hurry!"

They threw the iron masks in a locked case, as smoke wafted up in a column, and outside the city gate, they bound the case to a black mule. To the black mule they tied a flaming torch, and it galloped off, heading east, gods willing—away from Gallia.

And Gastreel, terrified by what he had witnessed, began to utter prayers, but all the cloaks in the world could not take away his icy chill of fear, and all the strong drink and pipeweed in the world could not assuage the dolor of what he had just witnessed, and of what was soon to come.

Chapter Sixty-Nine: News

Fortunato was walking to the Dragonpaw, awestruck by the size of the crowds in Galiope's streets, amazed that the city's population had almost doubled with refugees from the Vale of Ahorne, now, and also other valleys before.

And as he walked, he caught sight of men in green and brown dress, with bows strapped to their backs and swords at their sides: mountain rangers, sent to patrol the mountain way.

He stopped them, shouting, "Hail! Hail!"

And amid the packed crowds, they stopped.

Fortunato asked, "Have you been to the Vale of Ahorne?"

"We just got back," said one of the mountain rangers. "From Ahorne, and from the other valleys. You should be glad you were not with us."

"Have you heard from Edith of the House of Atheling?" Fortunato asked. "At Aerie Hold?"

"Aerie Hold has fallen," said the mountain ranger.

Fortunato's heart sank. "When?" he said, more softly. "When did it fall?"

"The rokahn broke through months ago," the ranger said, "the evening of St. Wolfrick's Night. The twenty-fourth of Brightleaf."

That had been the night Fortunato and the rest of them entered the Dim Roads, and Fortunato felt shaken at the news, shaken at the fall of the House of Atheling, shaken at the deaths of Cerdic and his family, and of Edith—once his love.

But Fortunato's long absence had caused him to realize who he loved most, after all. The one he loved was beautiful. The one he loved was kind. And he remembered her long, flowing dark hair, her bright eyes that glistened in moonlight. But the one he had loved had rejected him and fallen into the hands of his rival.

Ambrass—she worked at the Dragonpaw, and Nocturne wouldn't stop him. He would pursue her.

~

The news that Glenda told him—that the romance of Nocturne and Ambrass was no more—elated him only moments, before she explained the rest.

"She has gone back to Selwyn's Parish," Glenda said. "She is living among the gypsies now. She is marrying Gaius, her betrothed."

And Fortunato, standing there, cursed the night that Ambrass had sent him away, the night on the battlements, which surely now, she regretted. And he wondered if there was still a chance for them, a chance for them to be together, for Fortunato to have Ambrass—his love.

Chapter Seventy:
Forever Gone

In the cramped upper story room of her brother's flat, Ambrass was, for the first time in what seemed like years, trying her hand at the loom, spinning cloth in what—according to gypsy tradition—was to be her profession, when she wasn't wrangling her future children and taking care of Gaius's needs. Hanging over her, a memory, a bitter gall, she remembered the conversation she and Gaius just had, the dullness of it, the terrible mundanity. It was a glimpse of her future, becoming a mother and then a grandmother and then a crone. As she sat there, spinning the cloth, she felt her eyes water with desperation, and she knew she did not love Gaius— but she supposed that was not what marriage was about.

No, to him she would be wed, a bird in a cage, she and Gaius— forever—until she grew old and sick, and in that cage she would die. She stopped her spinning, and at last, overwhelmed, she realized she needed to rest, and what would she do?

In the distance was her deck of *tabbac* cards, sitting in a pile, and why not—why not now? Why not do something meaningless, and maybe get some false hope?

She laid them out, past, present, future.

The Lovers the past, *Death* her present, and what would her future be?

Her finger lingered on the future's card, but she realized that she did not care, that her future was what she made of it. It was she who had fled her old life; it was she who had run back into Gaius's arms.

Her finger lingered on the card, the past, and she examined the painting, two handsome bodies on the lovers' couch: man… and woman.

And her mind drifted off, to a new place, and she wondered what could have been, if she had not sent him away.

Chapter Seventy-One:
The Dream

The city was in peril, the government crumbling, but in the Dragonpaw Inn there was a fire in the hearth, and Reev and Wrinn were sitting in their favorite booth, and on the table Reev had stretched out the map he had taken from his grandfather's house. The contours of the island were drawn in black ink, and the name New Telantis brought questions, along with the coin necklace he wore—Telantis, the "True Empire."

And from the dark corners of the room, Fortunato strode toward them, a flagon of ale in his hand. And he said to them, "What's this?"

"New Telantis," Reev said.

"Where the Telantines lived, we suppose," Wrinn said.

"You're a Telantine, you say." Fortunato's smile grew. "You're saying we're related.

"And this… the shape of this island. It looks familiar. There was an island off the Imperial coast, near Ríva, where I grew up. Snakes and serpents lived there, and there was a legend that people once lived there, too."

"Maybe that's the one," Reev said.

Fortunato walked off, toward the table where he had been sitting.

Through the doors of the Dragonpaw came two figures Reev recognized, his Aunt Ramona, and his cousin, Ash. His aunt said to Glenda, "We came for the show." And they took a seat at one of the unoccupied booths.

From the darkness of the room came Dolley Wulfrun. Dolley, from Winter Ridge, whom Reev's aunt and father had known. In her hand was a harp. As she began to pluck the strings and sing, and music filled the room, the hearth flickered, and the din of laughter and clinking cups echoed, Reev looked to his cousin, Ash "Nax" Bensange, the son of the count, black-haired and gray eyed.

The city was in crisis, the government, it seemed, would collapse, and war was drawing near.

But Reev looked to Wrinn and was glad of his presence. He looked to Fortunato, and he smiled.

And Ash, his cousin Ash...

Dolley's music filled the room.

Reev stayed up until the dark hours of the morning. After Aunt Ramona and Ash spoke to Dolley and all of them had left, he retired to bed, glad to be in the Dragonpaw—an oasis in the midst of a storm, a candle burning brightly in a dark world.

He dreamed that night of a land of low purple mountains, a land raging with lightning. He dreamed of lakes of yellow sulfur and bubbling pools. And wandering that land was a black mule, on its back a case, delivering its load to some dark master.

Before a great and terrible tower, the Six Servants of Seymus appeared to him, the Servants of Seymus—their black robes seeming to suck in all light. They were riding great beasts—things half dog, half wolf, with human hands where feet would be... beasts larger than oxen—the dreaded barguest.

They rode, and the barguests howled, and their howl was one that curdled the blood.

"Reev!" the Servants were crying. "Reev!"

And amid this hellish land, amid these low mountains, amid the lightning and burning sulfur, the earth began to quake. "Reev! Reev!"

Reev woke in a daze, in the darkness of his room.

Gastreel was hovering above him, a terror in his eyes that Reev had never seen before. He had been shaking Reev, stirring him awake.

"Come with me!" Gastreel cried. "Come with me!"

~

Outside the city gate was that black mule he'd seen in the dream. On its back was that case he had witnessed. It was bucking and braying, and to its side a torch had been tied, which the night's rain had extinguished.

Behind them Fortunato had come running.

"What do you will of me?" Reev asked.

"Rebuke it!" Gastreel replied.

Words flashed, images—a flame of fire, a burning land, red-gold standards raised up, and a figure dancing in the flame. A vision—a thought. The words, "The Dark One's Hand is nigh!"

And Reev cried *"An, Abollari!"* though the words seemed to come from some hidden source, and what their meaning was he did not know.

"An, Abollari!" he cried again.

And the black mule, possessed of some dark power, neighed and whinnied, then turned and ran off.

"The Servants are reconstituting," Gastreel said, "we cannot stop it… only delay."

The black mule disappeared into the shadows of the night.

Fortunato stooped down, overcome by some strange agony. Gastreel fell back, seemingly buffeted by the wind.

And Reev knew the Servants soon would appear, and soon the Dark One's Hand would show his face.

May his house come to ruin!

Reev would crush Seymus under his feet.

THE END

Continued in Book Four, *Seven Against Seymus*…

Glossary

Dates and Times

Vardic Calendar	Julian Calendar Equivalent
Albos	January
Kaldsil	February
Primrane	March
Tidusca	April
Brenua	May
Aurelios	June
Odens	July
Sextil	August
Harona	September
Brightleaf	October
Anthanos	November
Candlebright	December

Elven phrases

Adari: "Helper."

Telantari: "Telantine."

Vadras Henion: "Henion Fortress."

Illunitari: "The Radiant One."

Illunaddori: "The Lord of Light."

Illuné vadila: "The Light guard (us)."

Velati Sonoren: "The Prince of the Dawn."

Ananda: "(You all) go!"

An, Abollari: "Go away, unclean spirit!"

Dweorg phrases

Khameirrat: "A way below."

Nirzun: "East Road."

Kharzun: "North Road."

Terms

Adamant: A blue-colored metal, hard enough to pierce stone, named after Emperor Adamantus.

Archwizard: The highest-ranked wizard. His duties include presiding over meetings of the Council of the Twelve and overseeing the maintenance of the Tower of Pythor.

Black Pass, the: A narrow gorge in the Dragonteeth Mountains. It is rumored as a haunt of ghosts.

Black Wolves: Large, intelligent wolves of the Dragonteeth Mountains. They are often captured and forced into the service of rokahn. They are one of the three divisions of Great Wolves, along with White Wolves and Brown Wolves.

Cambionia: The Imperial term for County Cambion.

Cathedral District: A large district of Galiope just north of the main gate, Godsgate. It is home to the city's churches and cathedrals.

Council of the Twelve, the: The ruling body of wizards, consisting of the foremost members of the twelve orders -- Green Robes, Blue Robes, Gold Robes and so on -- and presided over by the archwizard. They meet in the Tower of Pythor once or sometimes twice a year within the walls of the city of Galiope. Most of the Ruling Wizards live apart from the city, but many have a home in Galiope.

Dark One, the: A name for Seymus, the enemy of the gods, the king of the Abollaren or demons.

Dodoena: A goddess of light and abundance, favored by the people of the Lune Valley. Her symbol is the apple tree.

Doomblade: One of the original *estirion* blades, first called *Pelladrimas* ("Flame of Fire") and wielded by the elven warrior prince Camlon in the First Shadow War. Through many names and owners it eventually made its way into the hands of the human Simeon Nax.

Doomsday: The language of Shadow. Though when spoken, it sounds like formless whispers, the one it is directed toward can always understand it.

Dragonpaw Inn, the: A large inn of Galiope, owned and run by the half-elf Glenda.

Dragonteeth Mountains: Large snow-capped mountains, stretching from Gallia in the east to the ocean in the west, forming the border of the Northern World and the lands of the elves.

Dweorg: A race of metallurgists, smiths and tinkerers said to have been given powers of creation in ancient times.

Elves: Long-lived beings whose kingdoms and settlements lie in the north of the world. They are divided into several tribes, including the Lamen, the Umen, the Lonen, and the Nurnen. In recent years, the Lamen kingdom lost a war to the Kingdom of Zarubain and untold thousands of elves were brought into forced servitude.

Elvish horse: A kind of warhorse bred by the elves for speed and bravery. They are known by the bony horns that grow on their noses.

Empire, the: A vast state composed of seven provinces, ruled by an emperor and an Imperial Council. It is considered the foremost military power in the world.

Estirion: "Star-iron" is the hardest and sharpest metal known to man. The means of the making of star-iron swords are lost to history; they were said to be forged by Danthelon, the so-called "Wonder-Smith." Only twenty are known to exist; they are considered priceless.

Galiope: A large city of the Northern World, called by those that love it the Queen of the North.

Gallia: A region east of Zarubain and west of Kardir, a place of mixed forest and farmland. Its greatest city is Galiope.

Gallian League: A league of towns in Gallia which bands together in times of war.

Godsgate: The south-facing main gate of Galiope, serving as the major exit and entry point.

Greenwater: A district of Galiope built low to the ground, known as a place where sewers empty into the River Galios. It is known for its squalor and poor sanitation.

Gypsies: A wandering folk who traditionally roamed the world in colorful wagons. In recent years, they were welcomed by the Gallian government and allowed to settle in Galiope.

Hammond: A large town near Galiope. It is self-governing and outside the control of Gallia and Zarubain, located in an unorganized territory called the Northern Free States.

Imperial: To those outside the Empire, a citizen of the Empire. To those within the Empire, a man or woman originating in the coastal provinces associated with its founding.

Imperial City: The largest city in the known world, the capital of the Empire.

Kehrad: The most intelligent species of rokahn, they are thinner built than the other breeds, with angular facial features and often red or green skin. They often become leaders of rokahn warbands by force of will; however, their smaller size makes them easy targets.

Lindorm: A monstrous creature, a large legless worm of the ancient world, said to be the progenitor of a number of similar, lesser creatures.

Lonen Elves: A tribe of elves known for their atheistic beliefs and their advanced technology in war. They are often black-haired and pale in complexion.

Lonen Town: A district of Galiope in the city's western quadrant, home to elves of the Lonen Tribe. It features Lonen architecture and is almost homogenously elven.

Market District: A large district of Galiope, north of Middletown, known for its shops, mansions and financial institutions.

Middletown: A district in Galiope just north of the River Galios. It is home to many shops and market squares.

Murk: A swamp in the northern frontiers of the Empire, in the province of Gad.

Necromancer: A sorcerer with power over death and withering.

Norwood: A small village in the region of Noricum in the Empire, in the province of Gad.

Quick-blades: Easily-hidden knives with blades that, at the press of a button, can spring out or retract.

Rokahn: Humanoid creatures known to dwell in the Dragonteeth Mountains, considered creatures of shadow. When their population swells, they will often raid the lowlands for food. Breeds include kehrad, toltar, and the standard species simply known as rokahn.

Selwyn's Parish: A large district of Galiope named after Saint Selwyn, an ancient Gallian renowned for his piety. Decades ago, a fire swept through the district, destroying most of the buildings; around the same time, the gypsies arrived in Gallia and were welcomed. They rebuilt and settled the district.

Servants of Seymus: Six beings in service of the Dark One. They wear iron masks and are clothed in black.

Silver Drakes: Flying, silver-scaled draconic creatures known to inhabit the Dragonteeth Mountains.

Sindomas: A white flower renowned for its healing properties. It blooms in autumn.

South Weald, the: A large forest just south of Galiope.

Starstones: Shards of crystal, infused with magic to the point that they steadily give off light.

Strathbrad Gate: A gate of Galiope leading northeast in the direction of the town of Strathbrad.

Toltar: Thin, diminutive rokahn of tiny stature. They are nonetheless eager in battle and will fight to the death. They are used as scouts or spies in war or sometimes eaten by hungry rokahn as snacks.

Tower of Pythor: A tall tower in the center of Galiope, walled off to the outside world, where the wizards have their base of operations.

Vampire: In Elvish, *druen* -- a tribe of elves cursed in ancient times with a thirst for blood.

Vidowa: A sort of police force among gypsies, not sanctioned by the Gallian government but which nonetheless operates relatively unhindered.

Void, the: The dark side of magic, forbidden to use on penalty of death. They who use it eventually go mad, becoming wild purveyors of destruction.

Wall, the: A large wall forming the border of the Empire in the north. Only one gate allows northward or southward passage.

Wodenscross Court: The richest district of the city of Galiope, built on a high flattop hill. Its large mansions are passed down and usually remain within families; they are never for sale.

Wizards: Powerful magic weavers of the Northern World. They are governed by a council and have their own nation-state within the walls of Galiope.

Wizard's staff: An implement of magic that wizards use. Without it, their skill at magic weaving is weakened. The first task a wizard who has achieved full rank undertakes is the fashioning of a staff. They are constructed of crystal and certain types of wood.

Zarubain: A large kingdom of the Northern World, west of Galiope. Its legal ruler is the king of Zarubain, who dwells in the capital city of Zarubad; outlying regions are governed by dukes (duchies), counts (counties) and barons (baronies).

Zarubad: The largest city of the Northern World, far west of Galiope, by the sea, the capital of the Kingdom of Zarubain.

APPENDIX 3: BALA'S FIRST LESSON

The four easiest undead to create.

- **Ghul**

Appearance: Exactly as in the moment of death, except paler and more shriveled.

Characteristics: Under the direct command of the necromancer, no free will and minimal capacity to think.

- **Ghast**

Appearance: A ghost, partially transparent, of the version of themselves they least liked in life.

Characteristics: Cannot reach into the mortal world, except those of the most powerful will.

- **Strighul**

Origins: A thief who took a life.

Appearance: A man or woman with pale skin and bat-shaped wings, a mouth of yawning gummy strands.

Characteristics: Able to fly. Ineffective in direct combat, except for a stunning screech. Intelligent, but submissive to the necromancer.

- **Lamigha**

Origins: A person who killed an innocent.

Appearance: A tall woman seemingly formed of shadow, with red eyes.

Characteristics: Able to drain life energy. Bucks under the command of the necromancer, difficult to control.

About the Author

Cursed at birth with a wild imagination, Andrew Cooper spent his youth dreaming of worlds more exciting than Earth.

He is a graduate of the Odyssey Writing Workshop. His stories have appeared in Morpheus Tales, Fear and Trembling, Residential Aliens and Mindflights, among others.

He is also a graduate of the Creative Writing program at Western Michigan University.

Visit **www.aj-cooper.com** to sign up for the newsletter and stay up-to-date on new releases.

Find him on **x/Twitter** @ajcooperwriter.

9 781958 724248